DEAD END STREET

by
Dean McCormick

Order this book online at www.trafford.com
or email orders@trafford.com

Most Trafford titles are also available at major online book retailers.

Note for Librarians: A cataloguing record for this book is available from Library
and Archives Canada at www.collectionscanada.ca/amicus/index-e.html

Printed in Victoria, BC, Canada.

ISBN: 978-1-4120-7695-1

*Our mission is to efficiently provide the world's finest, most comprehensive
book publishing service, enabling every author to experience success.
To find out how to publish your book, your way, and have it available
worldwide, visit us online at www.trafford.com/*

Trafford PUBLISHING® www.trafford.com
North America & international
toll-free: 1 888 232 4444 (USA & Canada)
phone: 250 383 6864 ♦ fax: 812 355 4082

DEAD END STREET

DEDICATIONS

To My Mother

I NEED TO APOLOGIZE TO MY MOM for the torture and shame
I put her through for ten years and to thank her for sticking
by me no matter how bad I was.

I am truly sorry Mom. I hope you can accept my apology.
Thank you for being who you are and have been, I couldn't
be whom I am without you.

To My brother

Thank you for rescuing me from almost certain death and
devoting two years of your life to providing shelter, nursing,
companionship and, at times, laughter.

I also want to apologize to every mother, father, brother
or sister who lost someone due to drugs or prison.

PREFACE

THIS STORY IS BASED ON MY REAL life events, as one of the millions of "Baby Boomers", growing up in the 50's, 60's and 70's, In Orange County California. My name is Dean McCormick

Marijuana and psychedelics were introduced and becoming the drug of choice over alcohol.

This was the path I took, I lived for the today. A surfer on the southern California coast, trips to Baja Mexico looking for waves and finding endless supplies of Marijuana.

Thousands went from childhood innocents and law abiding citizens to felons and criminals.

1

Reality

AS SHERRI WHEELED ME OFF THE AIRPLANE, there stood my mother and brother. I tried to smile but, I could see the look. They were "freaked."

They gave me hugs and welcomed me home. I tried to act like I was fine but when they heard my slurred speech they started saying, "Don't worry Dean. We'll get you well."

Not a word was said to Sherri before they were whisking me out of the airport. Suddenly, Sherri was gone. I knew I'd never see her again. On the way down the freeway everything was hazy. I just wanted to rest.

We stayed at a Newport hotel for a few days. I was in agony and I didn't seem to be recovering but we had to stay hidden from the police.

Fortunately, my brother told my mom that I was going through heroin addiction withdrawal. Two weeks after I left Maui I was worse. The reality that I wasn't going to get better on my own set in.

My Mom set an appointment for me with a neurologist. His test results showed that my brain was fine, but my motor nerves were either damaged or destroyed.

"He must be wrong" I thought. I can think I just can't walk or talk.

The doctor couldn't say how long it would take to recover or any guarantees I even would recover. Which ever it would be it was going to be slow.

2

Innocent 1956

MY PARENTS SOLD THEIR FIRST HOME IN Downey, CA for
four thousand dollars and made a five hundred dollar profit.
They put a three hundred dollar down payment on a new single
family home, three bedrooms, in Anaheim CA. I was seven
years old and my brother was eight. Orange County, especially
Anaheim, was being carved out of orange groves; new homes
popped up every month, Disneyland had just opened. New
schools were under construction, roads widened, big grocery
markets and gas stations appeared everywhere to meet the
explosion of population filling the area.

The new neighborhoods were mostly young white working families with kids playing baseball in the neighborhood streets, occasionally brokrn windows, with a ball during a game of baseball, that was big trouble, hide and seek at night and sleepovers. Churches were full every Sunday and back then, kids learned morals. There was very little crime or bad influences. The worst violation of the law was people having firecrackers on July the 4th. We respected police and the law.

My dad was a hard working carpenter supporting a family of four. He was born in Oklahoma in 1925 to a very poor family that moved to Carlsbad California when he was a teen. He learned his carpentry trade building army barracks at Camp Penalton in Oceanside, CA.

My mother was born in Missouri in 1927 to a family of farmers and moved to Bell Gardens, CA at a young age to look for a better life. Somehow, my parents met in the late forties, married, and started a family.

We lived comfortably, my brother and I were into sports and were good students. My brother was a better athlete than I was but, I always made-up with hustle and sacrifice. I was the happy go lucky one. Our parents expected us to make something of ourselves. We were typical good boys and well liked in grammar school by our teachers. We were involved in all school activities and our mom belonged to the PTA. We were the all around American family.

One winter, when I was nine or ten, my dad decided to build a ski boat and trailer. He had never built one before but he knew he could do it and he did with the family's help. All four of us piled into the front of his work truck for the 700 mile trip to lake Shasta, pulling our new boat, with anevinrude motor, obviously too big for the boat. Dad bought the motor, the most powerful one he could get even if it sunk the boat.

When we got to Lake Shasta, we camped right on the water and hardly saw another boat for two weeks . I loved to ski, Dad would try to dump me so others could have a turn, but it rarely worked. Finally, he added another rope which was so much fun. The vacation ended when my dad fell on his homemade ski, busting it across his chest. He was a bit bloody but fine.

My parents square danced at Knott's Berry Farm with neighbors every Wednesday. Orange County was the white working class "American Dream". We were a happy family and my dad was game for anything, as long as he could make it.

A new junior high was built two years earlier, Volkswagens had just arrived from Germany. We loved to go to Huntington Beach and rent rafts to ride the waves. My brother was in junior high and I was going to be starting.

Junior high brought a new identity, no recess, no running, seven classes a day, and being told, "Now you are adults. It's time to buckle down. Things are going to get harder." We were adults but not to do what adults did.

I met kids from different neighborhoods, I was experiencing the world outside my own neighborhood and my parents. Orange County was growing-up and so were we. We went to school dances, the skating rink on weekend nights and Disneyland at night during the summer. Some of the kids we knew were starting to drink and smoke, I tried it but didn't really like it. That was seventh grade for me.

The next year a new sport hit big, surfing. I loved the beach and my brother and I were definitely sand crabs already. Up sprang music, clothes, and teen dance halls. Anaheim had Harmony Park, Newport Beach had Rendezvous and Huntington Beach had The Golden Bear. The Beach Boys, the Everly Brothers and Dick Dale all came out with surfing songs. Everybody was crazy about surfing. The eighth grade was molding me into a surfer and I loved it.

Orange County was blossoming its first teenagers. We had things to do and places to go, without our parents. Now it was girls, parties and alcohol. We were not as innocent as the year before and neither was Orange County.

The summer between eighth and ninth grade I spent at the beach surfing five wells in Huntington Beach. My friend Mike, and I, surfed and sometimes some of the older brothers came down with quarts of beer, definitely Ho Dads! Our parents would be furious if they saw us around these guys. We really did not want to be around them, but we couldn't tell them to split, they would kick our butts.

We usually shared a big board, catching a wave, or soup, for a ride and then giving the board up to the next guy. We learned to surf on big water logged boards. We started to wear surfer clothing, mostly big and baggy, and we started new lingo like, ho-dads (non-surfers, greasy hair and flat top haircuts), grimmies (to small to surf), surfs-up (big waves), flat (no waves), blown-out (bad shaped waves) and bitchen (great).

By this time I wasn't interested in school, my grades were falling and I couldn't wait to get to high school. The weekends were what I lived for, Harmony Park on Friday night, the beach on Saturday and then either the Golden Bear or Rendezvous on Saturday night. My brother and Mike had cars by this time so we were really experiencing all the different beaches, parties and nightclubs in our town. Ninth grade ended with a graduation and sending me off to high school.

Summer was great surfing at all the different beaches, Huntington, Newport, Laguna, Dana Point and Doheny, all the hot spots on the Orange County coast. Harmony Park on Fridays with Dick Dale was the happening. Harmony Park had good music, dancing, the surfer stomp and lots of girls!

By the end of the summer I was a fully devoted surfer, I talked the talk and walked the walk, surfboards, long hair, and baggy clothes. When I started high school there wa friction between surfers and Ho-dads.

My sophomore year, in 1964, was full of events. One good thing was I was in high school and about ready to start driving. The bad things were the angry parents and teachers, over our long hair and surfer clothes. We were different and all we wanted to do was surf. We had our own style of clothing, magazines, surf shops, music and surf movies shown at mom and pop beach theaters.

There were suspensions from school for violating their fascistic approach to the free of spirit of the day's youth and then that would lead to restriction at home. Clashes between college students and the campus police across the nation over the Vietnam war were on TV. Military recruiters, dressed in their best, came to the schools making sure we all knew to register for the draft when we turned eighteen or to enlist early, if parents allowed.

The changes that had taken place seemed to happen over night. The schools were against the surfers, police were against college students and the world reports showed thousands of people that hated Americans. I was always brought up to respect teachers, the police, older people and the government. Now there was mistrust and a wedge created between the young and old.

It became the norm to tell our parents what they wanted to hear. Our parents would give us money to go to the show on weekends but really we were going to parties. If we really told them what we were doing, they would have never allowed it.

This year in Balboa, the cops were mean to the long hair surfers, they had always been cool to us before. By the end of the school year many people were smoking marijuana but, not me or my friends.

When school got out for summer, we were excited for another three months of beach, girls and surfing. Some of our friends' older brothers had rented beach houses to party at. They smoked pot every night and one of my friends told me his older brother could get him some if we wanted. We told him he was crazy, he smoked it anyway, and after that, we stayed away from the beach house, we were too afraid of getting arrested. We spent the summer the usual way, on the beach, Harmony Park, the Golden Bear or seeing surf movies in downtown Huntington. The summer ended and I got ready for eleventh grade.

When school started, the surfers were rounded up and ordered to get GI haircuts or w be suspended. Bad things were happening the first day back, we were in the hands of the "Gestapo". The recruiters, were there asking us to sign up for military service so we could get first choice at jobs offered, since we were going to be drafted any way. This way we could be ahead of the game and telling us the army was great.

I asked them about the protesters on the TV, against the Vietnam war, they said they were communist and not to listen to them. With all the changes that had taken place the year before, the school was ready, and they really clamped down on us. We were the same kids, they just didn't like the way we dressed, our hair or the music we listened to. The school thought they were going to force us to change back. Changes were taking place whether they liked it or not. The main thing that was happening was pot, but the teachers had no idea, they were more concerned about trying to enforce their dress code.

All of this drove a deeper wedge between the people over thirty and the teenagers. Sometime that year I smoked pot for the first time, and I liked it. It was less harmful than alcohol and cigarettes that the older generation used.

On the weekends, we started buying ten dollar lids (ounces) of pot to party with at the beach. If you were caught with even a few joints you were sent to jail or even prison for years.

Now we had to deal with the cops, not just teachers and

parents. In one year a complete subculture developed within Orange County. The music had drug lyrics, the movies had drugs in them and people were starting to get arrested. I decided not to go back to school the following year. I just wanted to be left alone to smoke pot, surf, and hang out at the beach. I didn't trust the government, relatives, cops or the schools. Every night on TV thousands protested against the war.

My friends were all potheads, everybody smoked weed. We partied every night at different places and our first thought was to buy a lid of pot. We would usually score from somebody's older brother. The older guys sold us big fat ounces of pot for ten bucks.

We had become full blown pot heads and had sunken deeper into the illegal drug subculture that most seventeen and eighteen year olds had something to do with. And then there were psychedelics, LSD (acid) and Mescaline and they weren't even illegal. When they came around, we couldn't wait to try them.

Timothy Leary, a renowned doctor from Harvard University, was making headlines advocating tuning in and dropping out of society on LSD. The society was changing and we were part of it. We dropped acid at love-ins, concerts and the beach. Laguna Beach was the center of the psychedelic culture, artists and the new sawdust festival. Up and coming artists were there along with a lot of drugs and dealers. They had all the good pot, like Acalpuco Gold and Wahaka.

We realized that buying pot or acid, in quantity, was cheaper than by the dose so why don't we do what the brotherhood does. We started pooling our money together and bought kilos for one hundred dollars, which were forty ounces selling for ten bucks an ounce. Why work when we could make this kind of money. I started scoring either pot or acid every week, this made for lots of free drugs, money and girls. I hung out in Palm Springs, Laguna Beach, and Huntington Beach; went to concerts, movies, parties, Hollywood love-ins, and surfing.

My connections started deepening in Laguna. The dealers I knew in the Brotherhood would call me when a load of kilos or acid came into town. I had become a scammer, making runs to Laguna Beach to score. The Brotherhood started taking me to their connections, I was becoming a friend, and not just somebody they trusted and would sell to. I knew who the big dealers were, they wouldn't sell directly to me, but they knew I was okay. Buying stash every week and selling it to people my age, in Anaheim and Huntington Beach, I was making two to three hundred dollars a week, but I wanted more. Occasionally, I went down to Baja to surf and I knew I could get cheap pot there, but I didn't have a connection. The modern day prohibition was in full swing only instead of booze from Mexico it was Pot. Instead of "booseleggers" it was "potleggers" known as the Laguna Brotherhood made a lot of easy money from cheap kilos, right across the Tijuana border, and I wanted a part of it.

I asked a pot-dealing friend in Laguna if he could get me a connection in Mexico to score some kilos. He told me I could do some drug runs for him, that he had a connection there. I was ready to go; he told me how it would all happen. I would meet with his connection and pick up twenty kilos; he said he would show me how to stash it in my car to cross the border, when I got back he would give me 1 kilo for making the run. I thought why should I take all the chances and he gets all the kilos and money, did he think I was an idiot?

If I wanted a connection in Mexico I had to find one on my own. I went surfing in Baja the next weekend. I knew a Mexican kid I had surfed with. I heard he lived in a trailer park called Cantamar. I surfed with my buddies up and down the Baja coast that weekend and couldn't find him. I thought for sure he would have a connection or help me get one. We decided to go into Tijuana and see what was there.

When we arrived, we parked the car and started walking up and down the streets. There were lots of nasty bars with untrustworthy looking doormen calling people in off the streets. "Come see tits, come get some pussy". We decided to go into one of the bars, there was a nasty looking fat mexican woman dancing topless and immediately another fat mama came over and started grabbing my balls. I told her no and then she got angry and the mexican men were on us with knives. Luckily the police heard the fuss and came in and we got away. We started walking along and we spotted this taxi driver standing by his cab eating raw eggs, we watched in amazement as he downed about a dozen of them. He was a small guy with greasy jet black hair, gold chains, probably fake, and a pencil thin mustache. He spoke broken English exposing a few missing teeth. But, he did have a friendly face so we stopped and talked with him. He asked us if we wanted pussy, we told him no. Then he asked if we wanted yeska, spanish for marijuana. I asked him how much for kilos.

He told me he could get a kilo for twenty five dollars, then invited us to get in his cab, he would take us to his house and show us what he had, he said it was only about fifteen minutes away. We got in the taxi that had small balls hanging from the interior. As he drove it became apparent the steering was worn out from all the pot holes in Tijuana, but, he drove it like a Ferrari; we had quite a ride up a dirt hillside with shacks all around, we arrived at a little plain brick house with half a dozen chickens in the yard. He motioned us to go in with him. We were greeted by his shy wife and kids and then followed him into a back room, there he uncovered some kilos and invited us to smoke some with him. It turned out to be some good pot so we bought five kilos at twenty five dollars each. We learned the taxi drivers name was Herbie. He drove us back to T.J. and dropped us off on a side street, we didn't want him to see our car just incase he was a snitch. We got in our car and stashed the pot on the floor, covered it with a blanket and drove the forty five minutes back to the beach where we were camping. It was a scary drive traveling through the toll road stops but we made it back to our camping spot just fine. The rural beach camp was quiet, no one was out of their tents, we just sat there excited about all the pot we had just scored but then thought "what are we going to do now"? I hadn't figured out how I was going to hide the kilos in my car to get it across the U.S. border yet. We decided to hide the kilos under a small drainage bridge, we would come back in a couple days when we were ready to smuggle it across the border. We got our army shovel, dug a small hole under the bridge, put the kilos in it and then covered them with dirt and rocks. We quietly slipped back into camp to avoid anyone from noticing that we had been under the bridge. I kept a little bit out to smoke that night and the next day.

Sunday morning I awoke at six o'clock to the sound of the surf. I looked out of the tent, the water was totally glassy with four foot waves and no one was around. I grabbed my surfboard and headed for the water, it was just two pelicans and me. I had perfect waves for the next two hours, it was heaven. Teddy had taken the tent down and waited for an hour for me to get out of the water. The waves were so perfect I just didn't want to come in, even though I saw him waiting for me. We went to the cantina camp store and restaurant for some huevos ranchero and banana pancakes. The food was fantastic and cheap; this cantina was definitely a place to come back to.

We went back through Tijuana, when we got to the border it was backed up so we waited. When we got up to the customs agent, he asked us where we had been. I told him we had been at Rosarito beach surfing. He red tagged my car and we were sent to the secondary inspection center. As soon as we pulled into the inspection area, we were met by two custom agents who ordered us to the customs building where we were stripped searched while others proceeded to search my car. They removed the back seat and the entire paneling, checked under the hood and all around the engine. We didn't have anything on us, or in the car so they had to let us go. The guards had left my car a mess; we just threw it back together and left.

While driving back up the five freeway we decided we

needed to take two cars when we return to Tijuana. One car would carry the stash across the border, staying concealed at the beach while the other car would be used to make the score. It was obvious this trip someone turned us in, customs knew what we were driving, possibly Herbie the taxi driver.

After I got back I put together a smuggling kit that would conceal the kilos beyond even the most intense search. The only way I could get caught was if someone turned me in and knew where the pot was hidden.

Teddy and I went back to Mexico three days later. When we arrived in Cantamar, it was daylight so we waited until dark to retrieve the kilos. We spent the day surfing and keeping an eye on the little old bridge; it seemed safe. When it got dark we snuck over to the bridge, with our army shovel. This time there wasn't anyone camping on the beach so we felt safer going to the bridge. When we got under the bridge I noticed that the rocks had been moved and I could see part of the blue kilo wrapper sticking out of the ground, my heart skipped a beat. Were we being set up? We quickly crawled out from under the bridge to see if anyone was watching us. Everything seemed quiet so we returned back to the spot; I quickly uncovered the exposed kilo and looked underneath to see if the rest of the stash was there, luckily it was. We grabbed the kilos, put them in a burlap bag then headed back to our camp, by way of the brush. When we got back to our tent we opened the bag to check the kilos and realized that part of one kilo had been eaten. I knew then rats. We were lucky they didn't eat it all but after eating almost a third of a kilo they must have been pretty stoned and still wandering around out there.

In the morning I stashed the kilos in the concealed smuggling kit, went surfing and then ate breakfast. We headed back to the border, at San Diego, mid day and this time there was no line of cars, we drove right up to the customs agent. The agent looked in the car and asked the usual questions, where had we been, what was our citizenship and what were we bringing back? I told him we were bringing back a basket and that we had been down to surf. He asked me to step out of the car and open the trunk. I opened the trunk and he sifted through all the camping stuff and then closed the trunk and wished us a good day and off we went. We made it through without a hitch.

Talk about being excited, I had a connection in Mexico, five kilos for the price of one and I was going to make a big profit. My smuggling kit worked excellent, I could do this every week. I could surf the Baja. Now I was a smuggler, but I didn't consider myself a criminal, I was just a pot smoking surfer kid that was having fun and making money.

When I got back to Orange County, I removed the kilos, made some phone calls to set up some sells, then broke up the kilos in ten dollar lids. The kilo made thirty lids and by the time the night was over I had sold all thirty and made three hundred dollars and still had four kilos. This was big profit. Now the Laguna guys wanted to buy my kilos. After selling two kilos to them I split up the last two kilos into ten dollar lids and by the end of the week I had sold it all. In that week I made one thousand dollars with an initial investment of two hundred dollars.

I realized the possibilities were endless now, I knew how to smuggle. I was going to get rich quick and travel to Mexico and even Hawaii. I was spending money like water in Laguna's Mystic Art World Store buying expensive necklaces, bathing suits, rings and trinkets for my girlfriend.

My friends and I dropped acid a couple times a week and hung out at the beach. At night we would kick back smoking pot and listen to music. Two weeks flew by, I had spent five hundred dollars, I needed to go back to Mexico and score.

Back across the border we went, at night, with my surfboard and my girlfriend followed by Teddy, in another car with his girlfriend. We traveled a few miles down the baja to cantamar beach. Teddy and his girl headed for the cantina, my girl and I headed to T.J. to find Herbie. When we got to T.J. there was Herbie standing next to his taxi eating his raw eggs. He saw me and smiled, "taxi please", I said. Herbie opened the door for us to get in and we were off driving around town. I told him I wanted to buy more kilos and wanted to score regularly. I told him about the incident at the border and my concerns that he was possibly the one who turned me in, which he quickly denied. Herbie told me he would be happy to be my regular connection. He asked for half the money right then, I wasn't sure if I trusted him, but it made sense for him to go it alone. I asked him to show me where his house was again, which he did, and before we got out of his cab we had made arrangements to meet the next evening at eight o'clock at his house. I gave him one hundred dollars and said

"I'm trusting you, don't burn me." We had dinner and then drove the old bumpy road out to the beach by Cantamar and partied for the night.

The next morning, I was awakened by the sound of the surf and seagulls. The waves were perfect; I put on my wet suit, lit a joint and yelled for Teddy to get up. He poked his head out of his tent, I handed him the joint and said, "let's go surfing". We surfed all morning, just inside the kelp beds. The girls got up and laid towels out on the beach. They laid out topless, showing off their great bodies and wearing skimpy bikini bottoms. I paddled in and went straight to the car, passing by where the girls were sunning those great tittys saying, "this is great! What lovely bodies! burn those bras!", I got out some acid, we split it four ways, forty-five minutes later the sky was baby blue, the ocean was carbonated and we were psychedelic and digging it. We surfed and ate bananas and mangos all day. By evening we were crispy critters after being in the sun all day. We cleaned up and went to the cantina for dinner. When it came time to score, the girls didn't want to be left behind on the beach; they wanted to go to T.J. with us. I thought it would be all right, we were just going to Herbie's house and then back to the beach.

We drove up the side of the hill, past the shacks to Herbie's house right on time and Herbie was no where to be found. We waited for an hour and then we could hear a car coming up the road, it was Herbie in his taxi. He pulled up in his front yard, chickens scattered, got out of the taxi and informed me that he hadn't scored yet but that he could score right then. He told me to get into the taxi and he would take me with him. No one wanted to stay behind, it was freaky at night in Herbie's Tijuana slum neighborhood. We loaded in Herbie's taxi, he drove us to a motel down an alley and immediately the whores approached us. Herbie told them we were there for French movies not pussy. When they saw our surfer girlfriends there was definitely friction in the air. Herbie told us to wait there and watch the movie; he had to go around the corner to score. We walked into a little room with a projector showing nasty gross mexican women having sex with dildos. This was a French movie? The door of the room flew open and half a dozen mexicans came in and grabbed us, they were sent by the whores who were mad that we brought our women and insulted them. Just then Herbie got back, spoke to them in spanish and they let us go. Herbie got us all into his taxi and as we were driving away the whores were banging on the windshield and yelling profanities at us. We got back to Herbie's house; he had five kilos and also gave me a jar of whites and a jar of reds to show he was sorry for the delay and the scare. The girls had the shit scared out of them, I was never going to take them on a score in Tijuana again. We got back to the beach safely, the pot was great and I had the jars of whites and reds, which we each dropped a couple reds, smoked pot, roasted marshmallows and stumbled around the beach fire.

Sunday morning we got up early, still a little groggy, stashed the kilos and pills in the car, did some surfing, ate breakfast at the cantina and hung out on the beach until mid afternoon. We packed up the camp and then headed for the border. Teddy drove in a different line in his chevelle. I watched as he got to the border crossing, searched and then let across. Ten minutes later it was my turn, I got through without any problem. A few miles down the freeway we pulled off and met up with Teddy, picked up some stashed joints. "another successful scam," I said to Teddy with a high five, "see you back home."

When I got home, my mom had put a letter on my bed from the selective service of the United States. I opened it and boldly across the heading it said "You are hereby ordered for pre-induction physical to the U.S. Army," the date was three weeks away. This brought me to reality, I was nineteen years old, at twenty I would be fighting in Vietnam. Every night on T.V. there was news about the war, all those G.I.'s being killed for what? Protesters were all over the streets and my college. Normally I would walk past them as they tried to talk to me, but now it was different, I wanted to hear what they had to say. I explained to them I had just received my pre-induction papers. They told me that now the war involved me, my freedom, my life and now I had to think on my own. They said this was an unjust war, the American people needed to wake up. Also, the government didn't want people to think they labeled you a communist if you questioned the war. The war was all about money, not freedom and democracy. It is big business building a war machine, lobbyists in Washington wanted to keep it going, they were making millions. At this point in my life I didn't know how I felt, I was just a surfer kid who liked to smoke pot, the beach, Mexico and money. I was confused and worried.

Known as a supplier made sales easy. I had the smoke

and pills everyone wanted. I was hanging out in Huntington Beach all day surfing and then spent the nights in Laguna Beach among the art and drug underworld. The Laguna narcotic officers were notorious; they were like Elliot Ness, the untouchables on T.V.. We had to beware of certain streets that were being watched and the occasional raids. Laguna Beach was hot.

I was planning on going back to Mexico the next week but it never worked out that way, it always took two weeks. I was busy and my army physical was in one week, I had to get it together. I talked to protesters again at the college and they were telling me not to go, they would give me connections in Canada. I had some decisions to make.

Friday came and it was back down the five freeway to Mexico. It was the norm to stash a few joints on the U.S. side of the border for the drive back. I ordered my score from Herbie, in T.J. then headed to the beach to camp. Saturday I surfed most the day and met some guys from Garden Grove who surfed with me. In the late afternoon it was back to Herbie's. This time he had all the pot and pills at his house and told me it would be like that from then on. I said " muy bien gracious", we shook hands and then we headed out of the Tijuana slum and back to Cantamar beach, with five kilos and two jars of pills. We had left the girls at the cantina this time, we didn't want to chance any problems in T.J. When we sat down with them at the cantina there were four girls and no guys. I asked where the guys had gone and they said they were out on the beach building a fire. We all decided to go down to the beach. As I walked down the beach I could see the guys were passing around a joint. I walked up; introduced myself again and again they said they were Jon and Sammy. We sat around the fire listening to Bob Dylan, Jefferson Airplane and smoking pot. We really hit it off well with the Orange County guys, especially Jon. I told Jon I had some pot. We walked over to my car and I showed him a kilo and he was shocked. "What are you going to do with all that"? He asked. I replied, "smoke it." I grabbed a handful, gave it to him and then I grabbed another handful for me. We sat around the fire cleaning the seeds and stems out of the buds, listening to Bob Dylan's "Blowing in the wind". I asked if they wanted me to wake them up in the morning if the waves were good, they said "definitely."

The next morning I woke up around seven o'clock, the waves were two to four feet and the water glassy as usual. I woke up Jon and Sammy, my friend Teddy wasn't much of a surfer so we left him sleeping and we hit the waves, it was nice to have someone to surf with without begging. After about an hour I told Jon and Sammy I had to go in, I had some things to do. I came out of the water, dried off, and then headed to my car to stash the kilos for the ride across the border. As I was working Jon walked up with a joint and handed it to me. I confided in him, I was going to trust him, so I showed him my smuggling kit and said I was taking kilos across the border. I told him how easy it was and that the border agents had to know exactly where the stash was to be able to find it. Late that afternoon Teddy, the girls and I headed out for the border, but before we left we exchanged numbers with

Jon and Sammy. The border was crowded, as usual, but we crossed without any trouble.

Monday morning I went to the college to talk to some of the protesters, my pre-induction physical was the next day. They handed me a protest leaflet and informed me to carry it with me and that would cause me to be asked to leave the building. It sounded good to me that was my plan. When I got home from the school that afternoon my Mom came up to me and asked me what was going on. She said she had gotten over fifty calls for me over the weekend. I told her I had gone to Mexico surfing and people were just looking for me. She told me she didn't like me going to Mexico, she thought I might get mugged. She really didn't get on my case, because she knew I was going for my pre-induction the next day and that I was really bummed.

Tuesday morning I stepped on the bus with about fifty other guys and headed for L.A. Half the guys on the bus were yelling, "We're going to kill some comies!" I couldn't believe I was going through this. When we pulled up to the federal building we were met by an army sergeant, who boarded the bus. He instructed us that when we got off the bus we were not to speak with anyone or take any brochures "do you understand?" he yelled. Most of the guys yelled back "yes sir". "Now stand and when I give you the command march, and again do not talk to anyone," he ordered. The protesters had made it clear that it would be like this, and that it was my constitutional right to accept any information and if I did, I would be excused from my physical. They also told me I had to get them to write that I was being excused and if they didn't I wasn't to leave.

When I got off the bus I stepped up to a protester and took a brochure. Immediately the stocky little sergeant came up to me and ordered me to throw it away. I told him it was my constitutional right to read anything and with that he took me aside to a room and locked me in alone. Within an hour he came back with two other sergeants, they put a typed piece of paper in front of me and ordered me to sign it. I read the paper and it stated that I admitted to passing out illegal anti-war material in a federal building. I replied," that's a lie," I'm not going to sign it. I didn't pass out anything, I didn't even talk to anyone, and I just accepted a pamphlet. The little stocky sergeant got right in my face and ordered me to sign or he would kick my ass. I still refused. I wasn't going to sign anything that was a lie. The sergeant called me a "fucking communist" and then signed the paper with my name and the other two witnessed it. They had no problem perjuring themselves. They unlocked the door and ordered me to leave the building.

Outside I went up to a protester and told him what had happened. As it turned out the brochure I was given had been given to me by a professor from UCLA. He took me to the UCLA campus anti-war headquarters and drew up a letter as witness that I had received only one brochure and that I had reported for my pre-induction physical as ordered and was asked to leave. They sent one to the induction headquarters and gave me a copy for my records and told me that the army couldn't call me again for six months. He then gave me a ride home and gave me his phone number in case I had any other problems.

I went out that night to try to forget how crazy those army guys were. I realized I needed to do my thing so I could make enough money to leave the country, I didn't want any part of what the army was selling. This had been a growing up experience, yesterday I trusted the government a little, today I completely mistrusted them.

As the week progressed I was selling my pot and pills that everyone loved, hanging out at Orange Coast College, at the beach and eating avocado sandwiches and smoothies. When I got home my mom gave me a few messages and one of them was from Jon. I called Jon back and said I was the guy from Mexico. He wanted to buy a lid of my pot, if I still had any, I did and suggested he meet me at the Huntington Beach pier the next day.

The next morning I met Jon. We sat in his van watching the waves while smoking a joint. The waves looked good, we decided to go surfing. While we were surfing he asked me when I was going back to Mexico and I said on Friday. I asked him if he wanted to go. I shared my experience about my induction, what a bummer it had been. I was going to stay down in Mexico for a week and just drop acid, smoke pot and surf. I was bringing a girl and he should bring his. I said " Don't worry about the money, I have plenty of cash." Jon was interested in learning about scoring and wanted to know if he could get involved with me. I told him about Herbie, the whores, and the french movies and that we had to take two cars and he would have to drive me to T.J., normally I used Teddy's car. I would pay him this time and when we got back we would make a smuggling kit for his van next trip.

Friday night we crossed the border into Mexico. There wasn't any reason to see Herbie right away, since we would be there for a week, and we had lots of pot, acid and reds, we called them gorilla biscuits. We pulled up to the beach, at Cantamar, the ocean was florescent when the waves broke. We made our camp, went to the cantina for the evening. The next morning we all dropped a full tab of acid, since we didn't have to go anywhere, just hang out on the beach. As the week flew by Jon and I became better friends. We liked the same things, drugs, girls and surfing. Before we realized it the time had come for us to score so we all went into T.J. I met with Herbie and told him what I wanted. We bought baskets, blankets, watches and jewelry just for the fun of shopping and bargaining.

The next day Jon and I drove up to Herbie's house in the daytime. Everybody that was outside stopped and watched as we bumped and bounced up the ghetto dirt road, two surfers with California plates. It wasn't common for us to be in their neighborhood and we knew it. If the federally came along we would be pulled over for sure. Normally at night, no one would realize we were not one of them, but in the middle of the day we were a bust. We pulled up to Herbie's house and went inside. I introduced Jon to Herbie. Herbie offered Jon one of his eggs and Jon took it. Herbie sucked down one and then Jon did the same, I couldn't believe what I was seeing. Herbie took us into his back room and uncovered four kilos of pot, six jars of whites and one jar of reds. He told me he could only score four kilos this time so he got me some extra pills and hoped that would be okay. I could sell the pills faster and make more money but I liked to smoke the pot, I wasn't a pill popper but it was okay. When we walked outside of Herbie's we were carrying a duffle bag. The neighbors were staring and the kids were playing soccer, they knew what was happening. Jon and I just got in the car and drove away. The drive out of the neighborhood took about ten minutes but it seemed like an hour. I just hoped we didn't see a federally, since the stash was just in a bag on the floor. When we got on the main road Jon and I both took a deep breath, we wouldn't do it again in daylight.

When we got back to the beach we stashed the pot and pills and then decided to hang out on the beach for another day before crossing the border. The next day was Sunday and we had a forty five minute wait at the border. When I pulled up it was the usual questions, "where have you been? what did you buy? what is your citizenship? step out and open the trunk." This time the border guard tapped on the panels of my car and checked under the seats and glove compartment. "You're fine to go", he said. I wasn't worried, the stash was hidden well and could pass any search.

I met up with Jon at a restaurant down the freeway where we had stashed a few joints. I told him I would meet up with him that night and give him a kilo for helping me, he was happy with that. I dropped off my girlfriend and headed home. When I got home my Mom was right there wanting to know where I had been. I said I had been in Mexico, I had to get away. She wanted to know what about school. I only missed three classes and that I did all my work in Mexico. She didn't believe me but she was cool. Mom was happy with me because I was going to college. Again she told me the phone had been ringing off the hook while I was gone.

That evening I was all over Orange County filling orders, I was a popular pot dealer and now I had one dollar rolls of whites and reds. Everyone wanted a roll or two of pills to party with, sales were easy. I stopped off at some girls apartment, in Orange County, and called Jon to ask him if he wanted to come over and meet me. The girls were making pot brownies and I would give him his kilo. Jon came over and by the end of the night we were completely stoned on pastries. I liked Judy; she was a tall blonde with brown eyes, nice body, with long legs that intrigued me, not to mention her great butt. We hooked up that night and were a couple from then on. The next weekend I was going to go back to Mexico and asked Judy if she wanted to go with me. She had a job but said she could take some time off. Jon and I surfed everyday and at night built his smuggling kit.

Friday we were set to leave. It was Jon, Sharon, Judy and I on our way back to Mexico. Jon had sold his kilo so he had three hundred with him and I had five hundred with me, way more than we needed. Once across the border we stopped in T.J. to place our order with Herbie. When we found him he told us that we couldn't come to his house anymore, someone had turned him in and he had been in jail until two days ago. He told us we would have to score at the motel from now on. I didn't like that idea, but if that was how it had to be then that is what I would do. I ordered ten kilos and five jars to be picked the next evening, with that Herbie said he would see us tomorrow.

We drove out to Cantamar and stopped at the cantina as usual. We were drinking tequila and I said to Jon, "there must be a safer way to score." being in Tijuana, scoring at the motel and then driving back to the beach with the stash not hidden was just crazy. We needed to get a connection in Cantamar.

The following night we met Herbie and he took us to the motel. We gave him our money, he said he would be right back. It took hours for him to return, the whores were all over us. When he finally returned he only had four kilos and thirty jars of pills. He said that it was really dry for pot. We took what he had and drove back to Cantamar. When we got there the girls were really freaked out because we had been gone for so long they thought we had gotten busted.

In the morning Jon and I stashed the drugs and then headed out to surf. While we were out there a Mexican surfer and a guy from San Diego joined us. We started talking and made friends. After surfing I invited them to smoke a joint, they said, "sure, we have some too". I asked Miguel, the one from Mexico, if he could get kilos. He told me he could get twenty five dollar kilos in Rosarito. That sounded great so I asked him if I could get some next week. He showed me where he lived and where he surfed then gave me his phone number so I could get in touch with him when I returned.

Mid Sunday afternoon Jon and I headed to the border, in our separate cars, and inched our way through the line and

Mexican peddlers. We both had surfboards and pretty girls beside us. We were all sunburned from the beach and we each had pottery and baskets for a front. Though in different lines, we both crossed the border at the same time without any problems.

This was Jon and Judy's first time smuggling, both were excited about how easy it was. Now we had a connection out at the beach, no more dangerous trips through Tijuana, poor Herbie wouldn't be making money from us anymore, T.J. was just too dangerous.

When we got back home, I had people waiting for me who wanted pot and pills. Jon's people, in Anaheim, snatched up as much as he would sell; He was selling faster than me and then even started selling my stash. He was ready to go back to Mexico almost immediately.

Life in Orange County had shortly evolved into a drug and psychedelic culture for everyone, I knew, under thirty years old. The music had psychedelic lyrics like "Judy in the sky with diamonds", Donovan with "Sunshine", Peter Paul and Mary with "Puff the magic dragon" and then Cheech and Chong's movie "Up in smoke". I could go on and on. People were burning incense, meditating and the flower children drove around in their cars with big flowers on the sides. People over thirty didn't like us and the cops and narcs would search hippie cars for no reason busting people. We hated them and they hated us, the goings on the streets were "gastapo."

During this time Jon and I did multiple Mexico scams, with our Mexican friend Miguel, but pot was getting scarce and we could hardly score. There was plenty of pot in Mexico, just not at the border. We kept on smuggling pills, but I wanted pot.

Six months had passed and one day my mom handed me the dreaded letter from the draft board. I opened it and it read "You are hereby ordered for induction to the army". As I read on it said for me to bring only a toothbrush that I would be leaving from L.A. to Fort Ord. The date was three weeks away. I was expecting another pre-induction physical not and induction. At this point they weren't messing around with me, they were taking me.

Everyone I talked to, my mom, Judy, my brother, said the same thing "don't go". I was afraid if I didn't go I would be thrown in jail like Mohammad Ali. In three weeks I was on the bus with fifty or more other draftees. I went through the physical all day and at the last they noticed that I had had an eye injury and had limited sight out of that eye. That saved me from Fort Ord, they rejected me. At the end of a long stressful day I was back on the bus going back to my world in Orange County. When I got home that night I told my mom what had happened she along with all my friends were glad for me. They all thought the next time they saw me I would be in an army uniform fresh out of boot camp.

I stayed home with my Mom and Dad that evening, which was very unusual. I had the new surfer magazine and I wanted to read up on the main feature, which was San Blas Mexico, home of the second longest wave in the world.

The next day I saw Judy and asked her if she would like to go to San Blas, located one thousand miles down the main land in Mexico by car for three weeks. I told her I was dropping out of school. We could have a great time and when we got back we could move in together and have lots of money from the kilos we would bring back. That day I surfed with Jon; we talked, I needed a vacation after my near miss with the draft. I said I wanted to surf in the tropical waters down south and score some kilos. I asked him if he was interested in going with us but he said he couldn't go this time and wished me luck.

3

Tropical breezes

I PUT TOGETHER FIVE HUNDRED DOLLARS TO purchase twenty five kilos of pot down in San Blas Mexico. Judy and I applied for our Visas, car insurance, necessary documents to travel by car down the mainland of Mexico. I mapped out our trip down, the time it would take and packed our bags for our long journey into the mainland of Mexico to Mazatlan then onto San Blas to surf and buy cheap pot.

We left Huntington Beach, CA at ten o'clock pm and headed for Nogales, a border town crossing into Mexico. We crossed the border at five o'clock am, fifty miles past Nogales we were stopped at the checkpoint to show our visas and car insurance, we were on our way.

I didn't have a connection, just a general knowledge of where to get good kilos, for as low as five dollars to ten dollars and where to surf the best waves in Mexico. From the checkpoint, approximately seven hundred fifty miles to Mazatlan, it would be necessary to drive fifteen hours straight to get there by sunset. This was a long trip through perilous Mexican desert roads riddled with potholes, farm equipment, speeding buses, trucks, animals, washed out roads and bridges marked with black oil burning pots. We did hit a few custom checkpoints but sailed through without any problem. Occasionally small desert towns would pop up with people living in old abandoned railroad cars or just hanging out. These areas were desolate, never much traffic going north or south, how did these people survive?

We came upon Santa Ana, a desolate desert town, next to Hermisillio, a clean jewel of a town, stuck in the middle of the Mexican desert. This was where the road turns and heads toward the California Gulf at Guaymas, a well know sport fishing resort and shrimp boats fleets. Immediately after Guaymas, the road turns into a long desert drive again with occasional little side café's with meats and chicken hanging outside with flies all over them, for making tacos, next the road lead us through the capitol, Culican, which was big, ugly, and full of traffic and cops.

Our next stop was finally Mazatlan, which is on the coast. The road curves through dangerous mountains and lowlands. The road was riddled with dead horses and cows that had wondered onto the highway and were hit by speeding trucks and busses. Vultures were feasting on these animals cluttering the road. Two hundred more delirious miles to Mazatlan, we hoped to make it by sunset.

We made it to Mazatlan just in time for a beautiful sunset, drove on the main beach road, which was littered with six to fifteen story hotels right across from the beach. We found a safe hotel with fenced in protective parking and checked in. The luxury hotel was ten dollars for two persons, with balconies facing Mazatlan bay, opening to the sea breezes, a beautiful green blue ocean.

Mazatlan Bay is a tourist city with boardwalks and streets littered with cabanas, fishing boats and all sorts of locals selling their wares, looking to make a buck off the tourists. We changed into our bathing suits and hit the warm Mexican waters. The hotels offer tropical drinks on the beach at the cabanas so we relaxed with a tequila sunrise. Salespeople of all ages came up with puppets, jewelry, hammocks and much-wanted "yeska", marijuana. I was given some good green as a sample from a fisherman hoping to make a sale. He was eyeing us while leaning against his fishing boat on the beach. He was wearing huaraches, baggie old long pants and had his shirt open exposing his chest tanned from years in the water fishing. He offered larger quantities and better qualities, if I wanted, from a farmhouse in the country out of town. This was what I was there for. I was interested but we were cautious and I did not let him know we were continuing on to San Blas in the morning. I had heard I could score good large kilos there.

The next morning I awoke to the smell of the sea and a mild tropical breeze. I got out of bed, lit a joint and walked out on the balcony which looked down on the beach and over the boardwalk. The boardwalk was mostly empty except for the fishermen getting ready for their day of fishing. I turned to Judy, standing behind me, handed her the joint and told her we would stop here again on our way back home. We took our showers, put on minimal clothing, checked out of the hotel and headed south.

San Blas was one hundred eighty miles from Mazatlan over slow winding roads with an average speed of about thirty miles per hour. The roads were similar to African plains. It would be about a five hour trip from Mazatlan to the turn off to San Blas. When we reached the turnoff down to the coast, almost immediately, the drive and terrain made a drastic change into a twisty road winding down steep jungle terrain for fifty miles. Iguanas crossed the road everywhere; we could only travel fifteen to twenty miles per hour.

When we arrived near San Blas, we saw a sign for Manachan Bay; I knew there was good surfing there. We turned and drove down a two mile jungle road covered with a canopy of trees and vines tunneling out onto a beautiful bay. We sat and took in the beauty of the place, coconut trees, ominous green jungle mountains toped with white puffy clouds leading down to a white sandy beach and waves at the distance point. We drove slowly on the sand for a mile or so before we came to the point and I melted when I saw two white guys surfing perfect three to four foot waves alone. I asked Judy if she minded hanging out on the beach while I surfed. She knew I had to do it. I paddles out, they said they were from Florida, I said " I am from California." I asked them where a good place to stay was. They told me about San Blas, five miles away or Pepe's hotel, a small two story blue and white building right there at Manachan Bay, that was where they were staying. They went on to tell me that the staff was straight out of an old slap stick comedy. Pepe, the owner dad, wore his underwear way outside his pants, his wife was the cook and you never knew what you were getting to eat and then his daughter, nicknamed "I spy." They told me she was the maid and she would sneak around in and out of rooms all day, but the rooms were only one dollar and sixty cents a night for two and right where the waves were. After we surfed for a while I asked them about pot and kilos. They said there was lots of pot, excellent lime green and I could get it anywhere but to be careful, there were lots of bandits and federallys, who dressed like cowboys. The local federallys drove around in pickup trucks with men in the back dressed with belts of bullets and rifles in hand ready for a bust, a set up, to rob you, throw you in jail, rape your woman, make you confess to a crime or even kill you. Other than that, this was a paradise for surfers and smugglers.

Judy and I drove up to the hotel, went in, sure enough there was Pepe with his underwear belted outside his pants and his hair a mess. We paid for our room and then went up to the second floor to see what we got. The room was an even bigger joke. It had a tiny bed, a toilet under the shower and a tin can sticking out of the wall for air. We were the only guests besides the Florida guys and Pepe's family. We unpacked our bags, had great sex and then took a nap.

The next morning we drove into San Blas, five miles away, a fishing town of three thousand. We entered on a small paved two lane road passed the town square with a large fountain and a Kodak store we stopped in to get some film. In the store there was one camera for sale and maybe ten roles of miscellaneous types of film. There was a couple mom and pop cafés in town, the guys from Florida told me their favorite restaurant was McDonalds, not the same McDonalds we knew in the states. The menu was very limited, carne and beans, fish and rice, beer or lemonade. Dinner cost us three peso's, which at that time was about twenty five cents American money. The food was good, as long as you kept the flying bugs out of it. There were big ceiling fans above the tables knocking bugs down and right onto your food. We did see a few dingy hotels in town and decided that Pepe's was the best place for us to stay.

We stayed at Manachen Bay most of the time we were there, except when we would go into town to get away from the millions of mosquitoes that came out of the jungle every afternoon. Sometimes we drove halfway around the bay, to Santa Cruz, stopping off at a jungle path that lead to the most fantastic rainforest. The rainforest was complete with a river, pools, waterfalls and big warm rocks. The forest, in the shadow of the mountains, was cool in the afternoons so the big warm rocks felt so good after a swim in the river.

San Blas was a friendly town we liked to visit, but the federally racing around town in their trucks with their guns were freaky. Every evening was very festive. The people would all come out and socialize while the children would play foosball and scream with excitement. Every evening two men came rushing down the street with what looked like weed blowers on their backs, it was unbelievable, they were blowing poisonous clouds to kill the mosquitoes in town. The kids would stop playing their games and frolic through the clouds.

In the town there was an open air prison we would walk by and try to get a peek inside, but with all the federally around it was scary.

After two weeks of dodging federally and the spies at Pepe's hotel I decided it would be safer to score in Mazatlan. The waters in Manachen bay were shark infested but the surfing was great. One afternoon I helped some local fisherman pull a huge shark up out of the waters. They had an eighteen foot boat and this shark was bigger than their boat. I pulled open the jaws of the fish and there were rows and rows of enormous sharp teeth with a throat opening big enough to swallow a man whole. It was not a good feeling knowing this was the type of shark I was surfing with.

Packing up and checking out of Pepe's was a bummer but, it was time. Once back in Mazatlan, I decided to score from the fisherman I had met. Just as we expected, there he was by his boat and when he saw me he smiled, I smiled back. Later we discussed a buy of twenty kilos, the price and when we would do it. He didn't have a car so this meant a dangerous drive with him would be necessary. If the local police saw us traveling together they would stop us for sure.

The only way we could pull this off was to travel at night for concealment.

I left Judy at the hotel; it was much too risky to take her along. The fisherman and I traveled north of Mazatlan, past a check station, hoping not to be seen or randomly stopped. A mexican and a californian traveling together would be suspect of a pot score. We would get busted or robbed.

We made it past a desolate checkpoint thirty miles north of Mazatlan, and onto a dirt road heading into brush and trees. Shortly, a toothless Mexican stepped in front of my VW and gestured to stop. He quickly jumped in and started pointing and speaking quietly as we drove the dirt road miles, up and down hills. We came to a small village of about half a dozen mud huts, dogs were barking, the fear was whelming up inside of me, but I didn't want to show it. We made it through the village unnoticed.

Suddenly we made a quick turn, around some trees, and stopped, almost running down a barking dog, in front of a large mud hut with open windows and a tarp for a door. A pack of dogs came running up to the VW, the farmer came out and motioned us to get out of the car and follow him. We entered the two room hut where his family slept. Little ninos, ninas, his wife, dogs and birds. We went into the second room where he uncovered and revealed four hundred to five hundred kilos. At that moment I felt big time, even though I could only buy twenty kilos at ten dollars a piece. We sat around under oil burning lamps and smoked pot discussing me coming back to buy two hundred kilos, after I sold the twenty.

The fisherman and I hustled the twenty kilos out to the

VW, they filled the back seat area much more than I had expected. If you could imagine a bail of hay in the back seat of a VW, that's how it looked. I thought if we make it back to the hotel past the checkpoint, we would be lucky. As we drove out of the hills, on the windy dirt roads, we made several wrong turns, we didn't have the toothless Mexican to show us the way. Somehow, after about two hours, we found the road back.

We turned south and headed back towards Mazatlan. There was no one on the road except my VW, California plates, a white guy, a Mexican and a bale of pot in the back seat. When we were coming up to the dreaded checkpoint we were holding our breath that they would be asleep, drunk or something. The checkpoint looked quiet; we passed it going fifty miles an hour. Just as we passed, the patrol car next to the checkpoint hut turned its red lights on and then off, this scared the heck out of us. For some unknown reason, they didn't follow us but we were afraid they might have called ahead to Mazatlan.

At three o'clock am we drove into Mazatlan, half expecting the federally to be waiting and looking for my VW, which would be easy to see since the only things about were homeless dogs, cats and bums. The fisherman lead me up a little alley, to his home, he jumped out and I drove off quickly so as not to attract any attention.

I drove back to the hotel scared to death. As I approached the protected parking area there was a yard attendant half asleep at the driveway. I had to stop to be cleared before entering the parking area. I saw him look at the giant hump in my back seat, but what could I do. I drove past him and parked. When I got back to the room Judy was crying, she was scared that I had gotten arrested or killed. I was lucky to be alive, much less free. This amazing score was over.

The next morning I got up early to try and conceal this bulk of kilos in a small VW for the trip back to the U.S. through all the checkpoints, federally and towns. I hid the kilos behind the back seat, under the car and in a trap door, I had made prior to the trip. It didn't all fit well but it was all I could do. Our trip back would be non-stop, one thousand miles in one day, on mexican roads, stopping at check points and for gas only.

To say the least, this was a very scary trip back. The pot was not hidden very well, we were almost out of money and we needed to take an even more dangerous road, unknown to me, to avoid detection crossing the border to soon at Nogales. This made it necessary to take a little used road inside Mexico that skirted the U.S. all the way to Tijuana. The road nearly killed us many times. It was so treacherous through mountains, potholes, cliffs, a terrible rainstorm and driving for over twenty hours but we had no choice but to keep going, we couldn't take the chance crossing any Mexican mainland borders to the U.S. We would be certain to get busted; the customs officers know that most cars coming from mainland Mexico are smuggling drugs.

Somehow we made it to Tijuana and we were zombies from all the travel. We stopped at a dive hotel for the night, we just couldn't go on. After a night of rest in a broken down hotel bed, we got up early and headed for an area just south of Rosarito Beach to clean up the VW. We scraped off the tourista decals, which identify a vehicle that has been down the mainland, wash the car so it didn't look so traveled and buy some baskets before crossing the border.

The VW was shiny and clean, both of us showered, Judy put some make-up on and I shaved and combed my hair. Both of us tried to look fresh and well groomed. We hoped we were ready to pass inspection and be on our way to get rich. We hugged each other for luck and headed off to the border crossing forty five minutes away. The crossing of the border in San Diego was a nervous one. The kilos could be found with a minor search so we hoped to give a good impression of two people down for the day to buy a few baskets. When we reached the front of the line we were asked our citizenship, I replied "U.S.", and then we were asked how long we had been there, "one day," I replied, and we were asked if we bought the baskets in our car, which I thought was odd. Next the officer said, "Let me see the inside of your elbows". I had never been asked this before so I showed him the back of my arms, the top and the sides. When he realized I didn't have a clue what he was talking about he just laughed and said, "Go on." I thought to myself, thank you mama, we made it.

4

The plan

WE WERE EXCITED, BUT EXHAUSTED, WHEN WE made it across to the U.S. and now going home, after a three-week drive thru mostly desert wastelands on the mainland of Mexico. I was excited to have kilo's from deep down in Mexico; I knew this pot would be worth a lot of money. I dropped Judy off at her house and then headed home and slept until the next day. My Mom woke me up and again complained about all the phone calls. I jumped up and told her I had to go, I had to register at Orange Coast College, she didn't buy that and stormed out of my room.

Instead of going to Orange Coast College I went down to Huntington Beach and found a small little white beach house and rented it. I called Judy and asked her to move in with me. We bought furniture at the goodwill and started moving in the next day. I found a great hiding place in the garage for the kilos, ordered a phone and went shopping for food. I was ready to start selling. I called Jon first and told him where I lived and invited him over to smoke some pot. When Jon arrived I had a choice kilo picked out for him. This pot was loady, tasted well and the kilos looked like big loaves of bread, probably three pounds. I showed him pictures of San Blas, the great waves, the jungles and the big hotels in Mazatlan. San Blas was fantastic but the federally and the bandits are out to bust surfers.

The next day, Jon and I were at the Huntington Beach Pier, surfing as usual, Judy told me she had sold three kilos to my friends in Laguna for one hundred fifty each. She said they wanted to buy them all. She told them they would have to come back after I got home. That night so many people came by my house I started to get paranoid. I started telling my friends that I had sold everything, sorry.

A couple days' later things had slowed down to the pace I wanted. I sold fifteen kilos and broke up two kilos into ten dollar lids, I had made three thousand and I still had two kilos left.

My good friend Gary and his wife came by one evening, we were both potheads, and I showed him our pictures of San Blas and the mainland. He wanted to know how I did the score. I told him about the surfing and the prices of the kilos, seeing hundreds of kilos, and my connection. By the next evening Gary called me and said he had an offer. He asked if I was willing to let him bring his uncle over to meet me. He said his uncle was willing to drive back a load of pot from Mazatlan. I decided to meet his uncle and told him to come on over. When they got there I was surprised how straight looking Gary's uncle was and he was ready and willing to scam. He was perfect!

I thought, "We're on our way to big bucks!"

5

Unnecessary danger

THE PLAN WE MADE DURING THE EVENING was for them to take two days getting to Mazatlan, stopping half way down in the small fishing town of Guaymas, spend the night, then the next day complete the drive arriving in Mazatlan. They would check into the same hotel Judy and I had stayed at, park the sedan in the protective garage, to maintain it's concealment until the score was complete, and keep a very low profile until I arrived. I would take a flight from LAX to Mazatlan, take a taxi to the hotel and then call them. Once settled in at the hotel I would let the fisherman see me. He would know why I was there, and then signal me to a meeting place. I explained to my friends that I had to stay clear of the hotel, on these meetings with the fisherman, to avoid prying eyes, police and maintain security.

Also, my intention was to arrange a meeting at the fisherman's house my first night to set up the score and express my concerns. I wanted to hide the kilos in the car immediately after the score to avoid a dangerous drive back to the hotel. He would need his own ride back from the score this time; it was the only way to make the drive safe. If all went as discussed, with the fisherman, we would go ahead with the score the following night. I discussed this plan over and over with Gary and his Uncle and if everyone did as planned, everything would go smoothly.

Once the scam started, I was confident Gary and his uncle would take it slow and easy on the way down to Mazatlan, taking two days, but they didn't. For some reason they drove straight through arriving a day early, which I was not aware of. I figured they were still on the road and would arrive the same day I did.

This is the point the plan started to unravel and go bad. These guys were there a day early, doing their own thing and not keeping a low profile for themselves or the car as instructed. They did everything the opposite. During this one-day, they were making themselves known and seen together as they drove the sedan, with California plates, all day up and down the main strip. They even had the sedan parked out in front of the hotel instead of in the protected parking lot. Let me tell you, the local people are not stupid, they know or suspect surfer types of "pot smoking" and with a big car "smugglers." You can see the importance of keeping the car concealed in the back garage but they didn't. Not only was the car an issue, they also were on the beach in front of the hotel buying trinkets from the locals and smoking pot given to them by local peddlers. This was very stupid. Also, they spotted the fisherman, my connection, next to his fishing boat and even though I told them not to talk with him, they did. They approached him and told him they had a big car they had driven down and that they had one thousand dollars to buy one hundred kilos. These dumb guys completely blew it. They are probably the reason for the events that were about to unfold. They just didn't understand the importance of keeping a low profile and their mouths shut.

When I arrived on the second day, I saw they were partying, exposing themselves to the locals, driving the car, blowing their concealment and the plan. I couldn't believe what I was seeing; they just thought everything was cool. They thought they were big time smugglers from California. When they saw me they could tell I was very upset and asked, "what's wrong?" I told them I couldn't believe what I was seeing and that they were blowing it. They proceeded to tell me they had made contact with the fisherman, told him they had one thousand dollars to by one hundred kilos and that it was all set up for that night. This was all so unbelievable, they had disregarded the entire plan. They blew their cover, the concealment of the car, they had made contacts with the locals, there was no telling what they had said to them, and making contact with the fisherman and setting up a score.

They were exposing us to so many dangers. At this point what could I do but go ahead with the score, set up for that night, and hope we would be okay.

I went ahead and met with the fisherman, he was surprised I was back so soon, and I told him the two guys were part of my plan. He acted surprised that I was involved with their score; he said they were stupid and I agreed. I told him I knew they had set up a buy for that night and he confirmed it with a noticeably odd reply. I wish I could have told the future at that point; I would have known what his body language meant.

I told him what my concerns were during and after the score and that I wanted to avoid any unnecessary danger. I told him of my plan to conceal the kilos in the sedan as soon as we scored and that we would have to leave him behind when we hit the main road, south to Mazatlan, so as not to attract suspicion. So it was set, I decided to go ahead with the score Gary, his uncle and the fisherman had set up.

The score required the same drive as the first time. We drove at night so it would be easier to pass the checkpoint, with a Mexican, approximately fifty miles north of Mazatlan. Thirty minutes later we turned off the main road, onto a dirt road, into the brush heading into the mountains toward the farmer's house. The same dirt road up and down, around quick corners and then the terrain turns quickly into a mountainous jungle road filled with rocks, holes and occasional horses, rabbits or stray dogs, it was very dark and quiet. From what I remembered, we were headed for the farmers house, I wondered when the toothless peon would step out of the jungle trees to be our guide the rest of the way. Suddenly, the fisherman made an unusual request. He wanted us to back into some bushes and stop; we were half way in the bushes and half way on the road, which didn't seem safe. When the car stopped the fisherman jumped out, went into the bushes and came out with a sample kilo. I said," I don't like this, I want to go straight to the farmers house." Ignoring what I had just said he motioned for us to go ahead and try the pot. We opened the end of the kilo and started to roll a joint when all of the sudden we saw a car creeping around the turn on the dark road. Here we were parked sideways on the road like sitting ducks. The car stopped thirty feet away, turned its lights off and sat there for three or four minutes. Suddenly, they turned their lights on and crept forward towards us. All I could say was "oh shit! It's a bust". We threw out the kilo. The other car started to move up and around us. I thought they were going to go around us but they crashed into the front of the sedan breaking their own headlights. The car then backed up another thirty feet and stopped for another five minutes or so. This time they moved forward quickly and three Mexicans jumped out with guns, a uniformed federally with a pistol and two gruff looking peons with rifles cocked and aimed at the car. They closed in on us and motioned with their rifles for us to get out of our car.

The reality taking place was a true to life nightmare. Here we were three white guys out in the middle of nowhere, no one else, besides us, knew we were there besides these bandits with guns. What did they want, our cash, car or the kilo? Would we leave there alive? How were we going to get out of this?

It didn't take but a couple of minutes to find out what they wanted, after they got us out of the car. They started questioning us and wanted to know where the one thousand dollars was to buy the one hundred kilos. I wondered how they knew that information. The only thing I could think of, at that moment was, "no, we're here for a little yeska and women, were just tourists, nothing more". Their reply was they knew better, that we were there to buy kilos, that the fisherman sells kilos to surfers.

This questioning went on and on then the Federaly set his pistol on top of our car and got inside to search for guns, money and pot. Leaving his loaded gun on top of the car right next to me was unbelievable. Was this dumb luck or not? If I grabbed the pistol I probably would not be able to fire it or worse, I would miss and a gun battle would break out. When I thought about it, I thought no way! I didn't want to shoot anybody or get shot myself. I was just a scared pot smoking scamming kid of nineteen.

The standoff was going on and on and the bandits were getting less confidant that we were making a score or if we really had the one thousand dollars. Many times they asked us where the money and pot were and I just stuck to the same story that we were there for yeska and women and that we were just tourists, that's all. I could see that maybe they were starting to believe us so I bribed them with one hundred dollars. They grabbed the fisherman, pushed him aside and came back to us starting the process all over again demanding the one thousand dollars. We just kept to the story, we have no money, and we want no kilos, yeska and women only. Time and time again they would grab the fisherman, interrogate him, then push him back to us and drill us again.

After awhile it became obvious that the fisherman was in on the rip off. He kept reassuring the bandits that we had the money. Things were at a stand still of sorts when one of the guys with me showed me a gun. If the Mexicans saw the gun, they would start shooting for sure. I told him to throw that gun in the bushes quick, luckily he did.

Finally after the federally searched the car for the last time I could tell they were trying to figure out what to do next. They decided to separate us. They took Gary and his uncle and put them in the Mexican car leaving me outside to negotiate with them. It was obvious that they knew from the fisherman that I was the main guy. They only wanted to negotiate with me and the other two guys would be going to jail. At this point I knew the gig was up and they were going to get the money or kill us, they weren't going to take anybody to jail. I decided to give them my five hundred dollars and see if that was good enough. It seemed fine temporarily that is until that bastard fisherman started talking. Now they wanted the other five hundred dollars or else. I knew this was it; they would get the money now or kill us and search our bodies after we were dead. I told them to let me talk to the other two guys, reluctantly they agreed.

I stepped over to the Mexicans car where I told Gary and his uncle that the fisherman had set us up, he was in on the rip-off and that they knew we had the money. I told them I gave up my five hundred dollars and now they had to give up theirs or we would be killed. I got the rest of the money and went over to these bandits and gave it to them. Now they had the whole thousand dollars. I could tell they had never seen money like this before and they were freaked. I shouted, "now let us go, you got our money." I couldn't understand what they were saying exactly, but I knew they were deciding whether or not to kill us or let us go. I think the reason they didn't kill us was the fisherman's decision. He didn't think we were aware that he was in on the rip off so there was no harm in letting us go. It was good that we didn't let him know we were on to him. They finally let us go but said they were going to take the fisherman to jail. They gave us the kilo they had busted us with, a little gas money and told us to get out of Mexico and to not go back to Mazatlan.

Once we left them and found our way back to the road to Mazatlan, we parked our car at the hotel and went to our rooms thanking God to be alive. The next morning the guys were leaving at four o'clock am to drive back home. I told them to get rid of the kilo the bandits had given us that it was too dangerous to travel with and the car was possibly marked. I phoned the airport and changed my ticket so I could leave the next morning. I took a taxi to the airport at six thirty am the following morning, even though my flight was not until eight o'clock am, I had about an hour to wait. During the late sixties the Mazatlan airport was one building and one airstrip with a few wooden tables. There were no other passengers in the airport at that hour, I sat at a table by the window and then suddenly to my surprise John Wayne walked in, with a broken arm, and sat down. I later learned that he had been there on location filming and broke his arm and was going home to heal. We sat there all alone in the airport and we never said a word to each other. It was so weird, last night I was being ripped off in the Mazatlan mountains by bandits and the next morning, a few hours later, I was sitting with a legend.

The flight back to LA was uneventful. When I arrived and got through customs, I saw Judy waiting for me. I told her all about the trip, how the guys blew it and how we barely escaped with our lives. I then explained to her I advised them to get rid of the kilo, but that they probably didn't, they were so stupid. I was going home to Huntington Beach, broke and in need of a job, scared, but happy to be alive.

6

The decision

JUDY AND I WERE LIVING TOGETHER IN the little beach
house in Huntington, I was broke, out of stash and ready to
get a job. My dad was a foreman for a big contractor so I had
asked him for a job as a carpenter, I knew the trade, I had
worked many summers for my dad growing up. He told me
he would hire me but I had to pull my weight, I assured him
I would. I told him I was broke so he loaned me the money to
get my journeyman carpenters card from the union. Judy and
I were surviving on oatmeal for the next couple weeks until
I got paid. My first paycheck was for two hundred dollars, I

bought a kilo for one hundred dollars and made thirty-five lids out of it and sold them for ten dollars each. I was working as a carpenter during the week, making good money, while dealing at night making excellent money. Three weeks ago I was out of cash and now I was making five hundred dollars a week, had a house and all the pot I could smoke. Then the rain came and knocked me out of work, but the job was coming to an end anyway. I told my dad I was going to go skiing in Tahoe and when I got back I hoped there would be work for me on the next track.

I got back from Tahoe two weeks later and there wasn't any work for me on the job site, but, the job served it's purpose, I made money to start dealing again.

Now another new era was unfolding in Orange County. The brotherhood was bringing in a new smoke called hash. It was from Nepal, Afghanistan and India. They were bringing it in by the ton and making a lot of money. Some of the Laguna brotherhood were now filthy rich and Laguna was getting really hot. The Mystic Art World store was being watched day and night by the narcs, they knew some of the guys were the big scammers, they wanted them. The hillside homes back in Bluebird canyon and Thalia street were also being watched, you had to really keep your eyes open for narcs when you were there. My childhood innocents was long gone, I was a dealer of pot and hash and liked it. I figured I would be rich soon. Some of the big hash dealers slipped out of Laguna and moved to Hawaii and San Francisco. I was still scoring in Laguna, but at times it got scary, I wanted hash and that's where it was so, I had to take my chances.

The music scene was getting bigger with groups like the Beatles, the Stones and English groups galore. New names like Jimmy Hendricks, Janis Joplin and Jefferson Airplane came out of San Francisco. The groups were getting together and putting on a pop festival in Monterey California that expected to draw half a million people, Judy and I decided to go to this global event. I rolled at least thirty joints to last the two days. When we got within five miles of the festival people were walking to the concert area, talk about some psychedelic freaks, these people were definitely dropouts of society. We saw wild hair, wild clothes, people looking crazy high on LSD while pounding on tambourines, dancing in the streets throwing flowers, this was a hippie event. I had never seen anything like this before. We had a rendezvous place to meet some people we knew from Laguna, now living in Berkeley, who dealt pure mescaline. They said I could make a lot of money dealing it.

We met up with our friends, somehow among all the bizarre hippies, they said there was no way to get tickets or even close to the concert by car. We would have to walk five to six miles to even get close. I decided I didn't want to go, it was too crazy, I told my friends I was going to drive back home. Before leaving, my friend Rob told me that San Francisco was a psychedelic warehouse with large laboratories producing pure mescaline and if I wanted I could be their Orange County connection and make it big. He then gave me a sample I could make one hundred doses out of. He told me if I were interested to call him the following week and he would fly down a couple ounces. "Okay, I'll call you", I said.

When Judy and I got home we tried mescaline, just a little, and it was great. I called Rob the following Monday and told him I liked the mescaline and wanted to know how much it would cost me per ounce. Rob told me he would just give me an ounce and help me dose it up. He assured me that I could make big bucks. I picked Rob up at the Orange County airport. On the way back to my house he explained the laboratory procedures, the cut and size of capsule I needed. We set everything up, back at the house, and he showed me what to do. He said "have fun, now take me back to the airport."

Jon, Sharon, Judy and I started the tedious job of dosing up the mescaline; I realized why Rob wanted to leave before we got started. We had enough mescaline to fill one thousand caps. This was a very lengthy project and we were all stoned within thirty minutes because we weren't wearing protective gloves or masks. We only capped one hundred doses; we had nine hundred more to go.

Eventually we got it all capped up, one thousand doses just like Rob had said. He said it would sell for five dollars a hit or one hundred for three hundred. I was going to become a three-drug connection to all my friends, psychedelics, hash and pot. I was still running the border occasionally when I had the time, but had slowed down because President Nixon had invoked "operation intercept" at the San Diego/Tijuana border to stop drug smuggling. The customs agents searched every vehicle and the lines were backed up five to six miles and it was taking three to four hours to get across. The drivers were very irate and it was miserable, also, Mexico was getting really hot. Our government was putting pressure on the Mexican

President to clean up their border town drugs and corruption. This made scoring in Baja extremely dangerous.

When we did go to Mexico, kilo's were hard to get, I started scoring pills, whites and reds, there was a lot of money in them. Everything I did, I made money. Hash was my chosen drug of choice, but I sold whatever made money quick.

Some of my friends, I dealt mescaline to in Orange County, were now going back and forth to a hippie flop house on Oahu. All these guys wanted from life was to get high on LSD and now mescaline. Occasionally, they would ask me why I didn't take some mescaline to the islands. I wanted to go to Hawaii, but I couldn't find the time. I was flying to San Francisco every week to pick up mescaline, it was in such demand, and I was in demand. Jon wanted to go to Mexico, to score, and I could hardly find the time to do that.

The decision to go to Hawaii happened one night while hanging out with Judy, Jon and Sharon. We were looking over Surfer Magazine, after surfing all day at the Huntington pier, smoking hash and eating a vegetarian dinner. We decided that Judy and I would take an ounce of mescaline to the islands to sell at the "flophouse" and make a connection in Haleiwa with Jon's friend Smiley to buy hash. I flew up to San Francisco the next morning, scored two ounces of mescaline and flew back the same day. Judy went shopping for samsonite luggage. I asked Jon to stay at my beach house and he happily agreed. Judy and I were all set to go to the islands supplied with lots of cash, drugs and excitement.

7

"Wow!" Off to the North Shore

WE WERE UP EARLY, GOING DOWN THE five freeway from Orange County, with an ounce of pure mescaline taped to my body, on our way to LAX then on to Hawaii. Beautiful beaches, surfing and great days filled with pot, mescaline and hash. I had been a surfer since I was thirteen and this was my first trip to Hawaii, I had dreamed of this day and here it was.

We arrived at the Honolulu International airport at about

three pm. We took a taxi to Waikiki and checked into a hotel one half block from the beach. The room had a balcony looking out on the surfers at Waikiki beach and we watched our first Hawaiian sunset as we smoked a joint. That evening we took a swim in the warm Hawaiian waters, which were unbelievable. After our swim we walked up and down Waikiki, just being tourist, exploring the International Market Place and just enjoying our first night.

The next morning was spent in a taxi going to herb, health food and appliance stores. These stores carried the items we needed to build a laboratory for the processing of the mescaline. We purchased a dietary scale for measuring and a blender to mix in the cut. We bought one pound of carob powder, for the cut, and one thousand gelatin capsules. Once blended this mixture would be the ingredients for one thousand capsules, or doses of potent mescaline. Next would be the tedious task of filling the capsules, again we learned the reason chemists wear masks and gloves while doing this procedure, we were so high from the contact of the mescaline after doing caps.

We couldn't continue doing this tedious work any longer so we just went to the beach to gather ourselves. I ended up renting a surfboard and having a psychedelic fantasy. The process of filling the caps took us three days before we could cap all one thousand. We got a contact high every day at the end of our tedious work. When we were done I'd go surfing while Judy sunbathed.

On the fourth morning Judy and I rented a metal flake purple dune buggy to drive around the island. Our flop house friends, were excited to hear we were coming. They lived on the other side of the island from Waikiki, a very rainy but lush area. When we pulled up to their house, out came some long hair, bearded looking characters I hardly recognized. Immediately they wanted to try the mescaline, if they liked it they would buy three hundred doses right then, which they did. By the time the day was over they were totally psychedelic and reading Timothy Leary's psychedelic prayers and meditating. This wasn't really us, so we left to do some body-surfing at Sandy beach. We went back to their house the next day and they wanted to buy the other seven hundred doses. I only sold them five hundred doses at three dollars a piece. I was happy to sell almost all the mescaline but I wanted to save some for myself and for "making friends". This was great, two hundred doses left and plenty of profit to buy hash with, WOW!

The rest of the day our hippie friends showed us around the island. We were all high on mescaline, climbing ropes, and bunkers to get to water falls. Being so high made this a hair-raising trip. At the end of the day of hiking Judy and I said good bye and headed back to Waikiki. Now it was about time to go to the North Shore to see all the great surfing spots I'd seen pictures of, Waimea bay, Sunset Beach, Haleiwa and Velzeeland.

The next morning I was up at sunrise, smoking a joint on my balcony, watching Waikiki beach while Judy slept. The waves were only two or three feet and a few guys out. Just perfect for me I thought. I called the hotel desk and asked if they rented surfboards. They said they didn't but that one of the bellboys had gone back to the mainland and left an "old log" behind and I could use it if I wanted. "great", I said.

I walked down to Waikiki beach with this log on my head and paddled out. Waikiki, wow! I paddled, an old beat-up practically sinking board but, having a great time.

When I made it back to the hotel, Judy was up and had ordered us banana pancakes. We sat on the balcony looking over the ocean and enjoyed our breakfast. I got showered, Judy rolled some joints and we loaded up the buggy and took off to the North Shore.

Haleiwa was our destination. We were going there to find and meet a good surfer named Smiley who was a friend of a friend and hopefully, a good connection for me. I got the directions to his house before I left home from my friend Jon. He told me to tell Smiley who I was and where I was from and he would know it was all right to talk, he would help me score.

By mid morning we were driving through the pineapple fields, on our way to the North Shore, and then we crossed some final bridges and entered Haleiwa. It was a Hawaiian Knott's Berry Farm looking town that was filled with old store fronts with board walks, old locals, sandy surfers who looked like they just got out of the water, all wearing local made bathing suits and flippers. We stopped for a while to walk around, and then continued on. We passed unbelievable surfing spots that were so beautiful with palm trees, aqua blue waters and beautiful girls in bikinis. We came onto Sunset beach and decided to stop for a while. The sand and the water looked so nice; we laid out our towels, swam and just enjoyed the sun for the afternoon. We loved it!

About five O'clock we loaded up the buggy and drove back up Kam hwy, back to Haleiwa, to try to find Smiley. When we got into town we had to start looking for a dirt road that turned into a neighborhood of small wooden houses, made in World War II. Little Hawaiian houses. The road winds around for a couple blocks and dead ends at a red dirt driveway, which leads up to a little house that should be Smiley's house, according to the map. We found the road and house just as the map showed. It looked like a surfers place with surfboards outside and beach towels hanging here and there.

We pulled up in front of the house and out walked a young Hawaiian girl in a string bikini. She was a beautiful young girl with dark brown braided hair down her back, a Polynesian beauty with big round eyes, tight shapely lips, a figure beyond a young girl with big full breasts bulging from her suit top, ninty five pounds of a figure that might have been sculpted out of Playboy. I said "hi," but she did not reply. I looked at Judy and said "I think we are maybe at the wrong house," when out walked Smiley and said, "What's up." I started to say who I was and he said with a chuckle, "I know who you are, Jon's friend right?" I confirmed we were Jon's friends and he invited us in. I walked into a two-room house where they obviously lived on the floor. It was decorated by his Wahini with persian carpets, low tables with pillows and a mattress in the corner for sleeping. The floor was wood in some places and dirt in other places covered with carpets but, it was home to Smiley and you could tell he was proud of it.

Smiley was a short guy, about five foot eight, with short sandy colored hair, a real baby face but very good looking. He had the thin muscular legs of a true surfer, and mischievous light blue eyes, quick witted and a warm personality. When he was fifteen years old he had come to the island, from Orange County, California with his mother for a vacation and he wouldn't leave. His Mom finally decided to leave him there with some friends and one hundred dollars. All he wanted was the North Shore, perfect waves and girls. He lived a meager Hawaiian surfer lifestyle in old shacks and loved it. He became known as one of the best surfers on the Island, but he was never interested in being in surfer magazine, he was happy being a board shaper and a boxer fighter. He was one hundred and thirty five pounds of dynamite with two fists. Jon had told me that by the time he was nineteen or twenty he had established himself well on the North Shore. Smiley said, "grab a pillow and make yourselves at home". His Hawaiian beauty offered us freshly made mango guava papaya juice. I told him why I was there and what I wanted. "Jon said you would know the right people to get pounds of Afghani, elephant ears, known as hash, at a good price," I said. I wanted to score a pound or two depending on the price. He assured me that wouldn't be a problem. He said "this place has been flooded with hash for months" then he asked me if I wanted to try some. "Of course," I said ". He pulled out a bag and said, "Smell this.". He showed me two or three ounces of "Da kind, (good hash),". He then pulled out a hookah pipe and loaded it up. He heated up some coals and placed them atop the nuggets of hash and we smoked that hookah until our eyes ran, we coughed until we couldn't breath and drank gallons of his freshly made island juice. We got so stoned it was like taking LSD or mescaline. Smoking this way was the ultimate. When we took a break from smoking I asked Smiley about some surfing spots. He told me I should go out at Haleiwa where the surf was easy but good. He also told me I could borrow a board if I needed. He took me outside and showed me some fantastic boards. I thought to myself, if he only knew what I was riding that morning. He offered all but one for me to pick from. When I came back in the morning he would have a score set up for me. Before we left for the hotel I offered him some mescaline and he gladly accepted.

The drive back to Waikiki was a freaky trip. The roads were small and a bit treacherous in the dark and we were so stoned. It was late and we were driving this bizarre purple-flaked buggy through roads we didn't know but we made it back as usual, young, restless and fearless.

The next morning, after our banana pancakes and smoking some hash, we headed back to Haleiwa to pick up the board Smiley was letting me borrow. When we finally got down to the beach the waves were just as Smiley had said, easy and good, just right for me. I had a great morning surfing and afterwards Judy and I headed into town to have avocado sandwiches, Dr. Bronner chips and carrot juice at the local store. We sat on the boardwalk like locals. When we finished we decided to head back to Smiley's house to score.

When we drove up to Smiley's house, in our buggy, he

just laughed at us. Smiley said he had just returned from surfing at velzeeland. He also told me he had just talked with "Skinny" about the pounds I wanted to buy and that he was down to his last ten pounds and didn't think he wanted to sell any right now. I was bummed but Smiley said he would probably change his mind by the next day. That night we had dinner at Smiley's, his girlfriend prepared fish that Smiley had speared that day, in a tasty Hawaiian style.

The next day we drove back to Smiley's. He said Skinny had changed his mind; he would sell me a couple pounds. When we drove over to score I gave Smiley the money and waited outside, this I expected because scammers are paranoid of new people. As we were driving I pictured that Skinny lived in a house something like Smiley's, but, to my surprise, Skinny's house was and island paradise. He had a white house on about an acre of land with banana and Hawaiian fruit trees scattered on it. Half the grounds had beautiful green grass and a volleyball net. The other half had two horses, two dogs and a goat. The property sat about one half block off the beach. "He's just a casual guy" Smiley said, "who happened to make it big smuggling hash from Afghanistan and now is living out his dream".

After a few minutes Smiley came out of the house and said that Skinny changed his mind and would sell me 1 pound of hash for six hundred dollars but only if I paid him with one hundred doses of mescaline and three hundred dollars cash. Smiley had turned Skinny onto some of my mescaline while surfing and he loved it. That was the only way he would make the deal. He also said that if I came back next month he would have plenty of hash to sell and trade. I said "no problem." I made the buy.

After the buy we headed back to Smiley's place. I left the pound of hash at his house so I wouldn't have to be traveling with it. Smiley suggested we go surfing so we loaded up the buggy with a couple boards and headed off on the dirt road that lead us to velzeeland. It was beautiful with four to five foot bowls. I was a bit nervous but Smiley assured me that the surf was casual and he would stay right with me. I was surfing with the greatest surfers on the planet. Smiley cleared the way for me by telling his friends to watch out for me, he's from Huntington Beach and he'll probably run you down. This was Smiley's way, they'd know I was his friend and forgive inexperience and getting in their way. Before we paddled out, Smiley explained the break and reef we would be surfing over. "Be extremely careful on the inside of the big reef when the bowl sucks up the water over the coral it is only one or two feet deep. If you eat it there, it will slice you up like hamburger," Smiley smiled. We grabbed our boards and paddled out around fantastic bowls over treacherous reefs. My anxiety was pulsing through my veins until I dropped into my first bowl all alone. I was in heaven, this was paradise. This was the life I wanted to live.

Later that day we got back to Smiley's, I told him that Judy and I would be leaving the next day. I asked if I could call him to find out when the stash was in. He gave me his phone number and said "call me anytime." He then suggested that next time we came to the island that we should stay with him in the country, not Waikiki. He told me to just give him a call, and he would pick me up at the airport. Judy and I stayed for a few more hours smoking hash and listening to a Rod Stewart album. Smiley offered me the board I had borrowed for twenty doses of mescaline. I said "deal!" I gave him thirty doses, after that we bonded as friends. I told him our trip was over but I would be back, hopped into the buggy and drove away happy with a pound of "da-kind hash" and an island board.

8

Possibilities

WE ARRIVED BACK AT LAX EARLY IN the morning, after taking the "red eye flight", with a bit of jet lag. We pulled up to our little Huntington Beach house mid morning, excited to be home and to see our friends and tell them about our Hawaiian vacation.

The first person I saw was Jon. I couldn't wait to tell him about the beaches, surfing, Smiley's place and all the drugs. I showed him I had brought back a pound of the best elephant ear hash. He wanted to know if I got it from Smiley? "Yes I did, and there is plenty more at great prices." Jon wanted a few ounces.

Jon left and was back in less than an hour with his girl-friend and money. His girlfriend Sharon was a beauty. She was always dressed in black, her favorite color, and had that wonderful Marilyn Monroe hair, face and body. No one was immune to her when she wore one of her black bikinis, which was often. She would charge me up even after being around her a lot. Her sexiness was infectious and Jon always had her wear practically nothing. Everyone always told Jon to be sure to bring Sharon along. Jon sat down and I dropped the ounces in his lap, he smelled it and said, "It's Da kind." He wanted to buy half a pound. I invited him to smoke some with me while I thought about it. The hash was really loady stuff and Jon wanted it bad. I really didn't want to part with it so soon so I decided to sell him only a quarter pound.

Judy came in the room with cookies and tea and started telling Sharon, about the beautiful beaches we saw. I told Jon we experienced the Hawaiian daily life. "The North Shore was the vacation place for us, there was so much hash, big time scammers and beauties with bodies that you'd die for," I said. Then I told him that Smiley knew and surfed with the big timers, they were surfers just like we were. Those guys did big hash scams monthly and Smiley was in their inter-circle.

Smiley knew when the big loads of hash would come in from Afghanistan, India and Nepal. He told me it would sell quickly. As soon as he knew when it would arrive in Hawaii he would call. I had to be available to go back to the Islands at a moments notice.

The next week Smiley called and said a big load was coming in any day, I was on a plane back to Hawaii the very next day to buy ten pounds and to sell some more mescaline. Unfortunately, when I got there the hash had already arrived and was mostly gone. I was only able to get three pounds.

There was so much money to be made, middling pounds of hash at island prices, and moving it to the mainland, it sold fast! Big buyers were guaranteed one hundred to two hundred pounds each; a ten pound buy was peanuts. If I hadn't had mescaline as a bargaining chip, I probably would not have been able to get any at all. The Laguna guys, that were now island surfers, were bringing in up to a ton of hash per month. Most of the load would go to other parts of the country, fifty or one hundred pounds would flood the islands. These surfers were making hundreds of thousands of dollars a month.

These guys were buying island ranches, starting import export stores in malls and buying perspective land on other islands for future houses. They were no smarter than us only filthy rich, it looked so easy. I told Jon we could do a scam.

Jon and I were making a lot of money from mescaline and pounds of hash broken down into ounces. We were now taking trips to the islands once every month. We were making thousands and traveling every month, but we weren't getting filthy rich. We couldn't buy ranches or live on the island. "In-betweeners" never made the big bucks like the scammers who were bringing it in.

The multiple trips to the islands and never getting the amount of pounds we wanted was frustrating. Our appetite for big cash was at an all time high.

One of our trips to Smiley's was mostly just a three week vacation. While I was there Judy forwarded a letter to me from a friend in Germany that wanted some mescaline. That same week a load of hash came in and was sold to guaranteed buyers, even though we had been waiting for two weeks, we only got a few ounces. This was really frustrating. Smiley said, "You guys have the cash and a friend in Germany, maybe it's time to do your own scam". He suggested we buy a car in Germany and drive to Afghanistan to score. He told us that was how Skinny got started.

Our cash was close, but not enough for a big hash scam, maybe Germany was our break. If my friend in Germany was right, we could double our money easily and quickly. We headed back to Smiley's to talk it over and make plans.

9

Jon would go first

MY FRIEND IN GERMANY WAS IN THE Army, I had sold him pot, hash and mescaline when he lived Anaheim, but now he was abroad. In his letter he said it was like nothing we had ever seen, practically no laws against drugs. He said there was plenty of hash but no pot or psychedelics. He told us that our mescaline would be a good seller, better than Hawaii and more profit to be made. He stated he had a very good dealer friend there in Germany, he told him about our mescaline and if we could get some over there the market would be wide open for big profit.

Jon and I talked over this letter. Smiley thought this could be the break we needed to put together enough cash for an Afghanistan scam. It would be necessary to go to Germany anyway to buy the car we would need to drive to Afghanistan. We were banking on my friend, we needed additional quick cash.

Jon and I had fifteen thousand dollars but, Smiley told us we needed at least twenty thousand dollars to do an Afghan scam. Skinny had spent forty thousand on his last scam that netted two hundred pounds, this much is necessary for buying a car, traveling to and from Afghanistan, possible bribes to locals, police, customs and when we got back to Germany, buying a clean car to ship back to the states.

After talking over the possibilities, we decided that Jon or I should first go over there to see first hand how safe this could be done. We decided Jon would go first, see how reliable this dealer would be, how he would sell the mescaline, how much it would sell for and how long it would take. Also, he would go through customs in Frankfurt Germany to experience custom search. Once there he would find where we could stay and check into buying a car.

Two weeks went by while Jon was in Germany. I was in Hawaii selling mescaline and waiting to hear from him. When he did finally call he said, "Its good, looks safe."

Jon's report was that the customs were practically nothing landing in Germany. The dealers name was Russo. He was very cautious, low profile, and that most people didn't know he was a dealer. He had a network of clubs he general managed throughout Germany. He sold drugs to his club managers.

He had an apartment that we could stay at and he had a good source for buying cars. If the mescaline was good, it would sell quickly in his clubs. Russo would set up a tour of five cities, we would have prearranged meetings with club managers to deliver the mescaline and pick up the money. Each manager would buy two hundred doses of mescaline for one thousand dollars We would only see five people, go to five cities; drive approximately one thousand miles and net five thousand dollars in two weeks.

Russo also said that Morocco had hash that was good but inferior to Afghans, but it was only a couple countries away and if we wanted to consider doing a mini scam from there he would sell the hash for us as well the same way. We could make another twenty thousand dollars. Like Smiley said, forty thousand would be perfect. Jon and I talked it over and decided if the first scam went good we would do the Morocco scam.

Jon and I decided this was the time we had been waiting for to make the big one. Live in Hawaii, buy houses on the North Shore and live like Skinny. I already had my passport, it was just the matter of a ticket, so Jon would wait for me in Germany. I got on a plane from Hawaii to LAX, got picked up by Judy and drove home to Huntington Beach. I picked up a pure ounce of mescaline from my connection for four hundred dollars and was on a plane to Frankfurt Germany two days later. I landed twelve hours later, walked through customs, ounce of mescaline taped to my body, no problem at all, it was easy. I got my bags, walked out of the airport into

Germany, waved down a taxi and headed to a prearranged hotel to meet Jon.

I checked into my hotel room and as I opened the door to my room the phone was ringing, it was Jon, he had just bought the car and he would meet me in thirty minutes. I unpacked my things, took a shower, got dressed and was ready to go out on the town, ready to meet some German prostitutes, smoke some hash and eat some German schnitzels

Jon arrived, we were excited to see each other. The Afghani scam was on and we were going to be rich. Jon said he had been there for two weeks by himself and he was ready to party. He was excited to show me around Frankfurt Germany so we were off to explore clubs, hookers and drugs. We planned the next morning to drive to where Russo lived, about one hundred miles down the autobahn. The night was crazy. There were drugs and hash being sold on every corner by hippie long hair types, usually unkept teenagers or young people in their twenties. They sold to anyone that walked by, in America you would be arrested immediately, but not here. There were hookers on street corners and dedicated buildings full of women with hotel rooms located upstairs catering mostly to the women and their customers. The ladies of the night were all dressed up showing off their bodies with push-up bras exposing tits and partial nipple, short skirts showing off their tight butts through lace panties, with leather or suede boots. They were beautiful and young. When you entered the dimly lit interior, of the establishments, you could walk up and down the corridors and pick which beauty you wanted to spend some time with. These girls were ready to please, thirty marks, or ten dollars American money. We partook in everything that night and didn't get back to the hotel until late; needless to say, we didn't get the early start to Russo's house as planned.

Late morning we loaded up the new VW with our luggage and headed up the autobahn to Russo's, a four hour drive away, this gave Jon ample time to fill me in on Russo and what to expect. He told me that Russo lived in a small town, off the beaten path, called Bonninghoem that had a small American college housed in an old castle. Russo's house was located one mile outside town. He rented a room from an old German couple, actually the complete upstairs, and this is where we were going to stay. Russo assured Jon it would be safe and that the old couple never went upstairs, he had his own entrance to the room. He also told Jon it would be safe to set up a lab to mix the mescaline into caps. We planned to have Russo help in the preparation so he could experience how good it was and that we weren't exaggerating.

The four hour drive down the autobahn was great, porsches, mercedes and high speed European cars flew down the road like on a race track. We had to stay out of their way in the slow lane with the VW van. Jon said Russo had already set up the sales to his people. He mapped out our trip to Hilloersum, Stuttgart, Heidelberg, Manheim, Frankfurt and back. As we had discussed before, we would deliver two hundred doses to each of the five managers and make five thousand dollars with a one thousand mile round trip. Jon and I were a bit paranoid about meeting these people but Russo assured Jon his people would be the only people we would see and that this is how he does it once every month. The drive would take one week.

When we got to Russo's house, we went upstairs, Jon introduced me to Russo and we instantly hit it off. This had the feeling of something good. I looked at Jon and we nodded. This guy was a late bloomer but was made for us. Russo told us to make ourselves at home so, we unpacked and set up our lab.

It took us two days to cap up the one thousand doses and both days we got extremely zoned after capping and would go into Bonningheim. The town was filled with college students and townspeople by the afternoon. We hung out there for hours, meeting college girls, local pub owners and all Russo's friends. It seemed any friend of Russo's was a friend of the towns. We got along good there but after two days we were ready to make our city tours delivering drugs to people unknown to us. Jon and I were paranoid but Russo assured us again that it would be okay.

In the morning we took off, in our new VW, on our journey across Germany on the autobahn, hugging the right lane. When we got to our first city, Heidelberg, we were paranoid. We checked into a hotel, called our contact and set up the exchange for that evening. We met Russo's man at a park, he seemed as paranoid of us as we were of him, the exchange went smooth and we were on our way back to the hotel saying "one down and four more to go."

The next morning we set off for the next city to do it all over again. Everything went smooth in each city like clockwork. We sold nearly all the mescaline; collected four thousand dollars and we were ahead of schedule. Russo really had his people down.

We were invited to come back to the forth club around nine pm. The manager assured us it would be safe and the club would be full of desirable German girls. Jon and I replied simultaneously, "Okay!" When we arrived later that night the club was dark as we entered and it took a bit for our eyes to adjust. The music was loud with strobe lights flashing on girls dancing with girls in a very seductive style. The smell of hash was everywhere. We saw the manager, he motioned to us and sat us at a VIP table and brought by some beautiful German girls who proceeded to drag us up on the dance floor. No one could communicate but it was easy to get into the bump and grind with them. Later that evening we followed the girls a short way across town to a small flat they lived in. When we entered their flat the girls turned on low music, dimmed the lights and took off their nightclub attire revealing their lovely bodies and lace underwear. They started to dance together bumping, grinding and slithering up and down each other as Jon and I watched. This was obviously for our entertainment but obviously they enjoyed it also. We sat back smoking hash and enjoying the girls dance. This was live pornography at its best, these girls knew how to excite two guys to ecstasy. Eventually the evening turned into an orgy that lasted all night.

The next morning we awoke to the girls getting dressed and ready for their day jobs. We gave them a kiss and said goodbye. Hardly a word was spoken between all of us, animal instincts are universal. Jon and I headed back to our hotel, cleaned up, checked out and headed to our next stop.

After our last exchange we were ahead of schedule and Amsterdam was only a couple of hours away so we decided to go there, we wanted some club action now that we had a taste. We crossed the Dutch border and crawled down the autobahn.

We entered the city and found ourselves an expensive hotel in the center of Amsterdam. There were canals, bridges, brick streets and hundreds of mopeds and bicycles. Amsterdam was just like what everyone says a fairytale city. People were dressed in colorful swede coats, patched together like elves wearing funny wood shoes and buckled boots. Everyone going about his or her business. We wanted to find the drug nightclubs and the red light district, we heard about. Jon and I stayed in this fantasy land of a city for a week experiencing everything we could and dropping a couple thousand dollars but it was time to get back to Russo's and onto Morocco, we decided. We'll get back to Amsterdam next trip.

Once back at Russo's we let him know that everything went well and that we had decided to go to Morocco. We hung out with him for a few days and stayed high on mescaline. Russo loved it! He said he could shut his eyes and watch cartoons, Bugs Bunny, Elmer Fud, all the old favorites. Before we left, we told Russo the African scam should take us three weeks and asked if he could set up another scam with his managers when we returned. Russo said, "done deal, just be careful."

We stocked up for our journey with hash, to smoke, and

castellan wine to drink for our three day drive to Morocco. The first leg of the trip would be a ten hour drive to Paris on the autobahn. We got to Paris at night and checked into the Piccadilly hotel, in the middle of the red light district. Our overnight stay turned into one-week Two young guys exploring the bars and hotels filled with French, Swedish, German, Dutch and Danish women, selling themselves for ten dollars a pop. It was the equivalent to a human candy store and we were tasting the hot ones, the sweet ones, the ones in red, blue and black. This section of Paris was devoted solely to human pleasures, what ever you desired, you could find it here. We left there vowing to return on the way back.

We checked out of our hotel, loaded up the VW with our suit cases, looked around at all the women out in the morning and just shook our heads and said "see you in a couple weeks." We were on our way to Barcelona Spain, on the Mediterranean sea, another twelve hour drive. We told ourselves we would stay one night, that's it. We were already a week behind schedule and we wanted to stay on time, so we could have another week in Paris, which would make our trip two weeks longer than we planned. We didn't want to worry Russo, he was expecting us to be two to three weeks, that's all.

We arrived in Barcelona early evening and found a hotel we liked that looked out over the water. While unpacking we became aware of our surroundings, disco's with their doors open, loud music, dance floors full of people from many countries, young and old. The hotel sat at the foot of all this action and then up the hill from us was picturesque cobble-stone roads lined with more disco's.

After checking in, showering and resting, we left the hotel and walked into the cold Mediterranean night. We entered one of the busy disco's and realized immediately to move on. It was full of John Travolta types and worn out looking bar flies. We hopped from disco to disco winding up the hill on this cobblestone road that gradually changed to a cobblestone path. The nightclubs became farther apart, the crowds started dropping off and the clubs were more and more tucked in tight alleys, not open to the street but down steps. These clubs were more like coffee houses and small café's with just a few tables and a couple couches positioned in dark corners and maybe a bar. The music and lights were low and sometimes the smell of hash would come from the dark. These clubs offered coffee's and herb teas instead of alcohol.

We realized these clubs were where the Barcelona hash and drug people hung out, we luckily stumbled into them. We crept around in alleys, keeping a low profile, I could tell people were eyeing us. One of the café's we stopped in smelled of strong hash so we took a dark corner rolled our own hash joint and lit up. Shortly we were approached by two black guys who offered to share some Moroccan keef.

This is where we met our Moroccan connections, hanging out in these clubs for five nights smoking hash and getting to know these two Africans. These guys were tall, very black Ethiopian guys, about our age, with deep African voices. They were about 6'2" with afro style hair. They told us that they had been brought up in a small village being taken over by a renegade army and if they stayed, they had to join and fight, so they fled. They said they had been in Barcelona for three months scraping by and that now they lived in a beautiful flat just a few blocks away. They invited us to come and see their flat so we followed them around the small alley streets and then the area started changing to older dilapidated, three story rows of buildings up winding terrain. Their flat turned out to be really freaky. Entering ascending perilous stairs that were dimly lit and no railing. By the time we got to their third floor apartment we were shaking in our skin. Inside the flat we could see these guys were surviving on very little. They had two mattresses on the floor with sleeping bags for blankets and it was as cold inside as outside and there was no running water. We sat around and drank tea and smoked hash and listened to them talk about their culture, their parents, their schools, girls and how their dream was to get to California and become smugglers like us. We confided in them where we were going and they offered to go with us and help us score, they had connections, and after all they were Africans. Jon and I said okay, we thought what a stroke of luck meeting these guys. The next morning we checked out of our hotel, picked up the Africans, who had no luggage, what a surprise, and headed for Gibraltar, ten hours away, to catch a ship across the Straights of Gibraltar to Morocco. Let me tell you, the ten hour drive to Gibraltar was not fun. Almost immediately, these Ethiopians decided to remove their shoes in this crowded VW and they had the most ghastly stinky feet I've ever smelled. It was freezing outside and we were driving sixty miles an hour but we had to roll the windows down. The

African's in back were freezing and kept after us to roll up the windows. We told them only if you put your shoes back on, we were about to throw-up from the awful smell.

When we finally arrived at Gibraltar, we were nauseated and cold, traveling with these guys was the worst. We told them to hang out with the car while we booked our passages on the ferry to Morocco. The ticket person asked why we were traveling with blacks. That was puzzling to us since we were going to Africa.

The ferry didn't arrive for three hours, we walked around the area just killing time. We noticed the customs and their car impound yard, it was nearly filled. The most worrisome part of this was ninty percent of the cars had oval international license plates just like our VW had. Jon and I looked at each other and simultaneously said "let's not come back this way, oval plates are hot."

During our wait, we studied our map of Morocco. We found that there was another ferry crossing to Spain at the other end of the country from Melila to Malaga five hundred miles up the Morrocan coast. This would be our route back.

We took the ferry across Gibraltar to Africa, so we thought. When we arrived we still were not in Africa but a little Spanish province. We drove our car off the ship and fifty miles inland to the Moroccan border. We asked our African travelers what was going on, where do we go from here? Oddly they said, "we don't know." Jon and I looked at each other, we had made a mistake bringing them. We continued on, following Arabic signs, to Tanjier. When we reached the border, a small station manned by two customs agents with a lowered crossing arm across the road. We were the only car in sight. We stopped at the station, the guards motioned for our passports, which we gave them. Immediately they ordered the two Africans out of the car and took them inside their station.

Ten minutes passed, we were still waiting for clearance, we noticed hooded men just across the lowered arm motioning to us. They waved packs of something that looked like hash. Amazing, we were at customs and these Morrocans didn't care. Just then the guards came out of their station, gave us back our passports, raised the border arm and pointed towards Tangier. The two black guys were waving from inside the station as we drove off. They wouldn't even let blacks in Africa, their own country.

As we drove on through the border, one of the hooded men jumped on the side of our car grinning showing us a pound of hash. Speaking in Arabic he realized we didn't understand so, he spoke in Spanish "no", French "no, English "yes." Then he started speaking in English. This was unbeliev-able. In just twenty minutes we had lost our African guides, got a new guide and were looking at pounds of hash. We looked at each other, laughed, and the grinning Moroccan laughed with us all the way to Tangier.

We noticed as we traveled toward Tangier we were entering a land of no cars. There were occasional buses packed with people, suitcases and animals tied on top. There were small groups of hooded people, it was like we had just gone back in time two thousand years to bible times in just fifty miles.

The Moroccan parasite adopted us. He showed us to a hotel, which was not too expensive and then guarded our car as we checked in telling us he would wait. His boldness, we were afraid, was going to bring attention to us in Tangier making us very paranoid. We thought, " Oh no, how are we going to get rid of him?"

Our first excursion from the hotel was a smugglers nightmare. Our self-appointed guide wouldn't leave us, telling us do this do that. We were two six-foot guys, in American clothes, among these five foot hooded people. The local merchants saw us and came running from their shops, up and down the street, shouting "come, we have keef." Everywhere we went was like a shark attack; everyone wanted a part of us. Within twenty minutes a crowd had formed around us making us a spectacle, exposing us we were afraid, to cops and snitches. This can't be happening. We finally escaped from the crowds and got back to our hotel.

Back in our room safe, Jon and I talked. We could not go out looking like we did. We had to keep a low profile. We decided to dress like the locals with robes and hoods. We braved the crowds, found a couple robes, known as julavas, and got back to the hotel.

We put on the robes, over our clothes, we looked pretty good, besides being tall. The big test would be if we could slip past our self appointed guide. We walked out a side exit of the hotel, onto a side street and then emerged on the front side of the hotel. The robes and hoods worked perfect, our guide paid no attention to us. Now we could finally walk around Tangier experiencing the merchant shops without a crowd.

Most Tangier merchants speak Arabic, Spanish, French and sometimes English. If you looked at an item for more them thirty seconds they are selling it to you. They do not take no for an answer. They try bargaining with you, take you by the arm, showing you the keef they had to sell you. These stores were like small import/export stores lined up and down the streets of Tangier.

We got acquainted with a merchant who spoke English, we tried his keef, in the back corner of his store. We quickly found out it didn't get us high and that we didn't want to buy from him. The merchants would not take no for an answer so sometimes we would have to buy one half pound for ten dollars. We told them we wanted to buy good keef, called katoma hash, like we had smoked in Spain.

We went from shop to shop finding weak keef that didn't get us high. Finally we came upon a Spaniard, working and living in Tangier, named Eureka. Eureka was small in stature, but stocky as a mule and hairy as one too. He had long black hair growing out of his shirt onto his thick neck. It looked like a sweater until you got closer and realized it was part of him, two gold earrings and a full beard. He told us he had some real loady keef like we wanted at his house and invited us to his home under the city. We asked him what he meant by "under the city." He told us that most Tangiers lived below to get out of the cold winter winds and hot summer heat. We went with him.

Eureka walked very fast, we had to follow closely down steps, ninety degree turns down more steps until we came upon an underground market place filled with people. This was an underground city that foreigners weren't aware of.

Hundreds of merchants, were selling from wooden carts, birds, pigs, melons, a variety of foods, blankets, baskets, there were people smoking hookah pipes and playing backgammon, an Arabic past time, in this underground place stretching who knows how far.

No one noticed us. We were dressed in our robes and hoods just like them. We followed Eureka right through the market place to a narrow cave lined with doors carved into the sides. We followed behind, walking fast with our hands clasped behind our backs like all the others. About twenty minutes into the cave, Eureka stopped at a door, looks around and then made a series of knocks as a signal. The door opened to a family living pretty much huddled in a one-room cave with rugs, tapestries, pillows, mother, kids, babies, a grand-mother and not much else.

Eureka motioned us to enter quickly then bolted the huge door behind us. These people live in fear and don't even trust their cave neighbors obviously. The father of the family is the dictator, Eureka ordered his wife and mother to make tea for his quests.

In one corner of the room stood a hookah pipe surrounded by pillows, Eureka motioned us to sit. He loaded the pipe with a golden green pot, which turned out to be the loadiest pot Jon and I had ever smoked. Eureka said he could get us all we wanted at a small village a few hours away. We said, "let's go."

The next morning we checked out of our hotel and drove

to Tetawan, in the middle of Morocco, some four hours away, with our new connection Eureka. We checked into a sparcely furnished hotel where we stayed while Eureka went to his connection in the country. He told us strangers were not very welcome in Tetawan, especially Americans. He said he would be back in two days.

Jon and I stayed in our hotel for the next two days, leaving only occasionally. Tetawan was full of traditional Arabs, no frills. The people were suspicious, very spooky and there were no drugs in this town. No one was friendly, like in Tangier, we wondered what we had gotten ourselves into.

Eureka showed up two days later, and said it was all set up. We told him the quicker the better, we hated this place, the people were spooky. We immediately checked out of our no frills hotel, loaded our things into the van and Eureka directed us out of town toward some mountains. The drive to the village was taking us deeper and deeper into the Morrocan and back country. There were desolate hills, no cars and only an occasional hut on the side of the road. Once or twice we saw small villages alone on the sides of the hills in the distance.

When we finally came within a couple miles from the village, Eureka told us to turn off on a dirt road. The road went over a small mountain, down the side of a hill and then through a stream where Arab women, fully dressed in dark clothes with veils, were washing clothes.

As we came up the bumpy hillside toward the village, we drove through a goat heard manned by an Arab in traditional robe and a big knife at his side. He watched us intensely as we headed to his village. When we got to the edge of the village Eureka told us to stop and leave the van outside the village. He said there were no streets in the village, we would have to travel the rest of the way by foot. Eureka said were headed to Mohammad's house, he was an elder of the village. His house was located on the far side of the village passing over winding cobblestone walks. This was definitely national geographic territory.

We passed groups of men standing around their huts. They eyed us and knew we were strangers but we just kept walking following Eureka. Even though we were dressed in our robes, we felt the people knew we were westerners and knew what we were up to in their village.

It took about ten minutes to get to Mohammad's house on the backside of the village. A middle-aged man Eureka introduced as Mohammad greeted us. He had a friendly smile with dark skin and piercing eyes. He welcomed us into his house, made of mud and straw. The house was warm and air tight, to keep out the freezing mountain winds of winter.

Once inside we were offered the best pillows to sit on and we were served tea and arabic cookies, we were treated as honored quests. This was true traditional hospitality. Mohammad talked to Eureka in Spanish, French and some-times Arabic. He apologized to us for not being able to speak English. We were amazed that these men spoke so many different languages. He was apologizing to us and we only spoke English, how embarrassing.

Mohammad spoke and Eureka translated to us. He wanted to know if we wanted to smoke a sample of some marijuana we were buying. We nodded to Mohammad that we did. We were handed some great buds to smoke. I think he was impressed with us, we could hold our own smoking the "kind." We looked at Mohammad, nodded with approval, turned and looked at Eureka and said "let's do it."

When the price and the amount were agreed on, Mohammad got up and left the house. Eureka explained that Mohammad was going to set up the harvest and would be back that night, not to worry. He said we would stay in the house enjoying tea and hash.

Two hours later Mohammad returned and sat down with us. He spoke to Eureka in one of their languages and Eureka translated that the harvesting was happening and we now would eat dinner, enjoy music, smoke hash and the harvest would be in after dark.

Soon, after dinner, it got very dark and windy outside. There was a noise, Mohammad put his finger to his eye and he and Eureka peaked out a small opening in the doorway. They both nodded and Eureka said, "It's here!" They put out most of the lamp light, in the room, and opened the door facing mountainside leading out back. There stood six donkeys with bundles on their sides, tended by some dangerous looking men. This was the start of and adventuresome night filled to the brim with uncertainty.

The reality set in, we were in a remote mountainous village, alone at night, doing a scam, trusting strangers that looked as if they could be very dangerous and our car outside of the village. We would have a dangerous run if need be.

Each man outside carried a big knife. Jon and I looked

and thought, oh shit! Mohammad was a man of authority in
the village and when he motioned to the men to drop their
knives, they did. He could tell we were freaked out when we
saw them. The men entered the house without the knives, we
felt better. Although these men still seemed dangerous, even
without their knives, none of them smiled they were serious
village mountain people.

Each man carried a bale of pot as he entered the room.
Eureka spread out a big tarp and stood in one corner with
some big gardening sheers. Each man held steady while
Eureka chopped off the very tops of the pot spears, they
would discard the rest of the spear. They continued to shear
the tops and throw away thousands of dollars of perfectly
grown, dripping with pollen loady pot. It was obvious we
were in the growing fields where only the very best of the
plant is kept. The shearing was finished in about an hour. The
villagers bowed to us and Mohammad motioned with a wave
and the men picked up their machetes and disappeared with
their donkeys as quick as they arrived.

Mohammad dried a spear of a random plant and we
smoked a sample bud. We coughed and chocked like we
were smoking hash. The buds smelled like hash and there
was so much pollen on them, they were almost hash. We told
Eureka we would take it and he relayed that to Mohammad
who just nodded.

The next thing we had to do was package the pot for
travel. We pressed and packaged it in strong green plastic
to conceal its powerful smell during travel aboard ship and
through customs and countries. We pressed it into six odd

hotdog shaped packages. When we weighed it, it totaled fifty pounds. I told Eureka it would lose half its weight when dry and that actually it was not fifty pounds but twenty-five pounds, so the price should change. Eureka's reply was "no, it will not lose weight, its fifty pounds, the price does not change."

At daybreak I awoke on the floor next to Jon, I gently shook him. Eureka was passed out in the corner and when we looked for Mohammad, he was gone. We whispered to each other what should we do? We quickly decided to pay what was a fair price and get out without waking up Eureka. We left the money on the floor where they would find it and somehow stashed the bulk of pot under our robes and slipped out without waking Eureka.

We stood outside Mohammad's, we could see that villagers were up and we had to walk out among them to get to our car. We looked at each other and pulled our hoods over our heads and started walking as fast as we could, without looking like we were fleeing. The walk through the village was really scary.

We hoped we were going the right way that would take us out, we could only follow our instincts down hill. When we would pass through open areas we would be close to groups of villagers looking at us but none stopped us. The walk seemed like forever but was actually only ten minutes.

When we cleared the village, our van was surrounded by a heard of goats grazing. The herdsman was a kid of maybe twelve years old. We nodded to him, made our way through the goats to our van and unlocked it. It was freezing out and

I was afraid the van would not start but it did. We turned around among the goats and peering villagers hoping not to get stopped or stuck. Once we cleared the herd of goats, we headed up the dirt road towards the main road. There were herdsmen up and down the surrounding hills watching this VW with two strangers and all I could think was I didn't want to get stuck on the bumpy, pot holed road and need their help. When we made it to the main road, we took off knowing they couldn't catch us now, they didn't have any cars, just horses. The village had a bird's eye view of the road for miles so we knew they were watching us. Every time we reached the top of a hill we would look back to see if we were being followed. Mohammad and Eureka knew there was only one road, which way we were heading on it and they probably knew we were gone by now.

Fifty miles down the road we pulled off deep into the brush and stopped. Jon and I looked at each other and both said to each other "you've got balls!" I said to Jon " can you imagine the look on Eureka's face when he woke up and we were gone with all the pot?"

We hid the stash in compartments, built into the car. We looked over our map and headed for Melilla, on the other end of Morocco, to catch a ship the next day to Spain. Melilla is a small fishing village, on the Mediterranean, not many tourists and hopefully smugglers use. Our plan was to cross the Mediterranean further up Morocco crossing to Malaga Spain, thus avoiding a more dangerous search crossing from Tangier to Spain. Melilla was two hundred and fifty miles from where we were, maybe ten hours. We would be there by night and in plenty of time to catch the ship the next day to Spain.

We chose the shortest road, there were only two roads crossing Morocco's desolate countryside's and one gas station that we could see on the map. The map showed a moderate drive until we reached the east end of Morocco, on the Mediterranean sea. Our map was a combination booklet showing valuable information about roads, food, weather, accommodations and ship schedules. The road was cut into steep mountains overlooking the Mediterranean, beautiful, but dangerous.

We found out that the map didn't lie. The road was steep, twisty, un kept and with no cars, people or villages. We rounded a sharp turn cut into the hillside and there was this old lady slipping and tumbling down a ten foot embankment of the road, like a wild animal. She landed right in front of us. She had no legs, just stumps wrapped in rags and in her big ugly hands she held onto to wooden sticks she used to balance herself in this rugged terrain. I said to Jon, as we passed by at about two miles an hour, that was the most pathetic, miserable looking person I had ever seen. How could she be alone out here? Jon wanted me to turn around, he had to have a picture of her. I turned the van around and pulled up beside her to take a picture and this old lady roared and swung her sticks at the van. She wore a scarf on her head and under it you could see her round face covered with deep wrinkles, mostly toothless and dark squinting eyes full of pain and suffering. This was a close up of living torture that scared the hell out of both of us. I hope I never see anything like that again!

After the contact with the old lady we thought nothing could surprise us until, the road was blocked with mud ten feet deep. Here we had driven almost ten hours, almost to Melila, and the road was blocked from an avalanche. There was a bulldozer there but no workers in sight. We got out and surveyed the situation realizing how hopeless it was. One side of the road was a one hundred foot cliff that dropped off to the sea and the other side cut into a steep mountain and ten feet of mud. There was no possible way to get past this avalanche.

We looked at the map again and the only alternative route was all the way back, past the village we escaped from in daylight, a ten hour drive to catch the only other road, which was the longer route to Melila and would take twelve hours. On top of it all, our ship was scheduled to leave the next day. We would have to drive all night to make it in time, the next ship didn't leave for three days.

The decision to turn around took all our will. The trip back to Tetuwan took fourteen hours, now that it was dark. We were completely bummed when we got back to central Morocco, we had been within fifty miles of our destination and now we had another twelve hours to drive. We couldn't chance staying the night in Tetuwan, no telling who would be looking for us. The only thing to do was drive non-stop. Somehow the next evening, we pulled into Melila, the small fishing town. We had missed our ship but after a thirty six hour drive we didn't care. We were going to have to hang out for three days, until the next ship. We checked into a quaint seaside bungalow, next to the harbor, and slept until the next morning.

Melila was a quaint fishing village, small white houses dot the hillside above the town and the harbor people wore white cotton, not robes and didn't have knives. The docks were filled with working fishing boats and gulls. This was a nice place to wake up at after all we had gone through in the last forty eight hours, we were in heaven, we just hoped no villagers or cops showed up before we could get out in three days.

The first morning in Melila was casual, just getting familiar with the town and finding something to eat. We saw a small café across from the harbor serving food so we walked across the street and sat down at the outside table. The waiter appeared with small dried fish appetizers, which we devoured. We ordered breakfast and more fish appetizers.

We met a Swedish family at the café with two teenage daughters. These girls were teenage goddesses, seventeen and eighteen. They had lovely Scandinavian features, blue eyes, golden fair complexions, silky white blond hair and very beautiful. They wore summer shorts revealing long slender legs, thin ankles, nineteen or twenty inch waists, sexy hips and skimpy blouses showing pairs of firm breasts. It was nearly impossible to take our eyes off of them. They asked where we were from and we told them California. The girls immediately said, "California, you guys must be surfers." The Dad said the family had been traveling Mediterranean countries by ship starting in France, to Istanbul, Cairo Egypt, Algiers and now Melila, Morocco and their last stop was to be Tangier. We hung out with the family all day. They spoke good English and they were a great family with fantastic daughters that obviously liked hanging with a couple California surfers. Before we parted that afternoon, we arranged to meet for a sunset dinner and beer at the seaside café.

When we got to our room Jon commented that he wished those girls weren't with their parents. We smoked some hash and crashed for the rest of the afternoon, we needed it still.

It wasn't to smart to be out in the open at the seaside café. If someone was looking for us they could easily find us there. We took our chances and met the family for dinner anyway. After dinner we hung out and asked about each other's countries and how strange it was meeting here in this out of the way Moroccan fishing town. Later the dad said he hoped we weren't planning on taking any drugs on the ship. He said "I just want to let you know these ships are known to be used by smugglers of stolen diamonds, hash, heroin and espionage to the European market." He also said the customs agents were extremely tough on the European side. Jon and I assured him we didn't have any drugs. As it started to get late the dad said," I like you guys, do you mind if our daughters hang out with you, me and the wife are calling it a night." I told him, "not a problem." We found out sex is an expected pass time with Swede's, daughters included. We hung out with the daughters pretty much without the parents from then on. The parents didn't mind, they just did their own thing, their daughters were in good hands.

The cruise ship arrived on the third day, unloaded its passengers and a couple cars around noon. The ship would be ready to take on new passengers and cars at five pm for the eight hour night cruise to Malaga, Spain.

Now the reality started to set in. What the dad had said about how "hot" these ships were and the custom agents being so thorough. We could be looking at six years in a dirty prison. As the time got closer to board, Jon and I kept telling each other we would make it. We said our goodbyes to the Swedish girls and their parents and drove our van aboard into the belly of the ship. We parked our van, climbed the narrow stairs up to the deck and found a porter.

On board the ship we were issued a small room with bunk beds, not even enough room for luggage, it was sleeping quarters only. We went to the bar for a drink that turned into the whole night. We returned to our bunks at four or five am. The ship was to dock at six am and the bartender said the stewarts would wake us.

We were sleeping off a drunken night when our door opened and the Stewarts said, "you have to leave," in broken English. We got up quickly, thinking these guys were really bizarre, blurry eyed we got out. To our astonishment, everyone was gone and our van had been pushed off the ship into customs, where it sat alone waiting for us. Jon and I looked at each other, trying not to look worried about how it was perceived by the customs agents.

Immediately the customs agents came out when they saw us, abruptly took our passports, grabbed our luggage, sat us down and started searching our bags and van. Obviously, they did not like us for keeping them waiting. After an hour search, they couldn't find anything, we had hidden it well in the frame, they motioned for us to get our bags and get out of there. They still looked at us with suspicion but they had to let us go. Jon and I knew we were good but that was close.

We waited until we were about fifty miles away, drove off the highway to a campsite, cracked open the tunnel, got some buds, rolled a joint, lit it and high fived each other and headed for Paris, twenty hours away.

The drive up to Paris was a haze created by super pot. We would roll a joint, light it and realize two hours later there was still a half joint left in the ash tray. Russo's people will love this super pot. We figured it would sell for two thousand a pound quick!

The drive was long, all day through Spain with a hangover and no sleep. By night we reached France, the weather had turned nasty but we kept going, delirium was setting in but Paris kept getting closer. Late in my fourth shift of driving, entering the out skirts of Paris, it was ten pm and raining, I passed a truck on a two-lane highway and came face to face with another car going sixty miles per hour. Jon and I were so shaken by this near head on we pulled over and chilled for about thirty minutes thanking God we were still alive. I told Jon he had to drive into Paris, I couldn't. We arrived in Paris, checked into the Piccadilly hotel as zombies and without a word we went to our room and fell into a coma until the next afternoon.

When Jon and I awoke the next afternoon, we talked about what we had been through in the last four weeks. Things had not gone exactly as planned, but we made it. Our decision was to only spend a few days in Paris to recuperate and then head back to Germany. Russo probably figured we were in jail, because we were already two weeks later than expected.

We left Paris fairly refreshed, two days later, only a ten hour drive on the autobahn to Bonningheim Germany. On our way out of town we stopped to visit the Eiffel Tower and a couple of hookers. We arrived at Russo's, and just as we figured he thought we were in jail somewhere. He was amazed we made it. We told him "we're good."

The highlights of the scam were the topic. The hookers in Paris for one week, Barcelona clubs, Africans not being allowed in Africa, crazy Tangier shops, the score in the village, the escape from the village, the old lady, the Swedish girls, late sleepers and a near death collision.

When we told Russo we had pot instead of hash he was bummed, until he smoked some. The next morning we weighed what we had and it weighed twenty two pounds. We told Russo we wanted two thousand dollars a pound, he said "done deal." Russo said when ever we were ready he had another delivery set up. Jon and I said, " Let's go, we're ready!"

A one thousand mile drive on the autobahn, a couple of sex hunnies waiting for us to return to one of the clubs, good food and nice hotels was nothing compared to what we had been through in the past four weeks. Also, we were anxious to get going on our original scam to Afghanistan.

Everything went like clock work. Two weeks and we had collected forty thousand dollars. We started with fifteen thousand dollars and now we had almost fifty thousand dollars.

When we did get back, we bought a bigger car for our next
scam and gave Russo the VW.

10

"Ticket to Marseille"

WE SAID GOODBYE TO RUSSO. WE TOLD him not to expect
us until next summer, the drive to Afghanistan takes a month
each way through crazy countries. A Laguna brotherhood guy,
running from the law, was expecting us, he was our connection. We told him that the next time he saw us we would have
a quarter million dollars worth of Afghanistan elephant ears
hash, the best in the world.

All of us were a little edgy and melancholy the night
before we left. We had a long journey ahead of us and we had

already been on the road for four months but we were going to
be rich and buy houses on the north shore in a few months.

Jon and I left Germany on a cold snowy morning, in our
new Mercedes sedan, Rolling Stones playing on the portable
cassette player, lots of new batteries and entered the autobahn
headed for Austria. Our maps were charted, borders easy and
lots of money and smoke.

Three hours down the autobahn the Alps loomed
ominously and beautiful, completely snow packed from top
to bottom. When we got to the border, crossing into Austria,
the custom agents were friendly and asked where we were
headed. We told them we were going all the way across
Austria to Yugoslavia. The Agent said that this had been the
most snow they had seen in fifty years, crossing the Alps
would be dangerous, the country had been at a stand still for
four weeks. We told them we were good drivers and to please
let us pass. He said it would be risky and then let us pass. As
we climbed the mountains it got colder and icier, luckily the
weather was clear but the roads were treacherous, we could
drive off a cliff anytime. I went around a curve and a soldier
had his arm raised, for us to stop, I nearly ran him down, I
put the breaks on but nothing happened. The car slid on and
on slowly, the soldier leaped off the road and disappeared in
the snow down a cliff. We saw a three-car accident up ahead
thirty yards or so and it didn't seem we could stop. Finally the
car came to a stop, just before a collision. The soldier's superior officer put us under arrest for not stopping. We tried to
explain to him that we had tried but the slick road didn't allow
it. He didn't speak English and we didn't speak Austrian,

luckily the soldier climbed back up the cliff and explained to his superior that we tried to stop and couldn't so, he let us go. We had only been traveling about fifteen miles per hour.

We were hoping to make it across Austria and the alps in one day but after that incident we decided to stay at the nearest lodge until the next morning.

The next day we made it across the alps and dropped into semi flat land. We could see a lonely outpost with arms similar to Morocco's so we knew we were at the Yugoslavia custom check. We pulled up to the desolate customs outpost, our passports in hand, and waited for someone to come outside in the freezing morning. Finally, two customs agents came out wearing KGB long coats with high collars and fur hats. They spoke to Jon and me in Yugoslavian and we responded in the universal language of nodding our heads. They opened the doors of the car and signaled us to get out. They proceeded to search the car and abruptly grabbed the cassette player, tapes and batteries. One of the men spoke a little English and said "no TV allowed." We assured him that it was a radio not a T.V. Reluctantly, he handed the cassette player back to us. We got the point, western electronics were not allowed. We nodded to him that we understood and that we were traveling to Bulgaria and that we would not be staying in Yugoslavia, hoping he would understand. He looked at us again and said "Bulgaria" and stamped our passport visa papers for one day and we left.

Yugoslavia is a narrow country, we could drive across it in one day. The first fifty miles of road we traveled were only two lanes but later we came upon a concrete freeway with six lanes and not a car in sight. Jon and I looked at each other and said, " this is great, smooth travel." We got up to speed in a quarter mile, put music in the cassette and started to cruise until suddenly the road had a missing section, I slammed on the brakes and skidded off the end. To our amazement, the freeway continues just ahead maybe fifty feet so we bounced through the dirt and rubble and got back on the freeway; that was weird. We got up to speed again and we could see the road stretched for miles, this was an illusion, suddenly the road had another missing section and again we skidded off. Going off the road at these speeds we were bound to wreck or tear up our car.

The freeway continued just ahead again, we could see it stretching out for miles. This road was a nightmare of illusions. After hours of traveling we got off that incomplete Yugoslavian freeway. We were about half way across Yugoslavia, a desolate country without much structure. A gas station showed on the map about twenty miles ahead. We were hoping we could not only get gas but possibly some food.

The gas station came into view in the distance on the desolate landscape. Eventually we pulled up to the station, stopped and got out, it was so cold. A Yugoslavian peasant came out with a frown, pointed to our gas tank and we nodded that yes, we needed gas. After he filled our tank and we paid him we gestured that we were hungry. He frowned again and motioned for us to follow him around back.

To our amazement, there was a wedding party with maybe fifty people in a room behind this desolate gas station. Seeing a crowd was astonishing, where did these people come from? There were no cars, no means of transportation. The women were dressed in colorful long dresses, the older ones with scarves on their heads, the younger ones with long hair, bright red lipstick and large earrings. The men were dressed in baggy pants, puffy shirts, and large earrings also and some had long hair. These people were Gypsies and they insisted we join their party. It was fun, there were tables full of food, dancing and singing, I guessed, traditional gypsy songs. They grabbed Jon and me to join in their circle dance, we didn't have the slightest idea what we were doing but they could care less. They were all singing, dancing and laughing. This was a great party, not a sole spoke English. A wedding party for gypsies I'm sure last for days but, Jon and I slipped out in about two or three hours, stomachs full and full of amusement. Slipping out was the only way, otherwise these people might have insisted we stay and if we refused we were afraid of offending them.

The rest of the drive through Yugoslavia was cold but uneventful. We passed in and out of cities until we reached the border to Bulgaria.

This is where things got serious, another desolate outpost we were driving up to, we assumed was Bulgaria but it was still Yugoslavia customs. The custom agent took our passport, searched our car and bodies making sure we didn't take anything from their country. We did not take anything with us so, they gave us our passports and lifted the crossing arm to Bulgaria. Jon drove across six hundred yards, of no country land between Yugoslavia and Bulgaria customs and pulled up to the crossing arm and stopped. We sat there in our car for twenty minutes, finally two guards opened the door and looked at us as if surprised. No other cars were around but us. Both guards approached us, one on Jon's side taking his passport the other on my side taking my passport. The guard motioned for me to get out and step aside. He kneeled down by the floorboard, picked up the floor mats, shined his flashlight at the exposed trap door, opened it and saw money in bundles, drugs and a body car repair kit. He got up and motioned for me to get back in the car and then both agents went back inside their hut.

I looked at Jon and said, "We're caught, he saw everything." Jon asked me if I was sure and I told him yes because I saw it all too. We wondered what they were going to do. We just sat there for fifteen minutes.

It seemed like forever but finally they re-appeared. The guards came out with guns and removed us from our car. They opened the building next to them, it was an inspection garage. The guards pulled the car inside and we followed. They searched the complete car and at the end uncovered the trap door again. They emptied out our money, stash and smuggling body kit and set it beside our other belongings, cassette player, batteries, cigarettes and clothes. They motioned to us that they wanted our batteries for their flashlights. We motioned to them to take all they wanted, we could manage without music. They only took a few and then guestered thank you in their language. Next they pointed to the carton of Marlboro cigarettes, I handed it to them and they shook their heads and only took one pack. I couldn't understand why they were being so courteous to us, we were caught. They picked up four ten thousand dollar bundles of hundred dollar bills and pointed to our pockets and motioned for us to keep the money in our pockets not in the trap door. They loaded the stash and smuggling body kit back into to trap door, handed us our clothes, opened the garage door of the building and motioned for us to hurry and drive out of there. I said to Jon, " Let's go!" We pulled out shaking, not knowing what had happened? They let us go for some reason.

We had given them old batteries that only looked new, we had used them in the cassette player but, we were afraid to try and explain, they'd feel we were refusing to give them to them. We were not going to go back that way that's for sure. They knew what we were up to and we had given them bad batteries. We only hoped they wouldn't notify the next border. We wouldn't know until we got there.

Bulgaria is a small country and in just a few hours, even on terrible roads and passing through a few cities, we were at the border exiting Bulgaria. The exit from Bulgaria was much less stressful, the guards stamped our exit visa on our passports and lifted the cross arms. I drove the one hundred yards of no mans land to Turkey's customs outpost with its arms down.

Again, it took awhile for the guards to come out. Jon and I were still nervous after getting caught just hours before. This time it was more interrogation inside their building but in just a couple hours they stamped our passport and let us go. Turkey is a big country and Istanbul is a long ways from the border, Istanbul, the doors to the middle east, as it was known. Once inside Turkey, we knew we wouldn't see any more borders for at least a week. We loaded our cassette with new batteries, turned on the Rolling Stones, and headed toward Istanbul, a three day drive.

The roads were mostly one lane shared by both directions. There weren't many cars, mostly trucks and buses loaded with people sitting and standing. They have no definition of capacity in Turkey. The busses full of people, luggage stacked on top with live animals tied on top of that. It didn't take long on these roads to realize you would have to be insane to drive them at night. We looked at our map and found a town we could get to before dark, get a room and a room is just what you get, bare bones, only a bed. We didn't care, it felt so good to lay down and stretch out.

The next two days we traveled by day and slept at night until we got to Istanbul. Istanbul was where the embassies were for Iran, Iraq, Pakistan and Afghanistan where we could get our visas.

When we got to the outskirts of Istanbul, we knew we were approaching something big, trucks, buses, cars, motor-cycles, people and that old familiar smog. Driving in Istanbul is chaos at its worst. There are absolutely no laws or rules of driving, it was like a giant beehive of traffic except the bees drive cars and have horns.

Our first and most important chore was to stay alive on these roads and then to find a good hotel that would be comfortable, have good food and a protected garage for our car. Also, we wanted to be close to the embassies. I figured we would be there for at least a week getting our visas. We found a hotel that wasn't great but it would do, at least it had throw rugs, curtains and beds with lumpy mattresses but a nice view of the city skyline.

We woke up the next morning to Ali Bobba singing from high up in a big mosque. Our hotel room looked across the Istanbul city to a big magnificent dome and from it came the morning prayer. His voice travels across the city at daybreak. Our hotel got us a taxi, the front desk clerk wrote a note for us, in Turkish, explaining where to take us and to wait for us. The taxi driver took us to all the embassies on our list and we got all our visa applications. On the way back to the hotel the driver offered us some dark Turkish hash, we accepted.

After filling out our applications we decided to walk back to the embassies, but when we stepped out of the hotel, there stood our taxi driver, just like in Morocco, a self appointed guide. In his broken English he asked where we were going. We told him we were going to walk to the embassies, he insisted on driving but we assured him we were fine and took off walking. Each embassy told us it would be a three to four day wait to get our visas, which we expected. Each embassy was an extravagant small dose of its country, people were dressed in turbans, veils, and tapestries on the walls and incense filling the air in these places. Most of the people applying for visas were just ordinary people but occasionally rich looking government people, sultans, kings, and queens dressed in fabulous clothes, jewels, gold rings and bracelets and with body guards.

We walked outside, heading uptown, crossing the busy streets of Istanbul at our own risk. The streets were full of crazy drivers. The busy sidewalks were filled with thousands of five foot Turks. We found a restaurant on one of the busiest streets in downtown called the "Pudding Shop," funny as that sounds. This restaurant was well known to Europeans traveling by train to Asia. Everyone signs a big book, dates it when they left for Asia and then signed it again when they returned. This book, over one foot thick and many years old was passed around in the café for people to read or write in. I thought I had seen interesting stuff until I read the blank pages filled in by mostly European and American baby boomers leaving the modern world. Statements like going to Afghanistan, Nepal, India, Orient, back-packing the Himalayan's, find God, peace, love and never coming back! Every page was something startling but different. We signed the book but post dated it Jan. 12, 1971. We ate a Turkish sandwich and had some tea then back out to the chaos. Suddenly, we noticed the taxi driver on the corner pointing us out to two guys. We ducked back into the pudding shop. We figured that taxi guy was putting the finger on us to somebody, we stayed put.

While we were hiding in the restaurant we met a Dutch guy named Charlie. He told us he had made it across Lebanon and Syria without a passport, somehow, and got caught in Istanbul, on his way back to Holland. He had been stuck in Istanbul for one month with no passport or money, his embassy was going to help him, but when? He was living homeless in Istanbul. He told us that we were in a dangerous place, everybody was a snitch. He told us the police throw you into jail for anything, especially drugs. Jon and I were freaked out now, we told Charlie what we had just seen outside, the taxi driver fingering us. Charlie told us not to take drugs from the driver, or anyone else, he said the driver would turn us in for money. This city was turning out to be a nightmare. We left the pudding shop paranoid but, with arrangements to meet Charlie there the next day after we got our visas.

When we stepped out onto the sidewalk, we were approached by the taxi driver only this time he had another man with him. We asked the driver to take us back to our hotel. Jon and I spent the evening inside the hotel for safety, not stepping out for even a moment. We were afraid we were being watched and could be arrested.

The next morning we awoke, still shaken from the events the day before, and decided the quicker we could leave Istanbul the better. Jon and I decided we would get our visas, meet Charlie at the Pudding Shop and say goodbye.

We slipped out the side door of the hotel, avoiding the taxi driver, hurried across two busy streets arriving at the steps leading up to the Iranian embassy. Jon was turned down for a visa. The minimum age for a visa, without parent consent, was twenty one and Jon was only nineteen. I was twenty one so I got mine. Iran was a big country but I could drive it alone and Jon could fly over Iran and meet me in Iraq, on the other side, This put a real hardship on me but it was the only way to get our car to Afghanistan, and then on top of it all I would have to do it again on the way back. We were discussing this option as we passed through the rotation front doors.

As we stepped out of the embassy, there stood the taxi driver. He motioned to us to get in the car, we did out of paranoia. He offered us some hash, we said "no, take us to the pudding shop." When we pulled up to the pudding shop we told our driver we would see him later, we told him we were going to eat and shop. He offered to wait so he could take us back to the hotel. We lied and told him we had met some girls and would be with them, hoping to get rid of him.

From the taxi we could see Charlie through the window sitting alone waiting for us. He was six foot eight inches tall with stringy long hair a goatee and a mustache. Charlie was a Dutch citizen about twenty five years old, he looked like Frank Zappa but he was turning out to be a good friend, we liked him, and he was a wealth of knowledge for us. A police jeep abruptly stopped in front of the restaurant, piled with military police. They all ran inside, grabbed a guy sitting at the table next to Charlie dragged him outside and threw him into the jeep and they were gone. Our hearts were pumping, we thought they were going to grab Charlie. Charlie informed us, when we sat at his table, that happens all the time, they arrest foreigners for no apparent reason, torture a confession out of you, throw you in prison and then ransom relatives for years before they release you. This place was getting scarier by the day. We had to get out of Istanbul but, we were stuck without a visa to cross Iran. Charlie suggested we go to Beirut, Lebanon. He said they have excellent red Lebanese hash, he had a connection, a student of the University of Beirut who knew lots of people. He said he was there last month and it was only two countries away. Charlie said he would go back to our hotel with us, show us on the map the roads to take to Lebanon. "First," he said, "we'll go to the bridge leading to Asia which will be your escape from here." We could have some sandwiches there while he showed us the bridge. He was always ready to eat even though he didn't have any money but, we didn't mind feeding him, that was just Charlie.

We left the pudding shop, Charlie leading the way, through back streets filled with hundreds of street merchants with stores on top of stores. These side streets reminded me of Hong Kong. We emerged onto a main street about twenty minutes later, waved down a taxi, hoping not to be followed. The bridge was four stories high, a road on top, shops on two levels with backgammon cafes filled with old Turks playing and smoking tobacco in tall hookah pipes and drinking tea. The sea level, the bottom of the bridge, had small fishing boats anchored off it. The fishermen used small potbelly stoves grilling their fresh catch, selling fish sandwiches cheap, to the passing customers. It was cold out there but the bridge was like everything else in Istanbul, crowded with fast moving Turk's, but the sandwiches were great.

Once back at the hotel, Charlie told us everything we needed to know to get to Lebanon. He told us who to call, when we got there, and what to do. It all seemed to make sense so again I turned to Jon and said, "what do you think?" his reply, " let's do it."

Our escape took place the next morning at dark. We pulled out of the protected parking garage, in our car, hoping the taxi driver wouldn't be out there. We headed for the bridge, scared. There were hardly any cars on the road at that hour besides police jeeps, it was freezing cold so I think it helped our safe departure. We made it across the bridge to the Asian half of Istanbul and just kept driving. It took us about one half hour to clear the out-skirts of Istanbul and reach the one lane road leading to Syria two days away. Jon and I were so glad to be back on the road and out of Istanbul, which was a freaky place, a bust was certain, just a matter of time.

The drive through upper Turkey was fairly easy, just buses and trucks passing through little dusty towns. We stopped every once in awhile at roadside village stores to buy food, pita bread and cheeses, traditional Turkish food. There were not any restaurants or hotels in these areas so we ate and slept in the car.

After two an a half days we reached the Turkish custom outpost with two familiar sights, the arm down, a customs hut and then across no mans land to another hut that must be Syria. The only difference was that we were behind a bus full of people. All the other outposts we were the only car.

The border took a long time; the custom agents searched the bus thoroughly. This worried us, normally leaving a country is not that tough. Finally the bus left and it was our turn. I started forward and the arm came down. The Turks ran at us as if we were going to run their station. We told them we were just pulling forward but as usual, there was no communication. They pushed us in the station, took our passports, put me in one room and Jon in the other. I could see the guards looking at our passports and could tell they didn't like us by the way they threw the passports down. They searched Jon and me and then our car but found nothing after about an hour. They gave us back our passports and keys and pointed to the door.

We drove across no mans land to the Syrian guard station. The bus that had been in front of us was long gone. These guards were no nonsense guys, check the passports, inspect the car, search you and search your luggage. When you enter Syria, they want to know what you are all about. The captain spoke poor English but he was intense. He would say, "what are you doing here?" Jon and I answered "students," but he didn't accept our answer and just kept asking what we were doing there and wanted to know who we were. This went on for half the day, we thought we were arrested but eventually, he let us cross into Syria.

Shortly after we left customs we skirted the Mediterranean. It was beautiful, just like Bible times with sheep herders, white rocks, an occasional kid standing with wooden staff on rolling green hills watching over a heard of sheep. The road was winding around canyons and rivers and then back to the blue Mediterranean with its white sand beaches completely void of people or buildings. This was the most gorgeous place. The weather was mild, instead of cold winter, we were at the far east end of the Mediterranean where the climate gets warmer almost over night. We stopped off the road and went for a swim. The water was clear and warm without any waves. It was so quiet there all we could hear was the sound of bees and the seagulls, we were in paradise for sure. We got sunburned from skinny-dipping, feeling ourselves again, surfers who loved the beach.

Three hours later, we left the sea and traveled inland but the map showed the road would reach the Mediterranean many times from then on. The first town we came to everyone was wearing robes so we decided to put our robes and hoods on again to fit in. A car in this village town was rare, people hung out in the middle of the roads, like grazing herds of goats, so passing through was very slow and the villagers really looked closely at us hardly moving out of the road. This was very unnerving, stopping in these towns was not advisable so Jon and I decided to sleep in the car out on the road after dark, it would be safer we figured.

We reached the other end of Syria the following morning, after a few hours of sleep, freezing in the car, customs was no easier leaving than coming but we passed through and then continued driving across no mans land to Lebanon.

Pulling up to Lebanon customs was scary. There was a manned tank with its gun pointed right at us not fifty feet away. The guards took us inside and interrogated us wanting to know again, what did we want there, who we were, were we there to sell guns and did we have any diamonds? We told them no to all the questions and that we were there to go to the University of Beirut. The captain told us " alright, go straight to the university, do not stop anywhere!" He gave us back our passports and escorted us back to our car and watched us as we drove away.

Once through customs, we looked at the map and we were on the only road to Beirut. Shortly after the border crossing, the terrain again turned into green hills with big white rocks, occasional sheepherder, kids and peeks of the blue-green Mediterranean a quarter mile away. The road then turned toward the inland Syrian border. The area was dry but the snow capped mountains seemed close. We could see a village ahead on the road, as we were driving through we saw kids playing foosball. I looked at Jon and said " let's turn around and play. It will be fun, we'll kick their butts." We turned around and pulled up in front of the village square with one foosball table fully occupied by kids. We pulled down our hoods and smiled, hoping the kids would let us play. Within minutes I was playing. After playing awhile I noticed Jon was gone.

I looked around just as Jon was coming from a building with a small crowd of men. He walked up to me with a serious face and said "these men want our passports." One man spoke a little English but the crowd was yelling Arabic words at us. Jon said they wanted to know why we were there and why were we dressed like them. We got our passports out and he grabbed them, we looked at each other. "Hey" I said, "we just wanted to play with the kids, that's all, we are on our way to Beirut." His reply, " look around the village, these are angry Palestinians yelling at you." Jon and I kept trying to keep an eye on our passports, but getting very scared. The English-speaking guy said, "These brothers and sisters are dying because of you, your government supports Israel." We told them that our country was big and we had no control over our government. He translated this to the crowd and it infuriated them. About that time a guy with a machine gun was standing next to me in commando clothes. He was unshaven, black eyes and a deep scar across his face. His face was partially covered with Palestinian headwear, he had on a thick army wool shirt and pants, bullet belt around his waist and shaking a machine gun at me demanding something in Arabic. The translator said "because of you, his people must make raids every night against Israel." The crowd got louder and even the interpreter could not hear, he suggested that we go to a house inside the village and talk. I told him we could not do that, we were scared, I asked him to let us just have our passports and let us go. I told him we would meet with him at our hotel in Beirut and to please help us, he must of feared for us. He gave us our passports, walked us out to our car, we gave him the name of our hotel and he said "go quick, I'll meet you in Beirut." We started the car with the village people all around us and headed for Beirut hoping they wouldn't follow us, feeling like bullets would be flying as we drove away.

The road to Beirut was one hundred and fifty miles further, passing through small villages, we drove straight through with our hoods up. These people hated Americans because of our government. This was a shock, we thought Americans were liked.

Now we wondered what to expect when we got to Beirut. Ten miles outside of Beirut the two lane road almost instantly developed cars, buses and people. Finally, were driving along the Mediterranean. When the city of Beirut came into sight we saw many big resorts on the Mediterranean. There were high rises, big streets and a modern world, this was great, what a relief.

We drove into Beirut, heading toward the high-rise buildings on the main drag, across from the Mediterranean looking for a hotel with a private parking garage that looked safe. We found what looked like a luxury hotel and casino, pulled in, parked, stretched our legs from the long drive. and walked into the lobby. We expected a big luxury hotel to be active with people, but not so, it was run by a skeleton crew and very few guests. The man at the front desk said that two people including breakfast would be fifty dollars a week including private under ground parking, a phone and bathroom in our room, "fantastic, we'll take it," I said. He showed us to our room, on the tenth floor. It had two balconies, one looking out the front, the other looking over the alley behind the hotel. The room was clean and it had its own bathroom and telephone, just as he had said, which was a surpeise. This was fantastic, after four weeks of traveling long hours and sleeping in our car in mostly third world countries, who would expect a luxury room.

Our first evening was spent in our hotel relaxing, eating and going over our map, looking at ship schedules to Marseille because we did not want to return through so many borders. By ship we would only have one border to cross, at customs in Marseille. We would just cruise down the Mediterranean stopping at many ports like the Swede's but our car would stay on ship at each stop. We tried the number Charlie gave us but it wouldn't go through. We called it a night and decided in the morning we would go to the university and look up Michael, Charlie's student friend.

When we woke up the following morning the weather was perfect. I stepped out on the balcony to see the unbe-lievable green/blue Mediterranean sea with it's white sand beach. We ordered room service for breakfast and it was delivered by the same guy we had met the night before, we figured he was probably the cook too. We called down later for a taxi at the front desk and told them we wanted to go to the American university, that was one crazy ride. The streets converge upon each other and nobody slows down, they just honk, it was worse than Istanbul. Somehow we made it. The university was street level, on the side of a hill going all the way down to the sea, we could see why people go here, it was beautiful. We asked an American guy, passing by, if he knew Michael, he said no but asked what his major was? We told him oceanography and he pointed out the department we needed. We did find Michael there, he was very cautious of us until we described Charlie to him. We explained Charlie's situation in Istanbul, stranded, and that we were originally headed to Afghanistan but plans changed and Charlie had recommended Beirut. We explained that Charlie gave us his name, said that he could introduce us to some good people. This is when Michael got really cautious and asked personal questions about Charlie that only friends would know. Our answers satisfied him, he agreed to help us and cautioned us to be careful who we talked to, that there were a lot of snitches around. Michael took our phone number at the hotel, he would call us the next day, Jon and I headed back to our hotel.

When we got back to our hotel, a few hours later, Michael had already called and left a message for us to call him, we were surprised he contacted us so quickly. When I called him back he said we could meet with him the next evening, he would introduce us to a guy that lives in the mountains where the pot grows. Jon and I talked this meeting over and both decided we were going to be very cautious.

The next day, when we went to Michael's, there was another guy with him that looked like a student. Michael introduced us and said his friend lived in the hash village about three hours from the university. He had a sample of some red Lebanese hash and asked if we wanted to try it. Jon and I smoked some, it was good so we asked how much he wanted per pound. He told us one hundred fifth dollars per pound. I asked him what he would charge for two hundred pounds? His numbers changed to one hundred dollars per pound. He explained it would be necessary for us to take a taxi up the mountain where it grew. I told him we would not travel, he had to deliver it to us. He told us his people would not transport the hash and that we needed to give him a down payment if we wanted it. We compromised on the down payment and then agreed on the taxi, that was the only way, and set the trip up for the next morning.

We met our connection outside of town at a pre-arranged place. Jon and I wore our robes and hoods to blend in. We crammed into this old mercedes taxi with six other people and took off with this insane taxi driver who raced around curves, passing cars, honking, slamming on his brakes, dropping people off and picking people up. This was normal transportation up and down the mountain, to and from Beirut, it was unbelievably scary.

When we got to the mountain village there were a lot of armed commando looking types. We kept our heads covered with hoods, there would be no escape from this village that's for sure.

We met with the "hash man," his name Hassan. Hassan's house was very similar to Mohammad's, no electricity, plumbing, very clean, only the climate was warmer than

Morocco. We smoked his hubbly bubbly, a hash pipe stacked full of red Lebanese hash with the doors and windows wide open while we coughed our guts out. Hassan invited us to see his village and meet its people. We walked outside, into a beautiful morning, the view was breathtaking. Down the meadow, ten miles or so was the blue Mediterranean, turn around and in the distance were snow capped mountains. The climate was warming up but not hot, with crystal clear air and baby blue skies, I had never experienced such a peaceful place.

We walked down the stone street, greeted by everyone we passed, with a smile. A few people were wearing belts with pistols, but they were smiling. We stopped in a small café opening to the street and Hassan ordered us pita sandwiches, I think made with lamb brains, a delicacy we found out, with hummus and tea. After eating I tried to pay for the food and we were told we were guests and our money would not be accepted. The whole village treated us as quests.

We said "shu-krane, thank you" to Hassan and then ask when the taxi would be back to go down the mountain. Hassan told us not to worry, he wanted to show us the plantation working. He took us to a row of buildings with village men and women working in and around them. The first building was the curing building with hundreds of marijuana plants hanging upside down. There was some type of stone oven keeping the room very dry.

The second building was a room without any windows, only a door. Hassan knocked on the door and a young man in shorts, with a handkerchief over his nose and mouth, opened the door. We looked inside. The walls were lined with fine screen cloth or silk and the floor was covered two or three feet thick with spears of buds. Our translator explained that these two men collected hash pollen, first pounding the pot spears with bamboo, the hash pollen collects on screens and then they scrape it off and put it in cheese cloth bags weighing five hundred grams. In the third building men were pressing the cheese cloth bags, full of hash pollen, into hard placks

The final room was locked, with an enormous pad lock, Hassan had the key. He opened the big pad lock and inside was a dry room used to store the completed hash kilos. Ruben translated for Hassan, he told us that this room held up to a ton of red Lebanese hash when the season is at its peak. As we were leaving Hassan invited us to have supper with him, we accepted.

We ate a traditional Lebanese meal prepared by Hassan's wife and daughter. We had pita bread with hummus, stuffed grape leaves, olives, small portions of lamb and tea. For desert we ate homemade baklava made with nuts and honey. We sat around all evening smoking nuggets of red Lebanese hash and listening to Hassan's soft instrumental music until we all fell asleep.

In the morning Jon and I woke up with terrible coughs from that red Lebanese but otherwise a night to remember forever. Ruben entered our room with Hassan. We told him we wanted the red Lebanese hash and asked him how we could get it.

Ruben told Hassan we wanted two hundred pounds. He said his villagers would have to make it and it would take one week. He wanted the five thousand dollar down payment, said they would call us when it was ready and that they would bring it down the mountain to us to be safer. His men knew when the road was safe to travel and if there were any road-blocks they would know in advance. We nodded to Hassan, paid the money, shook hands and said, "Massalumi", which meant goodbye. The deal was set. On our way out of the village Ruben told us that Hassan liked us. He said he was taking chances by bringing the hash down the mountain. We got in our taxi and headed back down the mountain some-times as if on two wheels, back to Beirut.

Now it was all about hanging out in Beirut for a week waiting for the call. The only other business we needed to take care of was to rent a private garage, for concealment, at our hotel so we could load our car with the hash.

For one week Jon and I hung out with Michael at the university, smoking hash and meeting future leaders from Africa and Asia. This was an eye opening political experi-ence for us, what worked in our country didn't necessarily work for theirs. I was asked why our government meddles in so many foreign governments. I did not have an answer for them. The only thing I could say was that the general American citizen, did not make foreign policies, the govern-ment did that for us.

During the week Michael showed us Beirut, American movie theatres that played a lot of propaganda, sidewalk cafes serving sandwiches, carrot juice and many Lebanese foods such as falafels and baklava. There was an amazing open-air market we could buy local fresh produce. During that week we got accustomed to hearing aircraft and gunfire, mostly off in the mountains toward Syria. Sometimes it felt a lot closer but Michael assured us not to worry. He told us that most of the fighting took place at the refuge camps, PLO, what we were hearing was bombing by Israel in retaliation for raids.

The weather was a perfect seventy eight degrees. We went to a beach outside of town on the Island of Biblos, supposedly where the first Bible paper was made. The beaches were beautiful and the water very clear and warm. This was one of the few times we had taken our mercedes out of the garage and driven through town.

When we were driving back to the hotel, there weren't any cars on the road where normally there would be a hundred taxis, locals driving and lots of honking. We stopped behind an army truck, filled with some military soldiers armed with rifles, looking straight at us. All of the sudden the truck took off after a car skidding around the corner, shooting at them. Talk about scared, Jon and I had no idea what was going on. When we got back to the hotel we learned that the army had called a curfew and no one was to be on the streets. The desk clerk told us we were lucky we did not get shot. We asked him how were we to know about the curfew? His response was "didn't you see that there weren't any other cars on the road?"

Five days had passed and then finally one afternoon we got the call that our stash was ready and would be driven down the mountain the following day, if it was safe. We were instructed to be ready and that Ruben would take us to a house on the outskirts of town where the exchange would be made.

We knew now that in two days, we would score in Beirut, this would be a scary time for sure.

I booked passage for Jon and I on the ship we would be taking. In four days we would be cruising down the Mediterranean to Marseille, France, stopping in a few countries like the Swedes. We were looking forward to a five-day cruise avoiding all the radical borders and roads and no search until Marseille. We could casually get off the ship and visit places like Cairo, Sicily and Tunas.

The exchange went smoothly the next day. We were paranoid, to say the least, exchanging fifteen thousand dollars for two hundred pounds of hash and loading it into the trunk of our car and then having to drive back through Beirut to the hotel. The drive was the worst, getting lost on side streets, sitting in traffic for hours with horns honking, police everywhere and army jeeps following us at times. Finally we pulled back into our hotel and got to our room, it was intense.

The next morning we started working on stashing all the hash. It was a big job and took until evening and then we realized we had run out of room. As we were trying to figure out where to put the last seventy five pounds, gun fire started going off right outside the wall of the garage. We quickly stashed the last of the hash in the trunk, locked the garage and ran into the hotel. The hotel management had turned out all the lights and everyone hunched down while a gun battle went on just outside. After a couple of hours Jon and I crept over to the elevator and got up to our room. Shaken by all the commotion, we thought for sure we were getting busted. I peeked out over the balcony and down the alley, hearing occasional gun fire, and I could see, from my high advantage point, people hiding on roof tops by their cigarette light. How stupid that was, I thought, they were exposing themselves.

When we got up in the morning Jon and I finished stashing the hash, we were paranoid as hell. We got down to the last eighteen pounds and there was no more room to stash anything. This just made us sick; leaving this behind would mean a twenty thousand dollar loss. Jon and I talked it over and decided to give the eighteen pounds to Michael as a thank you for trusting us, he gladly accepted. We said good-bye and told Michael our ship would sail the next day.

In the morning, we checked out of the hotel and headed to the port to board our ship, we were both nervous but confidant. The ship was set to sail at twelve noon but we had to be there at eight am to go through customs with our car. We drove into the customs yard, there sat our ship directly in front of us with its big front open so cars could be driven into its belly. Finally we were on our way back to civilization and not expecting much search, if any.

Jon and I got out of our car, with one hundred seventy eight pounds of red Lebanese hash stashed in the frame, confident that even if the custom officers searched the car they would never find the trap door since we had sealed it and painted it, they could not get to it without a drill or a saw. We were the only car being shipped. Three customs officers walked out of their port headquarters and greeted us and asked for our passports and tickets. Two of the agents took out our luggage and placed it on a table to search. The third agent motioned for Jon and me to follow him into the customs building. Once in the office there was a forth agent sitting at a desk, he motioned for us to come in and sit down. His first question was why we were in Lebanon. We told him we were there to register at the university. He nodded and agreed that was a nice school. He then looked at our passports, turned to the visa page and stamped exit visa. We told him thank you and walked back to our car. Our luggage was finished being searched and the agents were starting on the car with a screwdriver and tiny flashlights. They gave the car a once over look, got inside, felt the headliner, under the seats, looked in the trunk and engine compartment and then stepped back. Jon and I put our luggage in the trunk and pointed to the ship for the okay to board. The agents motioned to us to wait there. The two other agents from inside the office came out and did the same search all over again, they found nothing. We knew we had done a good job sealing and hiding the stash, but this was still unnerving. All the agents were very polite but they wouldn't let us leave. the ship was right there. The agents had searched us three times but still would not let us leave. We didn't want to show how unnerving this was and we didn't want to look scared. The search had taken two hours and we still had two more hours until the ship was scheduled to leave.

Jon and I sat there looking at our ship for twenty minutes when all four agents came out and started to search again. They started with our luggage, tearing the lining loose, removed the car radio and even disassembling it, removed the paneling from the doors and took out the front and back seats. It was amazing what these guys could do with just a screwdriver. At this point I remembered what the Swede's had said, they were looking for diamonds, espionage, hash or heroin. We were in deep, we hadn't expected a big search like this until we got to Marseille, France. At this time the search had gone on for three hours, it was eleven am, we had one more hour. One of the agents took a small inspection plate off, under the back seat, and used a flashlight to look around. He then waved one of his comrades over and then they looked at Jon and me. I didn't put anything near that plate, I knew they weren't seeing anything. All the agents took a look and then the captain came over to me and said, "We see it, tell us how to get to it or we will blow up your car." I asked him what he saw. He took me over and shined the light on just a small corner of a pack of hash. I told him "that's nothing." He said he knew it was hash. At that point, I knew Jon and I were busted.

The captain took us back to his office even though the agents still had not found the stash and we had not admitted to anything. I figured this was the right time for a bribe. I pulled out five thousand dollars and put it on the captain's desk but he said things had gone too far, too many people knew. I put another five thousand dollars out and he said, "I'm sorry you are under arrest for drug trafficking". He asked me to show him how to get to the stash or he was going to blow up the car. Jon and I finally agreed and the trap doors were open just as our ship was doing its final boarding. My heart sank. I thought about escaping but had nowhere to run. It was so unbelievable, we were caught. When the agents weighed the stash there was one hundred and eighty one pounds. Greed had gotten to us by one pound we stuffed in causing the rest to shift and causing that little bit to show when they inspected the car. Jon and I sat there and watched our ship sail away without us.

We were detained over the weekend in an office at the port customs building. The custom agents were exceptionally nice to us, giving us drinks of R-rock, a Lebanese alcoholic drink, for our bad coughs we had developed from smoking hubbly bubbly pipes. An American assistant ambassador came to see us and gave us a list of attorney's, including their languages spoken and the school they attended. He said he could not recommend one, we had to make our own decision. Jon and I looked over the list and picked one that was educated in Oklahoma. The custom agents let us use the phone to call him.

We met with the attorney that afternoon, we had a lot of questions. He was a short man in his mid forties, balding, a bit pudgy, and dressed in a suit and tie. He spoke good English even though he wasn't too impressive looking, but what choice did we have? He just laid it on us. He told us we were facing five to fifteen years and that the American embassy would not help us. His fee to start was five thousand dollars, then he would go to court with us on Monday and see if we were being charged with possession or trafficking, he had to know which one so he would know how to help us. He told, " us not to worry." Jon and I looked at each other simultaneously and then looked at the attorney and asked if we could buy our freedom, his comment was "maybe." We hired him, gave him the five thousand dollars to represent us and hoped he was good.

On Monday morning Jon and I were hustled into an army truck and carted off to court. We had hardly had anything to eat for the past two days, we felt we were starving. We were put in a holding cell, partially below ground, with a small window at ground level. We anticipated going right to court but we were wrong, instead the cell kept filling up with more criminals until there was standing room only. We were in that cell all day, never saw our attorney, never had any food, there was no bathroom and no one spoke English. After many hours went by the guards opened the cell and took Jon and I out with no explanation as to where we were going but we didn't care, we wanted out of that cell.

The guards took us up some small concrete stairs, outside, and then into another building, up the stairs and into a small room. There sat our attorney. I started to speak to him and he motioned me to be quiet. There were three judges in white wigs and robes. The court was conducted in French, which we did not speak. Our Attorney motioned for Jon and I to stand up and one of the judges read off, I guess, our charges. Our Attorney replied to him in French and then we were handcuffed and hustled out of the building and back to the holding cell without even being able to speak. This all took about twenty minutes. Talk about being freaked out, angry and pissed. We had no idea what was going on.

A few more hours had gone by and the guards came in and hustled everyone out of the cell to waiting army trucks. Our attorney was standing outside the door when we emerged.

We started yelling, "What's going on? Where are they taking us? We need food." We had to yell loud to be heard over the Arab prisoners all screaming at each other, the guards pushing us and ordering us into the truck. All I heard was "don't worry," and something about being indicted. We were loaded up into the truck and whisked away.

We pulled into a prison yard and I was pushed off the truck with another prisoner but, not Jon, he was ordered to stay on the truck. We were being separated for some reason, why I didn't know, and no one spoke English. The truck drove off and I was put in a cell with no food, no blanket and no attorney for two more days.

I had not eaten in four days, I started yelling at the guards at this point, they would hit the bars for me to shut up and I would just yell more. That finally worked, they brought me an attorney, who spoke English, and he got me some food and told me I would be going back to court that day. I was ready to kill, I hated these people.

A little later, I was hustled out of my cell to an awaiting truck. I was handcuffed to a young Arabic kid, maybe fourteen years old, who was wild like a coyote, smelled and was dirty, I didn't care. I was out of the dungeon and assumed I was off to court. The truck pulled up to the court compound and we were actually pushed out of the truck like dogs, as if we had ignored a command. We were then rushed down to the same holding cell I was in before and there was Jon. We were reunited. I told Jon of the piss hole prison I was in. He told me of Ramal prison, also known as Sands, were he had been taken. He said it didn't sound much better than where

I was at except he occasionally got food and there were two Europeans in his room. As I was trying to talk with Jon, this Arab idiot I was handcuffed to kept jumping up toward the ground level window as if he wasn't even handcuffed to me. Finally, I started jerking his arm harder and harder, he looked at me as if I were the crazy one. This was the only way I could get him to stay still.

Here we were again on our way to court and we still had not communicated with our attorney. The guards came and grabbed me out of the cell, uncuffed me from the idiot and then grabbed Jon and cuffed us together. We were taken to the court building but this time to a different room where our attorney sat, a pompous little fat lawyer who had done nothing for us. We had been to court once and didn't know what went on, we didn't have food, we were separated and I had been handcuffed all day to an Idiot. He did not make any effort to contact either of us and he had our money. We were pissed. We wanted to know what was going on and what to expect in court, were we going to prison or being released? His reply was "don't worry." He said Jon had been indicted for trafficking, and he would go to trial. We were back in court to see if I was going to be indicted also. The attorney told Jon that since he had already been indicted, his only way out was the hospital as a psychopath. His only defense was to plead guilty and then get out by reason of insanity. I was instructed to plead innocent. The attorney would tell the court that Jon said I didn't know anything about the hash. He kept telling us this was the only way. He told Jon that if he didn't clear me then we would both be indicted and go to trial for trafficking, which meant five to fifteen years. He also said it was clear-cut, they would convict us for sure. The attorney told Jon he would have to plead guilty, I would go free today and he would go back to the prison and he would have him transferred to the insane asylum with the other Americans until he was released, again he told us this was the only way.

We walked into the court ready to follow our attorney's plan. There sat the same three judges in their wigs, looking real sixteenth century. Our attorney spoke in French as the judges listened. They looked at Jon, the head judge spoke in English to Jon and asked if his plea was guilty and if I was innocent. Jon's reply was " yes." The court proceeded on in French as our attorney translated to Jon. He told Jon he was being sentenced to five to fifteen years, but not to worry. Then I was told I was not indicted, and court was over. We were both rushed back downstairs to the holding cell with our attorney again saying, "don't worry, everything's okay."

In the holding cell Jon knew I was being released, this was the only way but, it was hard. When the cell opened the guards took both of us not just Jon, this was not what the attorney said would happen, "what's going on!" I protested. I was loaded in one army truck and Jon in another and off we went in separate directions. I wondered what was going on, my attorney said I was going to be released.

I was taken back to the dungeon of a prison again hungry, no blanket and it was freezing cold. On the floor there was shit and piss, I was ready to kill again.

The next morning I was taken out and pushed into another army truck with other prisoners and armed guards.

At this point I really didn't care I wanted out of that hell hole. The truck drove past the hotel I had been staying at just a week before living it up and free, now I was screwed. Maybe thirty minutes across town, the outskirts of Beirut, the truck slowed and bounced across tracks that guided a big gate. I was looking at orange walls covered with mold, topped with circles of barbed wire and manned gun towers. This was Sands prison Jon had told me about. I watched the big gate close behind the truck.

I was kicked from the truck and pushed inside. I had nothing but the clothes on my back. They took my picture and took me to a cell which was a room about sixteen hundred square feet in size and housed about fifty prisoners.

Once the heavy strong door slammed behind me I just felt despair. I looked for Jon. There was not a familiar face anywhere, just ugly unkept looking prisoners. This was living inside "One flew over the CooCoo's nest" and I felt like the big silent Indian . I felt so alone.

I was pointed to a spot to set my blanket along the wall. I sat there all day. An occasional breeze came through reeking of poop and pea.

I never ate anything. I just sat against the wall. Finally the door opened and I was motioned to stand up for the evening count.

After count everyone laid out their blankets, I did the same. After sitting up all day I was tired, I laid on my blanket and stayed there until five am the next morning.

The next afternoon I was switched to another room, again with about fifty other guys. When I walked in I saw

Jon walking around wearing his Jalave, I was relieved to see him.

Jon asked me where I had been and I told him I had been in the dungeons of hell. He began to fill me in on this prison. He had already fit in with some people. He told me the next day would be shower day and informed me I was lucky since it only happens once every thirteen days, I needed a shower and he could tell. He said the prison feeds on Wednesday and Sunday, that's all. I was so excited to hear that since it was Wednesday. He went on to say that there were two European guys in the room, one was friendly and the other was wigged. He said they had been in there eleven months and they were arrested at the airport. He had found out we were lucky to get arrested at the port, the courts were liberal. The airport court was a conservative one and that everybody gets five to fifteen years. The European guy told him that there were more Americans there but some had already gone to the nut house. The wigged out guy had been at the nut house but the conservative court had him sent back to the prison and he snapped. Jon had talked to our attorney told him I was coming and I would be released in two weeks at court. Two weeks in this room was not expected but Jon was looking at three months here and then three months in the nut house, I couldn't be bummed.

During the next couple weeks, I learned more than I wanted to know about Sands. The guards opened the big steel door in the morning for count and to issue medications then they were closed all day until the evening count.

The room was being run by the senior inmate. He was the

only one with a mattress. The rest of us slept on the cement floor on top our blankets.

The inmate that had been there the longest inherited the mattress and was in control of the room. If anyone of the inmates steps out of line, fights or is caught stealing the senior inmate reported them to the guards for punishment.

He was a King, over there on his mattress, being catered to by his servants. He sat there hairy belly sticking out of his stinky worn out pajamas. Obviously personal hygiene was not a priority to him. I thought to myself it wouldn't look out of place for flies to be buzzing around his head.

The punishment the guards deal out, I heard, was brutal. The offenders had their feet bound, leaving swollen skin openings and then their feet were horsewhipped.

Sands Prison held a mixed bag of personalities and every ones clothes were different. The Lebanese wore pajamas, the Africans wore white robes, the Europeans wore bellbottoms and Jon and I wore our javalas we bought in Morocco. The servants wore pajamas with holes in the knees and butts. The room was full of fifty of the strangest looking people I had ever seen.

The inmates walked around the room in one direction aimlessly in pairs. The room seemed to be in slow motion. I thought to myself, "Am I ever going to get out of here?"

The "King," senior inmate, sat on his mattress and held "court." He handled small disputes among the roommates while his servants would fan him. Whatever his decree, after listening to both prisoners, would be final and that's that.

The position of your blanket on the floor depends on

seniority. I was the last person to arrive after Jon, I was next to the shit hole and Jon was next to me.

The bathroom, if that's what you want to call it, smelled so bad. It consisted of a sink with constant cold water dripping from it and holes in the cement that were used as toilets, that was it.

We were fed rice and carrots in a big pot every Wednesday and Sunday. No food was given the other days. If you were lucky enough to have money deposited with the prison you could buy food every day and then you had a servant to prepare it for you, lay your blanket out and roll your cigarettes for just a bit of left over food in return. A tomato or a banana, whatever, if not for that he would starve.

On shower day, the guards opened one room at a time. This process took all day. Murderer's room first, thieves room, molester'ss room third and the drug users and trafficker'ss room last. Some prisoners chose not to shower and would stay in the room. Once every thirteen days was to often for them. We learned not to use these people as servants for good reason.

The showers were across the yard in another building. As I entered I saw a large concrete room with fifty one inch pipes sticking out of a moldy wall, cold wind blew threw the barred windows ten feet up. We were allowed a ten minute shower. When the water came on it was either scalding hot or freezing cold, no in between. I got wet, soaped up quick outside the water, stepped back in to rinse. It was hard to really get clean in the ten minutes.

The shower was finished in a flash it seemed. We were

marched out back across the prison grounds partially dressed and looking more like carnival workers than prisoners.

Once back in our room we used bottled water to brush our teeth, applied deordant but we didn't have a razor. Everyone wore beards in Sands prison. If you dared, an inmate would cut your hair.

Jon and I washed out our robes in the shower with us, these were the only clothes we had. We hung them to dry and wear our blankets around us for the day. By the end of the day they were still damp but we had to wear them to keep warm.

My first few weeks the days were so long and uncomfortable. I would wake up constantly at night because my arms would fall asleep against the hard concrete floor. I spent the nights feeling despair, lonely, and loss of hope of ever being released only to wake at daybreak to start it all over again.

I would sit against the wall with my eyes shut and think about my past. Warm summer days at the beach, being a kid and spending summer days exploring orange groves in Anaheim. How did I end up here among these walls with bombs flashing, gun shots in the distance, snoring and homosexual activity. Sometimes I just pull the blanket up over my eyes to shut out the reality and prisoners.

At daybreak a guard would bang on the steel door to alert us to get up. Jon and I look at each other but we no longer smile, we just shake our heads, fold up our blankets and place them against the wall.

After count the door shuts and we start our morning walk

around and around and around. Thirty two steps each way, turn around, until our breakfast.

Jon and I were fortunate enough to have servants. Our breakfast usually consisted of bread, cheese and maybe some bananas. After breakfast we would sit and talk for a bit and then walk some more. We could sit, stand or walk but, we were not allowed to lie down until dark. By mid morning sat against the wall with the other prisoners.

We talked about escaping but if we did we would be in the middle of Lebanon with no money, passports or transportation. If got caught escaping we would be gunned down by manned gun towers. It was hopeless.

We became friendly with some guys from Ethiopia, Europe and Sweden. Sometimes we would sit with them at meal time and pool our food together for our servants to prepare. Sometimes we had some pretty good meals. The servants waited on our every need and clean up all mess afterwards for just a few cigarettes and a bit of left over food.

After dinner time we would stand for the evening count. The guards would come in to count and take our food orders for the next days meal. When the doors closed the walking started again. Later there would be a loud bang on the door to signal the leader of the room to order us to stop walking, lie out our blankets and sleep for the night. Now all the snoring, farting and homosexual activity would start again. The lights were never turned off so I would just pull my blanket up over my eyes and think for hours until I could fall asleep.

This was all I had to look forward to day after day, week

after week, month after month and possibly year after year. I thought to myself, "this was going to be hard."

Wednesday's were special, we got a hot meal of rice, carrots and cheese. The guards would rush in the door with a big pot and put it in the middle of the room and rush out. We would all be ready with our bowls. Instantly there would be crowding, pushing and literally climbing over people to get to the food. The hunger brought out the "caveman" in you, it was strictly survival.

It had taken time but finally Jon and I started to get letters from our parents. We found that the United States Embassy told them to support us, that we would definitely be in there five to fifteen years with no food. We were completely blown away. Why would the embassy say that? They knew we had a chance of getting out.

It was common knowledge that some embassies would have their own citizen prisoners moved to their own countries for humanitarian reasons. Jon and I had heard nothing from our embassy since we had been arrested. We were told by the U.S. Embassy, in Beriut, we would get help with food, books and communication with our attorney and parents. Where were they? Other foreigners in the prison for drug trafficking received visits and communication almost daily from their embassies

Jon and I had been at the prison for weeks. The embassy knew we were there, they had notified our families with false information. We had sent so many letters and hardly got anything in return. Our nerves were almost shot and then we received a bundle of mail each full of letters of support and love. The embassy had held on our for some reason. The letters were from family members and girlfriends. We learned that they had put money on our books at the prison for food. We spent all day reading the letters over and over again, they were very precious to us.

Our families assured us they would do everything they could to get us out. Surprisingly I learned that our attorney had contacted our families asking for money for our defense. We were pissed. We had given that guy five thousand dollars to defend us and get us out and he hadn't done anything yet except ask our families for more money. We had heard stories of attorneys raping families for money, their homes and their bank accounts and then walking away and their loved on was left to serve five to fifteen years.

I wrote to my family and asked them not to send any money, I had already paid my attorney. Our attorney was our only hope, but now we didn't even trust him.

I went to the leader of the room, with the Ethiopian guy to translate for me, and asked him if he could find out what was happening with our court dates. He said he would write a letter to the commander of the prison and I would probably have an answer by the next day. I thanked him.

That evening the leader of the room invited Jon and me to join in on the button game, which he played every night joined by about fifteen chosen ones. Our being asked to join was an honor. In this game we all sat in an oval circle on the floor. One person was chosen to possess a button, all the others hold their hands clasped in front of them, the button man would go around to each set of hands and pretend to put the button in your hands. After he had gone to everyone in the circle he would take a seat and the person next to him would try to guess who had the button. If he was right, he would get to whip the hider with a knotted rag, but if he was wrong, every person in the circle would whip him with the rag. It was done all in good fun except with the Greeks and the Turks, they hated each other. The game continued from one person to the next around the circle. Each player normally gets whipped with the rag two or three times during a game. The Turks and the Greeks would hit each other so hard their faces would be red, finally they broke out into a fight that was broken up immediately but, the damage was already done.

The next morning, at count, the leader had to turn in the fighters. The guards grabbed the inmates and immediately the Turk started begging and sobbing and the Greek was begging and resisting. No amount of begging or sobbing would stop the guards for a second, they broke the prison rules and would be whipped. That evening the Turk and the Greek were carried back to the room, their feet whipped so badly they couldn't even walk. Their punishment for fighting had been carried out. The punishment was cruel and barbaric but it worked on most inmates who had seen it or heard of it.

Also, the guards brought back a written reply to the leader's letter on my behalf. It said I was scheduled for court the next week and my attorney had put in a request for me and Jon to see him the following day. I said, " thank you," and bowed to leader. Finally some answers.

Now that we knew we were going to see our attorney Jon and I had a lot to talk about. First, we wanted to know how he would like sitting in there not knowing anything that was going on. Second, we wanted to know why he was asking our families for money after we had already paid him thousands of dollars and nothing was happening. We had seen him only three times in four weeks and we were pissed.

The next day, when we saw our attorney, he said "how are things going?" I won't even say what went through my mind, let's just say we made ourselves clear that we were not happy. He told us not to worry, and again, that there had been a minor set back but that I would get out and Jon would get to the hospital next month. I asked him why we should believe him, we felt he was doing nothing for us except trying to rip off our parents. We told him that we wanted to be kept aware of everything and that we would be the ones to ask our families for money, not him. I demanded to know what was going on with my release, the anticipation of thinking each week I would be getting out was worse than just serving straight time. Jon wanted to know more about the hospital he was going to. This going to court and being taken back to prison, without a word, had to stop.

When our attorney left, we were returned to our prison room. We had been in there for four weeks and now one more week to go before court again. We agreed to just keep positive until the next week and hope that I would get released and Jon would go to the hospital.

Jon had a physical and mental evaluation early the following week just as our attorney had said. The Doctors evaluated Jon and diagnosed him a psychopath addicted to hash. According to our attorney the court would look at the evaluation and hopefully overturn Jon's conviction of five to fifteen years, to a three month stay in the hospital. Hopefully Jon would be transferred and I would be released the next Friday.

We went to court on Friday as our attorney had said. We were held in the same underground cell without food or bathrooms the entire day. When we were taken up to the court we looked pretty sad, in our robes that we had been wearing for five weeks, unshaven and unkept, next to our attorney in his nice suit and the judges in their black robes and white wigs. Our anticipation was high regardless. The court proceedings were held in French again and our attorney was presenting our case and the doctors evaluation, Jon's confession and my innocents. The judges looked at each other several times and talked over papers. I got the feeling they were in agreement with the way they moved their heads. The head judge had us stand and he pronounced a sentence. Our attorney looked at us when the judge was finished and nodded. He told me I was going to go free and that they accepted the diagnosis for Jon and he would be going to the hospital. He told us we'd go back to the holding cell, back to the prison and then I'd be released. After five weeks what he said was finally going to happen. He asked me if I had a place to stay until I got my exit visa, that could take three days, I told him I could probably stay at the university. He explained to me that after being in the prison for five weeks my visa had expired and that there would be lots of paper work but he would handle it for me, "don't worry," he said. I had learned now that meant to worry. Jon and I nodded our heads to each other and grinned, a resolution, things were going to change.

We were trucked back to the prison and back to our room. We told the other inmates what had gone on, that I was going to be released that night and Jon would be going to the nut house. We calmly sat back and waited for the door to open and call me out. The door did open, the guards took count and the door closed without me. We had our servants make our dinner and we ate in silence. The button game started but Jon and I just paced back and forth and never said it to each other but we both felt we had been screwed. The whole court thing had been in French and we were taking the word of our attorney as to what was said. That night was hopeless for me, things still went on as every other night, snoring, farting and the homosexuals pairing up. Jon and I felt like this was it, we would never see our attorney again.

In the morning, at count, Jon and I were called out to see our attorney. He was sitting in a room at a desk with no smile on his face. We sat down to listen to what he had to say. He explained that the court had released me but the prison would not until I had an exit visa. "How can I get one?" I asked. He told me I couldn't. He had set an appointment with the commander to explain that I could stay with him until I got my visa, I had to be there in person to get it. He then said that I would have to stay at the prison over the weekend because the commander was gone until Monday. I was trying to hide my anger of having to stay another weekend in that prison. We left our attorney and went back to our room. I was feeling so frustrated but, I didn't want to show that to Jon.

On Sunday morning we were called out again, this time for a visit. We didn't know of anyone who might visit us. We were taken to a building that separated the prison yard from the primary yard, just inside the prison walls. There was a set of bars and then a twenty foot opening and then another set of bars where the visitors stood. All inmates were crowding and yelling at their visitors and the visitors were crowding and yelling back. It was so loud with all the different languages being shouted back and forth. We looked through the crowd to see who might be there for us. Finally I noticed Michael, from the university. We couldn't hear each other so we just waved back and forth to each other until we were taken back to our room.

When we got back to our room it was time for the prison Sunday meal of rice, carrots and cheese. As we ate our meal we tried to figure out how Michael knew we were there and assumed he must had read about our arrest in the local paper, it was pretty ballsy of him to come there even though we did enjoy seeing him. His visit definitely raised our spirits. It had actually been a good day at sands prison. We walked pretty much the rest of the day and then played the button game. The Turks and the Greeks went at each other as usual. They hated each other so much you could see the fury in their eyes and they were so animated when they hit each other it was actually comical. There were very few laughs in a place like this, when it happened, it felt good.

Monday morning count came and went. Later the door opened, the guards said something to the leader and he came to me and said, "free free!" The reality of hearing "you're free" was bittersweet. Jon and I hugged, said goodbye, and I was rushed out the door. I was set free and Jon was staying behind, this truly sucked leaving my friend behind. The door slammed shut as I was looking back at Jon.

My attorney was waiting for me outside the visiting bars. He smiled and said "you're free, get your things, your staying at my villa, hurry."

When I got my personal things I had my passport, my watch, my suitcase and clothes but I did not have my return ticket to California on Lufthansa, it was missing. I complained but, it was hopeless.

Walking out of that prison was agonizing. I was leaving Jon, my best friend, but I had to go. My attorney said he knew how I was feeling but, this was the only way. The drive through Beirut was a shock, freedom so suddenly, I felt like someone coming out of a coma. We drove up the hillside to a villa looking over the Mediterranean. We passed through remote security gates, up a winding road, and then onto a cobblestone drive that took us to Hassan's enormous home built on a plateau sided by hundred foot cliffs overlooking a beautiful landscape. As we entered large brass front doors, he introduced me to the house staff. They were told I was a guest and then I was shown to my room. The room was one whole floor with a sunken bathtub, french doors opening to a large patio over looking part of Beirut and the Mediterranean. Hassan told me to relax, take a bath and eat some fresh fruit. As I sat in the tub, I looked around at this place. Just hours ago I was in a bleak place with nothing, now a mansion, free. While I was here, waiting for my Visa, I would focus on getting Jon out. Feeling this way made me feel better, not great but better.

That afternoon and evening I sat on a magnificent patio overlooking the Mediterranean with servants bringing me trays of fresh fruit and Lebanese pastries. I was treated like royalty all evening.

In the morning, when I awoke, I took another bath, put on some clean clothes and went upstairs and asked the house staff where I could find Hassan. They informed me he had gone to his office but he would be back for me at ten am. When Hassan came home he explained to me that I had to stay with him at all times so the police would not arrest me again, I was in his custody. He said, "now I will be going to the immigration building to get your exit visa." I replied, "the sooner the better!"

The immigration building was crowded but we went to the front of the line, my attorney I found out was a powerful man among common citizens and civil servants. Hassan had my papers for my visa completed and when the clerk told him it would be one month he demanded to speak with the person in charge and then he was assured the visa would be ready in three days.

After leaving the immigration building, Hassan and I went to the open air flea market, filled with thousands of merchants, buyers, bargaining, shouting, hugging and screaming. What a place! It was located in old town Beirut further up from the Mediterranean, Hassan purchased a ticket on Hungarian Airlines to Frankfurt Germany, a communist black market airline for me. He gave me two hundred dollars cash and I

was set to leave in three days. As it turned out, he wasn't such
a bad guy after all. It was just very different there and I was
amazed he put up with the way Jon and I talked to him in
prison. Nobody talked back to him in his world.

The next day I asked Hassan if he would take me to the
university of to say good-bye to a friend of mine. I told him
how Michael came to visit Jon and me at the prison. He stated
that was very brave of Michael and that he must be a good
friend, "yes he is" I said. Hassan took me and dropped me
off and told me to be very careful and be back at that spot in
two hours for him to pick me up. I went to look for Michael
at the dorms but his roommate said he was helping out at the
drama department and pointed me in the right direction. Still
feeling the newness of being free, the walk across the beautiful campus, breathing the sea air renewed my focus to save
Jon. I found Michael decorating the drama stage, he looked
up surprised to see me. We shook hands, and he wanted to
know how we got out, thinking Jon was out also. I explained
all the court ordeals, that Jon was held because, he had stash
taped to his body, and he had to go to the nut house before
he would be released. I told him I would be leaving the next
day, we exchanged addresses, his home was in Florida, and
I told him I would see him again sometime. It was time to
leave, Michael walked me out, we gave each other a big hug
then I stepped inside Hassan's big black mercedes and we
drove off.

This would be the last time I would see the University of
Beirut. Hassan took me back to his villa. He told me my visa
was ready but he felt it safer for me if he went alone to get

it, he had other business to do so he wouldn't see me till the next day. I spent the evening planning my return to Germany and feeling belly sick leaving Jon behind.

Early the next morning we were on our way to the Beirut International airport. When we arrived the only building standing had jeeps full of armed army soldiers protecting it. We walked past them and into the building, I showed my passport and ticket, then Hassan said something in Arabic and I was allowed to pass onto the airfield. I said goodbye to Hassan, thanked him and then walked to the only plane there. The pilot was standing at the top of the stairs and greeted me as I boarded. I sat by a window, looking at the runway guarded by army tanks and anti aircraft bunkers. There were maybe thirty passengers on the plane. The captain finally closed the door and the plane started moving. I thought to myself, please just hurry and get this plane off the ground. We taxied out next to a tank and sat there for twenty minutes. Finally we started down the runway, picked up speed and lifted off the ground. I looked down looking for sands prison where Jon was.

The plane made a stop in Budapest Hungry, but since I did not have an entrance visa, I stayed in the transient lounge for hours. Occasionally, I looked out the window at a dreary place, everybody dressed in gray. After a few hours my plane showed up and I was back on my way to Frankfurt.

When I arrived in Germany, I immediately tried to get a replacement ticket from Lufthansa back to California. They said they would work on it and gave me a number to call. I took a shuttle into Frankfurt and got a room at the same hotel I had met Jon at when all this had started. After checking in

I walked down the street to the train station to get a schedule and it was de-ja-vue. I was going to take the train the next morning to Heilbromn, close to Russo's. I went back to my room and slept through dinner until the next morning.

On the train, the next morning, sometimes passing close to the autobahn, I couldn't shake the melancholy feeling of Jon and me traveling on it talking about getting rich. Now, I was alone and Jon was in prison and I needed to make money to free him and I was homesick for Orange County. I was so engrossed in thought during the train ride I was surprised when the conductor called out "Heilbromn." I got off the Train with my suitcase and one hundred fifty dollars, took a trolley to the bus station and headed for Bonningheim. The bus climbed up and down rolling hills that Jon and I had driven, laughing and high on hash. Again that bellyache feeling overwhelmed me, I was feeling a real loss.

I arrived in Bonningheim mid-afternoon, got into a taxi, and in fifteen minutes I was walking into Russo's club. When I entered the club, there was Russo behind the bar giving instructions to a German cleaning lady. Russo saw me and gave me a big smile and then looked at my suitcase. I walked into his office and he followed me. Russo asked where I had been. I told him Jon and I had gotten busted in Lebanon and that Jon was still in prison there and I needed money to get him out. I explained the whole story of the car, the bust, the attorney and his plans for Jon. I told him I was practically broke and I needed to make money to pay Jon's way out. I told him that my ticket home was stolen by the prison. I asked Russo if he could help me make some money while I waited to get my replacement ticket. Russo said, " let's do it and get Jon out!" And then he informed me that he had totaled the VW in Spain. "No big deal," I replied.

I stayed with Russo at the club for a while and he offered me his old Peugeot to drive to his house. I took him up on the offer and left. When Russo came in that night we sat up and talked over what had happened to both of us in the last three months. I summed up the long trip, radical borders, how Jon couldn't get a visa from Istanbul thru Iran. I told him about meeting Charlie in Istanbul and he was the one who gave us the idea of Lebanon instead of Afghanistan. Russo said he had been vacationing in Barcelona Spain for a month and that he had just gotten back the week before. He said he had totaled the VW by running into a tree while high on mescaline. He got arrested and went to jail for not having proper insurance and damaging a tree. He had to pay heavy fines and was so broke he had to hitch hike back to Germany. I told Russo that I was hoping Judy would be able to send me one half ounce of mescaline to sell while I waited for my replacement ticket. We talked about buying a kilo of hash and sending it back to California by mail hidden in some speakers. I said when I got home I would sell the hash to make money for Jon's legal fees, then I would send the money for another kilo, so on and so forth until Jon got out. Russo and I figured it would take two or three weeks to sell the mescaline, buy and send the hash to California and get a replacement ticket from Lufthansa.

Just like everything else over there, everything takes longer than planned. I didn't take any extra trips or have any hookers this time as I waited and waited for my replacement ticket. I only had enough money after three months to buy a cheap ticket home and send a pound of hash. Judy had only sent me one quarter ounce, two hundred and fifty doses of mescaline, but it took her a month just to score what she sent. Lufthansa never gave me a new ticket either but with Russo's help selling the mescaline, dose by dose, all came together and I had a ticket home on Bohemian Airlines after two and a half months.

The flight home was booked from Frankfurt to Miami with layovers and plane changes but it fit my pocketbook. Once again, my return home was bittersweet with Jon in prison, I was free physically but not mentally. I had no idea what would be waiting for me when I got home but I called my mother and Judy to let them know I was coming home the next day.

My flight from Frankfurt was scheduled to leave at six thirty am. Frankfurt was a one hundred mile drive from Russo's so he asked if he could take me the night before, I would sleep in the airport. He had to be at work the next day and if he took me in the morning he wouldn't get back in time. I told him that would be fine. We headed up the autobahn at four pm and we arrived at the Frankfurt airport at seven pm. I told Russo he didn't have to wait around, I would be fine. I would call him when I got home and we bear hugged good bye. I entered the airport, checked my baggage, found a phone and made an international call to a hotel in Anaheim for a reservation the next day when I arrived home, and then found a place in the airport to hang out for the next twelve hours.

After a long uncomfortable night my plane boarded at

six thirty am, it took off on time at seven am, a half hour flight for a two hour layover for another plane in Brussels. I looked down at the patchy snow below and said to myself, " good bye."

The layover in Luxemburg turned into an eight hour wait for the plane. After being fueled and stocked all the passengers were finally boarded on this no frills aircraft with barely enough room for our legs. I was afraid I wouldn't make my connection flight to Miami. The flight to Nassau took only seven hours, instead of nine, due to tail winds, and landed at ten pm, my connecting flight was scheduled to depart at eleven pm. I hurried inside the terminal and handed my ticket to the counter person and he said, " we don't accept these tickets. You need to cash this ticket in and buy one of ours but, you better hurry, the plane leaves in twenty minutes." I grabbed back my ticket and ran to the Bohemian ticket counter, talked as fast as I could, telling them what I needed and to hurry so I wouldn't miss my flight. By the time I got back to the Miami airlines, I had missed the plane. I asked when the next plane was and I was told not until the next day at five pm, that was the last flight of the day. Now I was stuck in Nassau airport until the next day. It was eleven pm, I asked the counter girl where the lounge was. She stated that they didn't have one, it was a small airport and it closed at twelve midnight. At midnight I was asked to leave by a doorman, I asked him where was I to go? The airport was five miles from town and a taxi would cost fifteen dollars one way, I hardly had any money left. I told him I had to stay there and he walked away. The doors were locked and I spent the night in the

Nassau airport alone. New people opened the next morning, took one look at me and asked how I had gotten in there. I told them I had spent the night there and they were shocked. "Didn't the police escort you out last night?" I explained to them the doorman tried and they said, " That wasn't the doorman that was the police." I had to chuckle at this point, "your police dress like doormen?" I had now been traveling for forty one hours.

I landed the next day at the Miami airport, after a one hour flight, picked up money at the telegram office to buy my ticket to LAX on a direct flight. I had to buy a stand by ticket, unfortunately there was no room on the non stop flights so I took another plane from Miami via St. Louis to LAX, but was bumped in St.Louis, now fifty one hours of travel. I sat in a coffee shop at ten pm in St. Louis International hoping to catch a flight each hour to LAX. Finally the third flight I boarded was scheduled to arrive in Los Angeles at two am.

I arrived at LAX looking like a homeless person after fifty eight hours of travel, spending the night in two airports, being bumped from several planes and my bags were long gone. This had been the flight from hell.

Luckily my luggage had been stored in the unclaimed baggage lock up, I found a porter and showed him my claim ticket and he unlocked the gate and I got my bag and asked where I could catch a bus to the Anaheim hotel, it was four am by this time. The bus to Anaheim was scheduled to depart at five am via Long Beach airport; arrival at nine am.

I got off the bus in front of the hotel and the sun was

bright. I found a phone and called my friend Jerry, who lived in Anaheim, he told me he would be there in ten minutes. When Jerry pulled up and saw me he said, " you look terrible, just get in the car, I'll get your bags." I asked him to take me to a close by hotel to cancel a reservation I had made. I went up to the front desk and explained to the clerk that I had a reservation but my planes had been delayed, I had been traveling for three days and needed to cancel the reservation but I thought I might of gotten mail delivered there. The clerk looked and there was a package from Germany for me, I accepted it and thanked him.

I walked back out to Jerry's car and we drove to his house in Anaheim. He wanted me to stay there and tell him all that had happened on my trip. I told him I was too tired and just wanted him to take me home to Huntington Beach. I opened the package I got from Germany, which contained a German clock. I took off the back and unloaded a pound of hash. Jerry bought an ounce, for ninety dollars, then we took off for Huntington Beach.

11

A big dark cloud lifted

AS WE TURNED ON MY STREET I could feel my pulse
pounding. We stopped in front of my house, I gathered my
things from Jerry's car, told him thank you and he drove off.
It had taken three months and three days travel to get in front
of my house. Staring at the front door, I felt as if I wasn't
even there. As I walked up to the front door, I had thought
about this little Huntington Beach house hundreds of times
with Judy inside, now I was here. I tried the doorknob, it was
locked. I knocked and then saw the curtain move slightly and
I heard a loud scream, it was Judy and the door swung open.

She grabbed hold of me kissing and crying. We hugged for a long time. I looked over her shoulder into the living room and waved to some good friends. It felt good to be wanted, to be missed so much. She held on to me for a long time, I loved it and at the same time I hated it. How could I be excited with Jon still back in that Prison? It was a bittersweet time. I couldn't be truly happy until Jon was home too. Judy and I stepped inside, one of my friends grabbed my luggage, and I plopped down on the couch with Judy still holding on tight. The smell of home and seeing my friends was all so great. I was handed a lit joint and realized I really had made it home at last.

As I sat there looking around my friends were asking a lot of questions. How was the prison over there? How did I get busted? How was Jon taking being left there? What took so long for me to get home? It had taken me a year to get back home and they wanted to know everything that had happened. I told them that the prison and the legal system there sucked, we were hardly fed, sleeping on the floor, a shower every thirteen days, we shit in a hole in the floor. I filled them in about the bust, how it went down at the port shipping our car, the attorney's only defense for us, Jon had to plead guilty, because he had stash taped to him. I was innocent unless Jon testified against me..

Answering all the questions was very draining on me, I needed a shower and the reality of what I was now going to face sank in and I was exhausted. I asked everyone if they wouldn't mind leaving, I hadn't been alone with Judy for a year. They all politely got up and left us to ourselves.

After they left I showed Judy the pound of hash we would sale this to get our cash started. Judy smoked some while I took a shower. "After a long shower, I'll feel more like talking about the trip and what we've got to do for Jon".

Judy laid on the waterbed and I joined her, we just snuggled, it was so good to be home. I was ready to tell her everything, starting at the beginning in Germany, our adventures, smugglings, dealings, prison, court and the three months getting home. I told her about Russo, how much our friendship had developed and how we were going to work together to free Jon. Then she had a lot of questions of her own I needed to answer. She asked, "How are we going to survive? Will the police arrest you?". All I could say was, "I don't know".

I told Judy until Jon was free my total purpose was to free him. I called my Mom to let her know I was back safe and that Judy and I would see her the next day. She asked about Jon, she had grown fond of him over the years, he spent a lot of time with our family. I told her I would see her in the morning.

When we got to my Mom's house, she hugged me and cried. It was so good to see her. Moms are forgiving and I'm sure she thought she would never see her boy again. I told her the story, I was just a guilty as Jon, that he needed money to get out and I was going to help him, she understood how I felt.

My next stop wasn't going to be a friendly one, I was going to see Jon's mom. When she opened the door, she froze for a moment and then waved me in. We sat at the kitchen table and I tried to explain what had happened. She wanted to know where I had been for the past three months. "You promised to help Jon, he's really upset that I haven't heard from you or received any money," she said. I told her I was stuck in Europe without a ticket home. She wanted to know why Jon took the blame instead of me. I said I know Jon had written and explained everything to her. She told me that Jon needed me to payoff thousands of dollars to doctors, judges and attorneys. I agreed but, I didn't have the money now but I assured her I was going to get it. I was going to pay as soon as I could. I let her know I was sorry and Judy and I left feeling her disgust. I had been truthful to her and I meant what I said. I was going to help get him out of prison but, it would take some time.

When we got home, I told Judy I needed to write to Jon right away and explain. My letter started "hey bro, I want you to hear straight from me what happened, where I've been and what I am going to do. First, I saw your Mom today, explained that I had been stuck in Europe, without a ticket for three months, that the prison had stolen it and that Lufthansa would not replace it. You're Mom told me you finally made it to the hospital, that's great. She told me about all your expenses. Now that I am back, I can start making money and start paying for your release. Jon, I haven't forgotten about you, I promise. I won't have all the money at once but I'll get it. Hold on bro, I'll get you out. Write me and let me know how you are doing. What can I send you? I signed it, "your Bro and Sis".

After I wrote the letter I started weighing ounces of hash out of the pound I brought back. I made sixteen ounces which would net fifteen hundred dollars, enough to get started dealing again. I made some calls and set up sales. Within one day I had sold it all. I went by Jon's Mom's house and gave her five hundred dollars. She looked at the money and said, "What is this? I need thousands." I asked her to give me time, that I would keep it coming. With that she slammed the door in my face.

Now it was time to make calls to San Francisco for mescaline, even though the area was flooded with psyche-delics it was still a moneymaker. I called people I knew in Laguna and Hawaii to tell them I was back. People usually don't like to talk about drugs over the phone but I was sort of a celebrity in the drug world and everybody wanted to know the details of Lebanon. I met separately with my connections and then told them all the details of the bust. I told them that I needed to start scamming again to help Jon. Some of my connections gave me stash for free and some gave me money toward Jon's release, this was going to work.

The money started to flow in and I kept paying Jon's Mom for his expenses but she always wanted more. I couldn't give her everything, I needed money to exist and to keep on dealing. I started getting regular letters from Jon by now. I explained that his Mom was always angry with me and that she felt I should be giving her more money. I hoped he understood that I was doing as much as I could. In Jon's next letter he assured me that he knew I was doing my best and that his mom was just that way. He wrote that the doctors had committed him again as a psychopath and that he was hoping

to be released the following month. He had been there five
months, one more month his nightmare could be over.

When the next month came, Jon went back to court and
half the judges voted for his release and the other half wanted
more evidence from his doctors. This shattered Jon, his letter
was real depressing, his moral was gone. He said all they
wanted was more money and felt that he was never going to
be released.

Three more months passed, the holidays were coming
and Jon had been in prison for eight and one half months. His
defense had cost over thirty thousand dollars, every month it
was something else that kept him there.

One afternoon, a couple weeks before Christmas, I got a
call from a friend, he said; "Have you heard?" I told him "no,
what?" He then told me that he saw Jon, That he was home. I
was afraid to believe Jon had been freed but lots of my friends
started calling me and verifying the same info. Jon would be
staying at his mom's, I was sure of that, and I was also sure
I was not welcome there. Jon would contact me when it was
casual, maybe in a couple weeks, in the meantime a big dark
cloud was lifted off of me, it was time for a vacation and
celebration so Judy and I were off to Hawaii.

I made calls to my friends in the islands. Smiley was in
San Blas for a month surfing so I called another friend Mike,
who was working as a bellboy in Waikiki. When he answered
the phone I said, " Hey, what's up?" Instantly he recognized
who I was and asked where I was calling from. I told him I
was in Huntington Beach and that Judy and I were heading
over. He told me we could stay at his apartment but to be sure

to bring drugs, especially pills. I told Mike I needed a vacation and that I could bring some mescaline but what was the deal with the pills? He told me that jars of bennys (uppers) could sell for one hundred dollars to one hundred twenty five dollars a jar. I said, " I would bring them but that he had to sell them, I was on vacation". He said the surf and weather was great and he worked nights so we could surf every day and that he had three boards, I could take my pick, surf the days away and he would do all the selling.

Judy and I loaded up our bags, mostly with bathing suits and drugs and headed for Honolulu the next morning. We arrived around twelve noon, made it through the agricultural inspection, we declared nothing, and called Mike to pick us up.

Mike wheeled into the airport passenger pick-up area in a sixties something Hawaiian rust bucket, you would have thought he was driving a limo, he double parked and honked his horn when he saw us standing with our luggage. He jumped out of his car in nothing but a bathing suit, sandals, long hair down to his shoulders and a big smile. He grabbed Judy and I and gave us a big hug and said, "lets go!" We hopped in his car and off we went. The floorboard of the car was so rusted out you could see the street. I leaned over to Judy and said, "I hope this car doesn't break in half before we get there."

Mike told us he had a surprise for us. He got us two free nights in a suite at the hotel he worked at and if we wanted to stay longer we could for fifty percent off. He dropped us off at the front of a big Waikiki hotel, in his limo, told us also that his personal hotel staff would treat us like royalty. His shift started at three pm and he would come up and visit us then.

Sunset and Tequila Sunrise's on our balcony overlooking Waikiki was fantastic, only a few surfers left catching nice 3 foot waves with reflections of a beautiful Hawaiian sunset accompanied by warm trade winds. This was the perfect time to drop a mellow dose of mescaline and go for a sunset swim in the warm Hawaiian water. Judy asked which suit should she wear, her one piece or her bikini. The bikini was as far as she got, that red top and tiny white bottoms on her long legged body, wow!

Just as we were coming on to our doses of mescaline, and had on our bathing suits, Mike called from the front desk. I told him we were just getting ready to leave and go for a swim and he asked us to wait for him. Minutes later there was a knock at the door, expecting to see Mike, I opened it up. There stood a bellboy with a tray filled with exotic fruits and tropical drinks. "This is for VIP's, " he said, "compliments of the house." I accepted the treats, tipped him well and shut the door.

Just as I tossed a mango slice in my mouth there was another knock at the door, I opened it and there stood Mike in his bell uniform and completely groomed. I hardly recognized him as the same guy that picked us up at the airport three hours ago. He had a big smile on his face, I invited him in. He said he only had a minute, he was on duty, and he wanted to get some rolls of whites and some doses of mescaline. He said he had people waiting for the drugs. He then asked if I would front him a jar, one thousand doses, of whites and he would break it up and sell them. "Sure," I said, I handed him a jar and told him that we were just coming on to the mescaline and wanted to go for a swim, we would catch up with him later. He was on duty all night so he didn't mind. Judy and I headed for the beach leaving Mike in the suite to make up the doses he needed.

Judy and I took our pineapple drinks and towels down to a cabana on the beach, where we laid our towels, and headed for the water. The water was a comfortable and warm, we bobbed around in the water until dark and we got a bit chilly, then decided to take a jacuzzi back at the hotel to warm up. While in the jacuzzi I saw Mike, he motioned to me. I went to see what he wanted and to thank him again for setting us up at the hotel, it was great. He wanted to know if he could go up to our room again and get some more pills, he had sold all the ones he got earlier. "Mike, I can't believe you sold them all already," I said surprisingly. "These are night people here, they love speed," he said. He wasn't kidding, he had sold a jar of whites, three pills for one dollar and mescaline for ten dollars a dose. He was selling to his co-workers and to people partying in the hotel. All that evening we had continuous visits from Mike and we were starting to get a really paranoid. I was afraid people would start to realize Mike's connection was in the hotel. The last visit from Mike was at one am, I told him that was it for the evening and from then on he had to sell jars only. I asked him to call me in the morning and we would go surfing. I could tell Mike was high on the speed. His eyes were wide open, his pupils were dilated and wild looking, there was hardly any color left in his Iris. "I'll see you in the morning, good night," I said.

The next morning I figured Mike wouldn't be calling until late so I headed to the beach for some surfing. After surfing I could see Mike and Judy on the balcony, of the suite, waving to me. I waved back and headed up to the room. When I got in the room Mike was still in his bell uniform, he hadn't gone home or to bed yet. "How's the water?" Mike asked. "Like heaven," I replied. I sat Mike down and explained that last night was like a Chinese fire drill. There was too much coming and going from our room, people were going to figure out who had the drugs. I could get busted or ripped off. "Mike," I said, " sell jars from now on." Mike told me he had already pre-sold the jars and the rest of the mescaline. He took all I had left and made a great profit.

I realized that this side of the island was a complete different world than the north shore. Waikiki was a nightlife town full of action and needed pills whereas the north shore was laid back, slow paced country life that enjoyed hash.

Mike returned later that day with all my cash. I had made nearly two thousand dollars in one night with just a few drugs. I saw the demand, I could make a fortune. Mike said he could sell at least ten jars of whites a week, maybe more. That could make me over one thousand dollars a week, not including the mescaline I could sell to him and friends on the north shore. I could see a new scam starting.

While Mike and I were surfing that day, talking about all the money we were going to make, he suggested that I move to the island. He knew of a house available that was half way between Waikiki and the north shore. He told me of an old lady writer that had a house in the middle of five acres in a rainforest, which needed a caretaker for the numerous animals she sheltered. He said the area was like a jungle and very private. A friend of his had lived there but moved back to the main land, it had been vacant for a few months. He offered to introduce me to the lady, she just wants somebody there. The rent would be free and I would have five acres with a giant trees like avocado, mango, guava and banana that were all organic. I thought it sounded great, I always wanted to move to the islands. I couldn't wait to get back on the beach to tell Judy about it.

Back on the beach I thought Judy would be so excited to hear about the house but to my surprise, she started crying instead. I didn't say anymore about it until we got back to our room and we were alone. I asked her what was wrong even though I already knew. She couldn't leave California because of her job. I told her this might be a great opportunity and we should at least look at the house the next day, no commitment.

The next morning was a beautiful December Hawaiian morning with tropical rain flurries, intermittent sunshine, trade winds, palm trees swaying and a beautiful rainbow. Mike pulled up in his sixties something rust bucket to take us across the island to the old Hawaiian woman's house. "She might not even like me or I might not even like her," I told Judy. "Mike said she's an eccentric writer, you can never tell about that type," I said. We drove up to the house located on the country side of Oahu. Her house was fifty feet back off the main road. Mike pointed up the hill, "that's it," he said. It was a big house, from what I could see, among morning glories waist high with lots of jungle type vines and trees, built on stilts on the side of a hill. When I saw the house my heart leaped, it was a true island setting, now Judy was excited.

We opened the old rusted gate and walked up to the old woman's door where we were greeted by a three legged, half blind growling dog. "Wait here, that dog bites," Mike said. He opened the gate, called the dog by some Hawaiian name and the dog kind of mellowed. Mike then walked up to the front door, keeping an eye on that mangy mutt at all times, and knocked. He waited and then knocked again and finally the door opened and there stood a heavy set woman in a Hawaiian Moo-Moo. Mike talked to her awhile, she motioned the vicious dog inside and then Mike motioned for Judy and me to enter the gate. I walked up to the front door and Mike introduced me to her as an encyclopedia salesman looking to locate on Oahu and that I did a lot of traveling. "This is Tutu," he said to me, "That means grandmother in hawaiian". I was looking in a face that was so big and round her eyes, nose and lips were all close together in the middle, she looked like she had been hit in the face with a frying pan and to top it off she had wild permed hair and I would swear there was no neck on top of her plump five foot body. Immediately she said to me, "You must never bother me, our only communication will be by note in my mailbox. Do you understand?" she barked. "Okay, can I look at the house?" I asked. She gave Mike the key, he turned to her and asked if the chimpanzee was chained? "Stay on the path and he won't get you," she barked.

We left her house and started on the path leading up to the jungle house. On the way up the hill Mike told us to watch out for the chimp, he was near by. Halfway up to the house we spotted the chimp peeking over a log right at us. He was hooked to two trees by way of a locked belt around his waist with a cable attached to another cable with a ring that slid giving him an outside perimeter to roam. He could not get to the path we were on but he was sure watching us with his beady little eyes. He was ready to attack if we stepped off the path into his reach, we made sure we stayed on the path.

When we walked up the stairs, maybe ten feet, out of the jungle and opened the door we heard a scrambling noise. "What was that?" I asked. Mike just laughed, "This is the jungle and no one has lived here for two months," he said and left it at that. The place was big inside, two bedrooms, two living rooms and a big kitchen looking down the hill onto the path and road. The building was made of wood, tin roof, no ceiling and no glass on the windows, just screens. "Years ago this was a chicken house," Mike said, and now to me, a place with island charisma and a lot of potential. The back door opened to tall jungle grass maybe three feet tall. Mike said the vegetation in the area grows five inches a day, there were lots of critters and that there was no hot water. "Who needs it here anyway," I thought to myself. I looked at Judy and said, "What do you think?" "I want it," she said. "I'll fly back once a month, with some stash and stay for a week, and you fly back with me each month for one week, we'll keep both houses," she said. We had always wanted to move to the islands and this could be our first house. "It's decided, we'll take it," I told Mike.

This vacation turned into a move, not just a vacation. I went to Mrs. Tutu and told her I would take the house and that I would be a good caretaker when she needed me. She agreed and then asked when I could move in, I told her, "starting tomorrow."

Most of the next week was spent going to second hand Hawaiian stores, rather than the beach, these were the best places to outfit a surfer's pad.. We found everything we needed cheap. Someone had turned in a fantastic bamboo style full set of furniture for a living room and bedroom with matching seashell lamps that sold for a couple hundred dollars. At our next stop we got two used large asian rugs, one for the living room and one for the bedroom, a clunky refrigerator, a T.V just to have, Mike said we probably wouldn't get any reception, an old stereo, for seventy five, which worked great and all our basic kitchen items. Our Island paradise was completely outfitted for just a few hundred bucks. At the local market I hired two Samoan women to make the house more livable by sanitizing toilets, sinks, floors and debugging the place, it was full of hundreds of jungle critters. I hired their children to machete back the jungle, this would keep a lot of the bugs away from the house and give me a back yard. The last thing I bought was an old Hawaiian rust bucket from a used car dealer in Honolulu for three hundred bucks. It was a sixty one ford falcon and what a mistake, it was a real piece of shit but, I was stuck with it. Now we were islanders in just one week.

Mike agreed to stay at the island house for two weeks while I went back to the mainland to score more drugs and get my clothes. Judy and I checked out of the suite at the hotel, which we had hardly used the last week we were there, and headed for the airport. We said goodbye to Mike. I would call when I got back in a week or two.

Our flight home was uneventful. Judy's sister was there to pick us up and told us that Jon had been trying to get in touch with us. She told him that we were in Hawaii and he wanted us to contact him as soon as we got back, but not at his mom's house. Jon said for us to call Randy and he would get the message.

We pulled up to our Huntington Beach house and every-thing was great. I had a house in the islands and a house in Huntington Beach, I had a lot of money, Jon was out and I would be seeing him the next day. I could tell it was all bitter-sweet for Judy, I knew that feeling all to well, she had priori-ties that would keep her here, but that would all change. I sat down and called Randy and left a message for Jon to call.

Jon called almost immediately. When I heard his voice I got chills down my back. Jon was really back, the Beirut bust was history and we were still partners, bros, and things were going good. "Come on over, I've got some fantastic Afghanistan elephant ear hash we just brought back from the islands." Then I proceeded to tell about the rainforest house, the monkeys, tropical birds, waist high morning glories, beau-tiful fruit trees, the five acres of paradise and the best part, rent free. He said he was at his mom's house in Garden Grove and he would be there in about thirty minutes. I reminded him to bring a board.

I was in the front yard when Jon drove up in his mom's old Buick cruiser. I yelled to Judy, " Jon's here!" she ran outside. There was the same big familiar smile that was Jon's trait, prison hadn't changed him, he was the same old Jon. He opened the big cruiser door, we high fived, hugged and then he hugged Judy, we were family united.

We all went in the house, locked the doors and closed the curtains. I handed Jon the hash pipe and we both laughed at each other. It had been quite awhile since we parted at sands prison. I was anxious to hear everything, what caused his sudden release, his flight back and the nut house. He told me there had been a shake up in the judicial government and that our lawyer took advantage of the corruption and got a judge to release him. He told me then the attorney drove him straight to the airport before anyone could stop him. "I was out of court and on a plane to Germany within an hour luckily," he said.

The next week was just like old times, Jon and I surfing, getting loaded, more surfing, getting loaded again. I scored a keg of whites, fifty jars which could make over six thousand dollars in Hawaii. I told Jon I would be going back to Hawaii in a week to sell the pills. I asked Jon to come and move to Hawaii with me. "We'll have a great time." Jon said he had taken a job at his mom's work and was starting the next week. Jon and I had a great time that week surfing and now all was going to change. I was moving to the islands and he was getting a job. I let him know that if he ever changed his mind and decided to come over I had plenty of room, an old rust bucket surf wagon and plenty of money, all he had to do was give me a call.

I wasn't going to see Jon for a while so I suggested we go down to the pier and get ourselves an avocado sandwich, strawberry smoothie, some Dr. Bronner's chips and walk on the pier. I wanted to give Jon some money to hold him over so after our walk, I handed him ten one hundred dollar bills, "I hope this will hold you over till you get paid." Jon just smiled and said "thanks!"

A couple days later I was on a plane to Hawaii with a keg of whites, an ounce of mescaline, moving to Hawaii, how things change. I had always wanted to make this move but now I was melancholy but resolved. My consolation was Judy sitting by my side. I had decided I needed her to come back with me to help decorate the house and stay a few weeks; she didn't seem to mind a bit. When we arrived in Honolulu Mike was there waiting. How different this time was, only two weeks had passed since we left and now we were going to be taken to our surfer pad instead of a big luxurious hotel on the beach.

As we crossed the island and approached our house, the first thing I saw was my rust bucket parked at the bottom of the hill. As we got closer, we could see our Hawaiian jungle house in paradise. We pulled up, got out, stretched, got our suitcases and walked up the path to the house. Carrying the suitcases up the hill, through the thick jungle air, we were drenched within five minutes. We reached the house, climbed the wooden stairs and opened the front door. This was our new beginning.

Mike said he had to get going, he had to get to work but he needed ten jars of whites and one hundred doses of mescaline. He already had people waiting for the stash. I had to package them up. He helped me get the baggies made and then was off and said he would be back in the morning with the cash.

That evening, after unpacking and settling in, Judy and I walked up to Tutu's mailbox and left her a note letting her know I was back and to let me know if she needed me to take care of anything for her. The note let her know I would be around for the next three weeks. We then walked down to the local store, about two blocks away. She saw us and said "Aloha," I replied back the same. I gingerly opened the old screen door at the entrance and walked in, followed by Judy and the Hawaiian mom. She introduced us to Pop, who was behind the ancient cash register, these two were meant for each other. They were both about two hundred and fifty pounds, he wore a Hawaiian shirt, baggy shorts and old worn out sandals and she dressed in a traditional moo-moo, also old worn sandals and a flower in her dark hair. They were a perfect example of old Hawaii, probably born right there.

The little Hawaiian store was crammed full. It served as a hardware, grocery, sewing, bakery and produce store all in one. They had giant avocados, papayas, mangos and guava's really cheap; they were picked off trees behind the store. We bought some fruit and an avocado, the size of a small cantaloupe, and headed back up to the rust bucket hoping the battery wasn't dead and it would start. To my surprise it started, and we drove out on Kam highway and parked next to the bay to watch the sunset. Judy opened her purse and pulled out a joint and fired it up. We talked about our future, fired up another joint and pulled our clothes off for a skinny dip in the bay. Judy's body looked fantastic as she walked naked to the water. I thought to myself, "This is what I have been waiting for all my life." In the water we bobbed face to face talking. We figured we would mostly stay in the country and when Judy moved over we considered moving to another island and buying some property on the beach.

In one month the simple life in the islands agreed with me. Judy had been gone two weeks and I really missed her. Mike's nightlife people had bought all fifty jars and one half ounce of mescaline. My phone seldom rang, it was either Judy in the evening or Mike in the mornings. Smiley was still in San Blas and then going on to Europe and Asia, obvious a hash scam, he wouldn't be back for three months. I saw Mike every other day while I was holding but now that I was sold out I didn't see him. He would call and ask me when my next supply was coming, he had people waiting, and the demand was giant. I spent my days smoking hash and surfing excellent velzeeland waves, enjoying the scenery of beautiful girls in their bikini's, but I yearned for some company, even in paradise, I needed someone to talk to. Each day for weeks I would paddle out, alone, high on pot, hash or sometimes mescaline. I felt full of insight surfing, especially if I were loaded on psychedelics, I felt one with the water, waves, sun, sky and birds. I went for days using mind altering drugs, alone, hardly interacting or speaking with anyone. I thought and wondered, philosophically, about everything.

I decided to go back to the mainland and get some more jars and mescaline so I called Mike and asked him if he would watch the house for a few days. Mike was glad to watch the house, I said, " I will be ready to leave for the airport in the morning would he come and get me?" I called Judy next and told her I'd be in the next day, "I miss you, will you pick me up?" I asked. She responded "yes."

When I walked off the plane there stood Judy and Jon waving. I went through the agricultural inspection quickly, kissed Judy and high fived Jon. I asked Jon how work was going. He told me he quit after two weeks, it sucked, and he punched out his jerk of a boss. "So, you coming back to the islands with me in a few days?" I asked. "You know I am," he said. I told him I just knew he would hate surfing everyday and making tons of money. We all laughed.

When I got back to Huntington Beach, I realized how much I had missed it. I gave Judy a few thousand dollars spending money, called my connections and set up a score of a keg of mini whites and an ounce of mescaline to be picked up the next day. Jon took off to start setting things in place for his move. He was going to tell his mom he was moving to the islands with Smiley and that he had a job building surf boards and free rent. Jon was going back with me, the demand for my drugs was "BIG" and things couldn't be better.

Within days Jon and I were on a plane on our way to the islands. We had stash, which conveniently fit in my suitcase inside a bathing suit. Mike was selling ten thousand dollars in one month. On the five hour flight I filled Jon in on Mike and his duties at the hotel, how he sells most of the drugs to his co-workers, hookers and hotel guests. Waikiki was just another concrete city but it is situated in paradise. Like in any big city it has its night people which include drugs, sex and crime of all types. The people want to stay up all night and party, this creates a big demand for whites. "I only sell to Mike, I don't trust the other people I know in Waikiki."

When we arrived at the airport Mike was there as planned to pick us up but this time he was in my old rust-bucket with a shiny new set of surfing racks on top. He explained that his car had broken down and so he had been using my car so he thought he would surprise me with a new set of racks, sounded like a good deal to me. I introduced Jon to Mike as we loaded up the car with our luggage and then I jumped into the driver's seat. Jon started to laugh and when I asked him why, wasn't he impressed, he just laughed again and said, " Yeah, I'm impressed, I just hope I get one." We all laughed and took off for our drive to the rainy back side of the island. As we got closer and rounded the final corner I told Jon, "There she is, on stilts on the side of that hill." We parked at the bottom of the hill, got our luggage out and headed up the path. Once we got inside I showed Jon his room and the rest of the house. I asked him what he thought. "It beats sands prison and Smiley's house," he said. I could tell he was stoked, he was an island guy like me.

Mike was waiting in the living room while Jon and I were getting settled. When we were done I went in and sat on the floor pillow next to him and asked him what he needed. He told me he needed ten jars of whites and one hundred doses of mescaline. Mike had to get to work, so Jon and I drove him back to Waikiki. He said he would be back the next day for some more. After we dropped Mike off, at his apartment, Jon and I headed straight for Ala Moana park, took our surfboards, off my shinny new racks, and paddled out in the warm four foot waves. We didn't talk much for the next few hours, we were busy doing what we felt we were meant to do, surf in paradise. We surfed until sunset and then drove around the island to the North Shore, stopping to get a shave ice, and then to Smiley's house. We wanted to find out, from his girlfriend, an update on his where abouts but she was nowhere to be found. We decided to get a hawaiian pizza, we were so stoned and tired we devoured two pizzas on the drive back. When we got back we stumbled up the path to the house, we really needed a flashlight, I could just imagine that chimp watching us, and if we got off the pa, he would nail us for sure.

The next five months were filled with great surfing, late afternoons eating shave ices on the porch of the old Haleiwa store, hanging out at north shore surfer's houses smoking hash and occasionally dropping mescaline, very mellow. When we felt the need for some excitement we would head over to the city and hang out with some of Mike's friends. Jon and I tried china white heroin a couple of times until one night we got really sick in a bowling alley. On some other occasions we went to drug houses and smoked cocaine but we weren't impressed.

I had flooded the Waikiki, Honolulu market with whites, sales were slow but it was still easy steady money. I was always hankering for bigger money, now that I had a taste of it from the Morocco scam.

Tutu would leave notes on my door every once in a while. Sometimes she wanted me to hike up the mountain and pick bananas for her or move a tree or tend to one of her caged monkey's. It was always trivial but important to her. Tutu was kind of like a mother but also a little weird. Our relationship was usually pretty good.

Finally Smiley returned from Asia, not looking good at all. He had a broken foot and arm. His car collided with a truck, in the mountains in Afghanistan. It hit on his side and he was partially crushed. He lived on opium for three weeks, because he was in such pain, and he got addicted There was no way to get medical attention in the mountains, only drugs. His foot and arm had to be re-broken to be properly set when he got back to the city three weeks after the accident. I think the experience changed him, he wasn't the same old feisty Smiley. He was really pale and using china white, we were stunned. Smiley didn't talk about the scam he had been on but for sure it had gone bad. That was the last time I ever saw Smiley, he moved to an outer island.

The North Shore had changed a lot, the big scammers moved to private ranches on the outer islands, keeping a low profile. Their scams were tons nowadays and it never surfaced on the North Shore, it was to hot, hash was now more expensive here than in California.

Supporting two houses was expensive but Judy had to stay

in Huntington Beach to maintain her job. I loved my island house but I was spending a lot of money in hotels and flying people back and forth bringing me kegs of whites, mescaline and now hash. My relationship with Tutu was souring, mostly because I wasn't there much during the day and at her beckon call like before. One evening, after surfing all day Jon and I came home and a pad lock was on the front door of my house. This was unbelievable! I went down to Tutu's house, knocked on her door but she didn't answer. I went around back and yelled to her through an open window. Finally she came to the back door and handed me the key to the pad lock and shut her door without a word. I walked back up the path to the house and showed Jon the key. We opened the door, wondering what to expect to see inside; to our surprise everything was intact. From then on I avoided Tutu but I could tell this was the beginning of the end.

The new surfer magazine came out with an article of Biarritz, France, showing pictures of beaches, great waves on the Atlantic coast and spoke of topless sunbathing women. This was the Frenchmen's Rivera from August tenth through September tenth. The article said the airfares were at an all time low price of just two hundred and fifty dollars round trip on Air France. I said to Jon, "We've got to go there. I'll finance the trip and we'll do a safe hash scam from Europe. Are you game?" Jon said "definitely!"

The next day I called Mike and told him I was moving back to Huntington beach, but I would be back the next winter, and that he could have my car, furniture, carpets and anything else he wanted. I would be leaving in a week.

The next few days dragged, we were anxious to leave. Mike took a lot of stuff and I was leaving everything else. I wasn't going to tell Tutu a thing, I was just going to leave, and that was that. Mike took us to the airport, we were only taking our surfboards and suitcases.

Judy picked us up at the airport, we drove Jon to his mom's house in Garden Grove and dropped him off. I said, " call me or I will call him in a couple of days." When Judy and I got back to the Huntington beach house she was bummed at losing the island house and wasn't to excited about the article in surfer magazine and that I was going to finance a European trip she wasn't to sure of.

12

Artifacts

WHEN JON AND I MADE THE DECISION to go back to Europe, we agreed this time no dangerous countries. We were going to sell mescaline in Germany and then buy hash, already in Europe, selling at much lower prices than Orange County. Sending the drugs from Europe to the United States was easy. The profits weren't as big as from the hash countries but there was little danger. If we hurried, we could surprise Russo with the mescaline, purchase a vehicle, go on a road trip unloading the mescaline and still make it to Biarritz France on the Atlantic coast to surf between mid Aug and Sept. We knew it was going to be great spending the summer in Europe, surfing in Southern France and making lots of money.

We bought tickets on Air France for only two hundred and fifty dollars round trip on a twelve hour non-stop flight to France. We landed at the International airport outside Paris, walked through customs with two ounces of mescaline taped to our bodies, no problem, French customs just checks passports, no searches. We got our luggage and surfboards, took a shuttle to the train station and caught the overnight train to Stuttgart Germany. The train ride was kind of a drag because it was so crowded. Once in Stuttgart we rented a vehicle and headed for Bonningheim and Russo's, just one hundred and fifty kilometers away.

We drove up to Russo's club early evening, sat down, ordered a beer and waited for Russo to see us. We could see him in his office doing his books looking very business like, the club wasn't up to full swing until later in the evening. He still looked the same, goatee, semi cropped long brown hair and sort of pudgy. I asked the waitress to send vodka with tomato juice to Russo, this was his drink of choice, she said sure. When she delivered the drink, Russo looked up to see who had sent it to him. When he saw Jon and me he freaked and ran out to us from his office. He said he never thought he would see us again. "It's really great to see you out of prison Jon." He leaned over to me and said, "I hope you brought mescaline." "Yeah, we did," I answered, then he wanted to know what was up with us, he knew we were scamming again.

We told him we wanted to get a VW camper van and

we hoped we could sell the two ounces of mescaline we had brought with us. We asked him if we could do a club trip again. "Sure!" he said. He wanted to know if we were going into Asia again, Jon and I both answered "definitely not." We told him that after we sold one thousand doses we were heading down to Southern France for a month to surf. Russo looked at us funny "who do you think you're kidding, there's no surf in France.". "That's what you think," I said. Biarritz is invaded by surfers from around the globe between mid Aug. to mid Sept. It's a surfing paradise for one month then the current changes and the cold water returns. We would head back to Germany to sell the other one thousand doses that we would leave with him. We wanted to buy twenty or thirty pounds of good black hash while in Germany and start sending it back to California "can you set it up for us?" Russo said he probably could but that the price now was about three hundred dollars a pound, before we had paid three hundred dollars a kilo. Jon and I agreed that was still a good price.

I asked Russo if we could hang out at his house and set up our lab. "Does a bear shit in the woods," he replied. Russo couldn't wait to get started and get high, so he could see cartoons again.

Russo set up our deliveries and warned us to be careful; the drug laws had gotten stricter in the last year. Jon and I picked up some smoking hash in Heidelberg, on our first delivery, then visited some familiar prostitute areas, otherwise it was strictly business this trip. We made all our deliveries to the club managers, collected five thousand dollars and was back at Russo's in just over a week. Although we did notice

drug use in the clubs and streets it was very subdued compared
to a year and a half ago.

When we returned, the van, we had purchased, was ready.
It was perfect, we had an icebox, stove, cupboards for food
and a bed. Jon and I went to a camping store, got a tent, some
sleeping bags, pots and pans and some food and we were all
set to hit the autobahn to Amsterdam, our first stop on our
way to Biarritz's. Amsterdam was out of our way but we had
two weeks to make a three day drive and it was only mid
July. Once again we said goodbye to Russo but no dangerous
countries this trip just camping, surfing and then we would
be back.

Up the autobahn, across the border to Holland in five
hours, our van was great. We stopped at a campsite just
outside of Amsterdam, littered with European campers and
colorful tents of every shape. We put up our tent and made
camp, so no one could take the spot we picked, then headed
into Amsterdam, two miles away, for the evening. A week in
Amsterdam is to die for, beautiful European girls wanting
sex and drugs. The hookers in the red light district stood in
their windows, next to their beds, just waiting for a "John"
and a chance to close their curtain for ten dollars. Driving
into Amsterdam at night was like having a pass to drive down
main street in Disneyland, we parked close to the central city.
The clubs were alive with bizarre crowds and loud music that
blasted right through you as you entered the doors, every floor
had different happenings. We bought some hash cookies and
tea at the concession stands, they had an array of hash and
opium. We went to a few different clubs, dropped some opium

in our tea and drifted into the scene. Somehow we drove back to the campsite that night and the next morning we barely remembered anything from the night before.

Jon and I managed to recover enough to try out our new propane stove. We had pancakes and coffee. This was going to be great camping all over Europe. We took our showers and headed for the giant flea market in Amsterdam. The flea market was as remembered, a major happening not to be missed. There were permanent stands and booths loaded with antiques from China, carpets from Persia and tapestries in excellent condition. I bought two fantastic carpets for less than ten dollars. The carpets, artifacts and tapestries were worth almost nothing there yet some were from the 1400's to the 1700's. The Dutch people wanted modern things now, not the old stuff. As we were walking around I noticed a person's head sticking above everyone by a foot and a half that looked like Frank Zappa. "Jon look there, its Istanbul Charlie," I said. We kept our eyes on him and worked our way over to him through the crowd, sure enough it was Charlie. The last time we had seen him he was stuck in Istanbul and trying to get back home to Holland. Charlie was as surprised to see us, as we were he. His first question to us was "How did the Lebanon scam go?" We told him we got busted and filled him in on the story. He asked about Michael, I told him Michael was fine. Charlie invited us to his houseboat for some food. We walked three blocks over canals, down canal streets and past many old black barges. We came to this one funky one with pot plants growing on the open deck, Charlie said, "come aboard!" We followed him down in to the cold steel belly of the barge where Charlie's living area was. It wasn't much more than a few chairs, a bed and a hot plate but Charlie was comfortable. It was so cold in that belly, outside it was sunny and sixty five to seventy degrees but in there it was maybe fifty degrees. "Charlie, your place is great but why don't we go up on the deck", we said.

From then on, whenever we were at Charlie's we would stay on the deck, and watch the tourists pass by, or meet him at his girlfriends funky apartment. They took us to some small coffee and teahouses, off the beaten path run by Turkish men. Charlie told us that this was where we could buy kilo's of good hash, cheap.

We bought one quarter ounce of hash to take with us to Biarritz surfing and told Charlie that we would be back in Amsterdam in September or October to score big. We asked Charlie if he could find a small apartment for us. He said we were more than welcome to stay on his boat, which we appreciated but declined, it was to cold on his boat for us, we needed an apartment. He said he would do that for us.

Everyday while we were in Amsterdam we would go to the flea market and buy fantastic rugs, tapestries and small antique clocks then mail them to California and Hawaii. This was our way to find out if customs or mail inspectors were opening the packages. If they weren't opening the packages then we had found a gold mine. Every evening, after rocking nightclubs and beautiful prostitutes, we would meet up with Charlie and go back to the Turkish restaurant to eat and drink tea laced with opium.

Another week wasted away and it was time for us to

continue on. Charlie's girlfriend had a going away party for us at her apartment with friends and some beautiful prostitutes. It was a great time of sex and black opium, supplied by the girls. We said goodbye late that evening, we'd be leaving in the morning.

The next morning we broke camp, rolled a joint and headed to Belgium on our way to Paris. A couple hours up the Dutch autobahn and we were at Belgium's customs, showed our passports, no search, no problems. Less than thirty minutes we were in Brussels, the capital city, and then about thirty more minutes further Jon lit a hash joint as we were sitting at a stoplight. I was thinking that the light seemed to be a few minutes longer than usual when all of the sudden an officer walked out of a little building towards us. "This must be the border to France, put out that joint," hoping the officer wouldn't smell it, but he did. The officers searched our van well. All they found was a pipe, we had hidden our quarter pound of smoking stash well. We needed that to party with new friends coming from Hawaii, and girls we met in Biarritz.

We barely got through customs and were on our way to Paris about two or three hours more of a drive. We were going to stay at the Piccadilly hotel for one week, in the middle of the red light district, then planned to go on to Biarritz by August fifteenth.

Paris was fun, the hotel, the food, the prostitutes everywhere and still only ten dollars. We stayed high on hash and hung out in the outdoor cafe's, living the life of internationals, the world was our oyster. It wasn't Amsterdam but it was fun.

A week passed by quickly, we were anxious to leave and get on to Biarritz, surfing was eating at us. We used the hotel phone and called ahead for camping reservations at La Bar beach, a surfing spot pictured in surfer magazine.

In the morning we left heading south to the French Atlantic coast, a six hour drive. We were excited, to say the least. On the way there we came upon a carnival so we stopped to walk around and stretch. There was some wild bumper cars and some wild drivers, especially one guy who was demon driven. Jon and I each got in a car and we were nailing this guy and he us, no bad intentions. He got me when I was taking a rebound and just about broke my neck. I got a bad whiplash and that ended my ride. When we finally got to Biarritz I was injured, but didn't want to see a doctor, I figured surfing would help. It was late afternoon when we arrived so we just drove around checking out the beaches, they were beautiful. This was the Frenchman's Rivera. It looked just like the pictures in surfer magazine, rental cars with surfboards stuffed in them crowding the quaint French city. Here it was mid August, we were in the South of France and people were out enjoying the sun and beach. We drove right up to a seawall off the parking lot and there we were staring at topless sunbathers wearing tiny bikini bottoms. We got out to stretch and take in more of this amazing sight, I looked at Jon, "I love this place," I said, Jon licked his lips. We walked down to the water to touch the Atlantic ocean, it was a bit cold but it would be fine. There were about twenty guys still out surfing nice bowls. It war hard to believe we were in Biarritz France surrounded by semi-naked girls, this was going to be fun! We decided to find our campsite before it got dark. We found it one half mile off the beach. It was a great campground, full of campers, tents of many colors, trailers, clotheslines with bathing suits and towels. We checked in and were assigned a camp site, made up camp, rolled some hash joints and got ourselves prepared for the beach in the morning, expecting waves, chilly water, topless women and a great day.

Our first morning we drove about half a mile down to the beach looking at three foot waves and no crowd. The water was glassy, about sixth five degrees, blue, white sand, high tide and waves a bit close to the rocks. Within two hours a beach appeared, there was a seventeen foot tide, this is when the local people come out to enjoy the water and girls appeared topless.

After a couple of days, getting to know the area, we found another campsite that suited us better and was closer to the beach. The campsite was full of surfers from Hawaii, Australia, New Zealand, England and the east coast.

In our new campsite we met a couple, he was from Florida and she was from New Jersey. They told us they had met at the Paris airport a month earlier. They stayed in a Paris hotel for a few nights and then traveled together to Morocco and accidentally came upon the beautiful Biarritz beaches, on their way down, saw what a happening surfing scene it was so they decided to spend their vacation camping together. The guy's name was Rob, he had some good Moroccan catama hash that he was smoking and selling to the surfers. I asked him where he got it and he told me he bought a kilo in Morocco, bought a Hassock stool, hid the kilo inside it and then mailed it to his hotel in Paris. When they left Morocco and got back up to Paris, they stayed one night and the package arrived, they bought some camping gear and here they were. Rob was only maybe five foot seven, square and stocky, sandy colored hair with a big walrus mustache, a great conversationalist. Rob didn't surf but we still became good friends and Lani wore see through bathing suits. Lani was really sweet along with having a great body, about five foot five, and a pretty face. She had short brown hair, a smile with perfect white teeth, a great ass, nice legs and small boobs with great nipples that showed through her bikini tops.

We surfed Hosseger, Biarritz, Anglet and surrounding areas. These spots were wave rich and ultra fun. The waves we surfed each day ranged from thrilling perfect, waist high rippable bowls, to hard pounding wedges that could knock your head off, powerful backdoor barrels. We met girls on all the beaches each day then partied into the nights.. Biarritz was a huge happening, wine, women, drugs and sex, on an international level.

Within two weeks we got to know a lot of beach people and surfers from all over the world. The water had warmed up to seventy to seventy five degrees and the weather had warmed up to eighty five degrees on the sand. Everyone we met either had rented a fantastic villa or was camping at one of the campgrounds and every night up and down the beaches from Biarritz to Bayonne great parties were happening. There must have been two to three thousand surfers. We discovered a great well-known restaurant called the Steak House that made the best apple pie ever. The pie sold out every night, everyone loved it and would even line up to order some. Jon actually twisted the waiters ear one night because he didn't serve us our apple pie we had ordered first and instead served the people that ordered after us. Besides the apple pie they served a great tuna steak but the pie brought in the crowds. Every night after dinner we would go to the boardwalk there were arcades, pastry stores, foosball and girls still in little bikinis, or very short skirts, hanging out on the breakwater wall, making it hard to concentrate playing foosball.

During the day, at low tide, the locals would come on to the beach fully dressed, put a pullover robe on, strip down to bun huggers, neatly fold their clothes in a small bundle and go for a walk. Sometimes, the tide would come in before they came back and wash their neat little bundles of clothes away, if we couldn't save them.

By the third week we were very tight with Rob and Lani, his girlfriend, we were a camping family. One day Rob said he had to leave the next day and take Lani to the Paris airport that she was leaving, we were surprised to hear she was leaving. Rob was gone the next morning. Jon and I were lying on the beach, a couple days later nursing hangovers from cheap Portuguese wine, when Rob came up to us and introduced us to his wife. Talk about a shocker, this guy was a true gigolo. She was a stewardess, they had been married for twelve years.

By the end of the third week things were really winding down, people were leaving, the water was cooling down overnight to about sixty five degrees and the familiar summer breezes were getting a little chilly. The waves grew to about twenty feet and the ocean looked like the inside of a washing machine. surfer magazine photographers were at every beach, this was the hot spot on the planet because of the big waves.

Rob's wife only stayed a couple days and then Rob hung out with us. We made a three day trip with him to Portugal and Madrid, just to see the places. When we got back Rob told us he had to get back to Florida, sold his camping gear and left just like that. Rob was a mysterious guy.

The fourth week we were getting anxious to leave, the season changing and the water temperature was now about sixty degrees. Most of the people had left, there were just stragglers. Biarritz had been fantastic but it was over now and it was time to get back to Russo's and make some money. We went for our final apple pie at the Steak House, the owner had become a friend so we sold him our surfboards for three hundred dollars each. We told him we were leaving the next day and maybe we would see him again the next year.

The drive back to northern Europe was like driving into a refrigerator. We were very tan and our bodies were in shock going into the extreme cold weather. We drove straight through to Russo's, about thirty hours. When we got there Russo said we looked like we must of had a good time by the looks of our tans. We told him how great it was and that next year he had to go with us. I told Russo it was time to get back to business and make some money and he handed me five thousand dollars, he had sold the other ounce of mescaline.

We told Russo we saw Charlie in Amsterdam and that he introduced us to his friends who had connections for hash at good prices, better than Germany. I explained they had offered their houses, connections and services as a base for our scamming. I felt it was time to sell the van, it was much to cold for camping. We would drive it back to Amsterdam, get an apartment, sell it and commute from then on, the van had served its purpose. We told Russo we would get in touch with him after we had settled. Before we left, we dropped doses of mescaline and went clubbing in and around the college, a final night with Russo.

When Jon and I arrived in Amsterdam we found a hotel and spent the night clubbing and literally fucking around. The next day we went to Charlie's houseboat, climbed on board and knocked on the door. Tall lanky Charlie peaked out and said, "come on in." He offered for us to stay with him again, we thanked him, and told him it was to cold for us, we were hoping he had arranged an apartment for us. He explained that he had arranged for us to rent a flat at his friend's house and that we could use his friends shop to prepare the hash for transport and shipping.

Charlie took Jon and I to the flat, it was located only a few blocks from his place, near central Amsterdam, a house only walking distance to clubs, the flea market, the food market and the red light district. We came up to a brick building and knocked on the door, probably five hundred years old. Simon answered the door, we had met him a couple months before, he invited us in out of the cold. Inside the flat wasn't much warmer than outside. Simon took us up to the third floor and showed us a room, he referred to as a flat with two beds otherwise unfurnished. The room was very dusty but, it was secure and private. The view, outside the large window, was a brick street lined with trees and a canal down the middle passing through fairly small bridges at each end of the block. Simon stepped up and pointed across the canal to a row of brick three and four story residences, "That's where Ann Frank hid from the Nazi's for a year," he explained. I was amazed. Simon then told us that the first floor was his, private, but we were free to use the rest of the house, kitchen, bathrooms and shop. Simon and Charlie left us to check the place out and decide if we wanted it.

Jon and I sat on the beds, it was so cold in the room we could see our breath, but it was perfect for what we needed. The international market place would have everything we would need to make the room comfortable, carpets, blankets, curtains, chests, anything! We got up and decided to check out the rest of the building. The bottom floor was once a print shop complete with a book press, woodworking hand tools, power tools and a lot of privacy. We could easily convert it to a smugglers shop. Simon had also told us that there were many spirits living in the house. He said it was once a tavern in the 1600's and that most of the spirits were old merchants, "some are evil so watch out!" he said. Jon and I looked at each other and frowned.

Now that we had an apartment we sold the Van, to the first buyer, bought some hash and started to plan. I felt the best way was to experiment with a variety of shipping and mailing of the hash in small amounts, and see what way worked best. We set up the work shop and oiled some old book presses to use to press the hash for shipping. Just about everyday you could find us at the flea market buying different items we could use for shipping purposes. We took them back to the shop and took them apart looking for hiding spaces in them. It took us a few weeks to get good at disassembling artifacts skillfully enough so we could put them back together perfect without a blemish.

By the start of the second month we were becoming highly skilled, after destroying a lot of Chinese antiques, now we created hidden spaces, pressed hash in different sizes and shapes and then reassemble the antiques. We even became good at matching the finish on the antiques so no one would be able to tell they had been tampered with. We shipped off two kilos total and they went right through the mail within a few days.

When we weren't working in the shop we spent our time partying at the clubs and the red light district, always ending up at the Turkish restaurants drinking tea laced with black tar opium and smoking hash. Amsterdam was cold and the sun never came out but, neither did we. The city didn't come to life until ten p.m. but it didn't take long for our biological clocks to adjust. We stayed up all night and slept late, we were beginning to experiencing some opium withdrawals by mid day. We weren't too worried, when we left Amsterdam we wouldn't have any more opium.

We heard from Russo. He wanted to come up for the weekend to party land Amsterdam. I said, "great! I'll pick you up at the train depot in Charlie's citron," which was a cartoon looking car built out of, it seemed, a trash can, it fit Charlie. We took Russo to Charlie's houseboat on Princengrath canal,

the first thing he saw was pot growing in the windows, and
Russo loved it. I introduced Russo to Charlie. Charlie said,
" I was just leaving for the flea market, do you want to come
along?" This was his daily routine. We went along, Russo
and Charlie bonded well, typical Russo. When they left the
flea market we took Russo to show him the apartment we
had rented and to introduce him to Simon. We showed the
shop to Russo, and demonstrated how we hid the hash in the
antiques. The only problem was getting good addresses to
send the hash to. Judy had two different addresses for me to
send to her. She had already received four pounds of hash that
I bought for two hundred dollars a pound, already sold for one
thousand dollars a pound in Orange County. It was a good
profit but we needed more addresses so we could send maybe
ten pounds a week. Russo was impressed but he wanted some
more mescaline. "Okay, I'll call Judy in the States and have
her send a couple ounces."

    We were invited to Charlie's girlfriends flat for dinner
that night and then out for our usual clubbing, smoking hash
and ending up at the Turkish restaurant so Russo could have
a taste of Turkish tea with opium. We were up most of the
night. Russo's first night in Amsterdam left him with a huge
hangover but, he said it was worth it, he had a great time.
Russo stayed another day but then had to get back to his club.
I told him I would call him when the mescaline came in. Jon
and I dropped him off at the train depot and said goodbye. It
seemed like he had only been there two hours, not two days.
We had smoked a lot of hash and drank black opium tea,
which makes everything seem like a dream.

The following two weeks flew by. Now we were having trouble scoring hash from the Turks but the mescaline did arrive with Judy and money from the last shipment. I was happy to see Judy but it didn't go over to well with Jon. What was I thinking? We only had this one room between us and Judy was invading Jon's space. I apologized to Jon but Judy was there and there wasn't much I could do. We needed to get the mescaline to Russo, Jon said he would go to Germany, it would take him a couple weeks, we made plans to take him to the airport the next day. After Jon left Judy and I traveled around Holland by train, trolley and bicycles seeing the country.

I contacted Jon and he said everything was going fine and he would be back the next week by plane. The next Saturday Judy and I went to the airport to pick up Jon. The passengers unloaded the plane and no Jon. This wasn't like Jon at all. We went back to the flat figuring Jon had called Simon or would be there waiting for us but when we arrived, no Jon. I sent a telegram to Russo asking him where Jon was. Russo called me the next day, said he hadn't seen Jon in a week, that he was traveling by train delivering the mescaline. He had planned to take a flight from Frankfurt back to Amsterdam. Russo said he would check with the different clubs and see who had seen Jon last and would call me the next day. The following night Russo called and said Jon might have gotten busted, that one of the clubs got raided and after that no one had seen Jon. I told Judy she cried and prayed he was just hiding out.

Days crept by, Judy and I were sick with worry about Jon until, I telephoned a friend in Orange County. He said he had seen Jon the night before, that Jon told him he almost got busted in Germany, so he took a flight to Paris and split. It was unbelievable, we had been terrified and he hadn't even tried to contact us. We figured he had freaked out but, why didn't he contact us? Now we were relieved but pissed. I knew Jon was upset and this was an opportunity for him to go home with some cash but I didn't think he was that way.

Now I was down to five thousand dollars enough to make things happen still but I needed more addresses to mail to. The hash came in abundantly and the addresses started increasing. Anyone who let me mail hash to them got to keep an ounce for free so, everyone wanted some free hash. Each package contained a pressed three and a half ounces hidden perfectly. I was sending to twenty five addresses a week, which was seventy five ounces and was making thousands in profit each week.

I sent a telegram to Russo and let him know that I heard from friends that Jon was in Orange County safe with the money he collected. Russo couldn't believe what Jon had done either and said that he would be coming to see me again in a month, "It will be great to see you, just let me know," I said.

Judy and I settled down in Amsterdam. Everything was going smooth and our cash was building, we made over ten thousand dollars the first month, the only thing holding us up was more addresses to mail to. The second month of mailing went perfect. If only I could get more addresses, I thought I could make ten thousand dollars a week.

Russo came to visit and we went to Charlie's girlfriend's house for a fondue dinner. This was a very international dinner, Russo an American Russian, Charlie a Dutchman, Me an American, Judy an American, Simon German and Charlie's girlfriend Dutch. I talked with Simon that night and proposed a deal. I would share the scam with him if he would press the hash into artifacts, I would go back to California, get more addresses, he could keep up the mailing and we could all get rich. I was really homesick, I had been in Amsterdam for five months and away from home for nine months. Judy had a kid at home she wanted to get back also. Simon didn't hesitate a minute, he knew the whole scam. We were set, we would do a final mailing, I told Simon I would leave him with five thousand dollars and twenty pounds of hash for the next two weeks mailing. I knew, that would give me plenty of time to get set up more addresses.

I felt Russo was being left out so I asked him if there was anything I could do for him? He just wanted us to keep in touch with him. Judy and I made our reservations to fly home, feeling a little melancholy but, I knew I would be back the following summer and we would all be rich.

Now that I was almost on my way home, I couldn't wait to go surfing in Huntington beach, go down to Laguna beach to feel the sun again and get healthy. After months of late nights, all kind of drugs, I was ready for just pot.

We arrived at LAX and went home by taxi. I was anxious to pick up my first mailing, see friends and definitely see Jon.

13

Home

AFTER NEARLY A YEAR IN EUROPE PARTYING, I was unhealthy, pale and nearly addicted to opium, sleeping all day and living the night life in Amsterdam. In the past three years I'd hardly seen California. I had lived in Europe twice a total of twenty one months, traveled to sixteen countries, some multiple times on four different continents, eight months in Hawaii living a surfers dream and gone through over two hundred thousand dollars.

Now I am twenty four years old and back in Huntington beach pretty much starting over. I had changed in the past three years. The good was the knowledge I gained, the geography, the politics, cultures and meeting people all over the world. I always thought we Americans were a lot smarter than other countries, especially third world, but not so, Europeans speak two to three languages and are very knowledgeable. The third world people speak three to eight languages and are very knowledgeable about the world around them. I realized the other countries viewed Americans as arrogant people. This made a major change in my belief of American citizen's intellectual superiority. People here only speak one language, on the average, and are only interested in their own city or state, not the world. I cherished my American privileges compared to anywhere else, I realized America is the greatest country on earth, but we are not perceived as the good Americans who stick up for small governments everywhere. I saw graffiti on walls saying, "down with American imperialism." Worldwide Americans are perceived as "bullies" pushing our weight around.

The bad is I had blown so much money, I was nearly broke, my health was terrible and I needed a change in my life, a new focus. I had always been a morning person and stayed away from addictive drugs. I had slipped so far, this was going to change, never again. I needed some sun, good food and from then on I would have just pot and hash, no hard drugs. Judy and I kept to ourselves for a few days until the hash started rolling in, along with money, then our spirits lifted. I decided to contact Jon and ask him what had happened.

Jon answered the phone at his mom's house. I asked him how things were going. He told me he was scraping by living with his mom and driving her car. I just asked him, "Jon, what happened? You scared the shit out of us! We didn't know what to think, you just disappeared and then a week later I hear you're back in Orange County. What is this all about?" Jon told me he almost got busted in a raid at one of the German night clubs in Hamburg. The police were everywhere and he slipped out of a window. "I just freaked out and headed for the airport, " Jon said. Then he continued on, "I got a flight back to LA, I wasn't going to go to jail." I told him I was glad he didn't get busted but he could have at least called us and let us know what was going on. I ended the conversation there, I could still remember walking out of sands prison and him staying. I wasn't about to carry a grudge or ask him about the mescaline money he had collected. I told Jon that we should get together, I didn't mention anything about the present hash scam and he didn't ask. It was unspoken knowledge that he was out of it by going home in the middle of a scam.

At first I had success receiving hash, I got more addresses. It got harder to score in Europe and the expenses were eating up the profit, I needed a weekly shipment. Gradually the scam was falling apart but once a month still was profitable.

Simon scored and sent the hash. This time the shipment was late but it had been late before so I wasn't too worried until a friend contacted me and said he had a visit from a FBI agent regarding his mail. At this point I knew the scam was over and I figured I was going to get busted. Judy and I burned our passports, cleaned any and all paraphernalia, relating to Amsterdam, out of our house.

The next few weeks were filled with paranoia, I thought I

was being watched. I was afraid to deal any drugs or contact anyone that was involved in the scam. All the FBI would have to do is see me at one of the addresses, I had been mailing to, find out I had been in Amsterdam and then that would be it. I would be busted.

The weeks passed by and nothing happened but, I was still paranoid. I asked my dad for a job as a carpenter, he hired me and I was back in the construction racket.

I made pretty good money as a journeyman carpenter but, I couldn't stand it. I grew up working for my dad and uncle's as their laborer, I learned the trade the hard way. My Dad knew he could put me on any job and it would be done right. Generally old time carpenters were rednecks, and I was a long hair "hippie" type, which caused a lot of friction even though my Dad was the foreman. I was teamed up with my step moms son-in-law, he wasn't too bright but he wasn't a redneck. After a while we were doing siding and decided we could make more money going out on our own so we went out and found another job.

While working with Rob the rainy season set in and money got tight. In the past six months I had gotten to know Rob well. I told him about Lebanon and he told me he had a connection in Tijuana for heroin that would deliver to San Diego. There was no running of the border but still at good Mexico prices. I told Rob I was clean and that I didn't use heroin or associate with the people who do but I was interested in getting cocaine. Rob said he could get it. I knew I could make a fortune, I had the connections to sell and I knew a lot of people. A friend of mine had sold me some cocaine a few months back, it was the new drug of choice, very popular but hard to get. I told Rob that if this was real prove it and call the guy. Once again this news was hard to believe, Rob was just barely getting by working as a carpenter, why?

Rob made the call to his connection named Marcus, in Mexico, specifically Tijuana La Playa. Rob set up a meeting for the next Saturday at the Mexican's house in Tijuana La Playa, I was truly amazed!

The next Saturday Rob and I were on the five freeway heading for Tijuana to see Marcus. I didn't know what to expect. We crossed the border, skirted Tijuana heading towards Ensanada, getting on the toll road and shortly exiting at Tijuana La Playa. We traveled a mile or so further into an exclusive beach neighborhood and then stopped in front of a home surrounded by a tall wall with a massive steel double gate. Looking through the massive gates with a fifteen foot wall was a fantastic compound complete with a swimming pool, tennis courts, horse stables, Mexican gardeners tending to large rosebushes, small kids playing and dogs. The house was a three story Spanish style with large balconies on the second and third floors affording ocean views above the protective walls. This was unbelievable, beyond any of my expectations and certainly a far cry from Herbie the taxi driver eating his raw eggs. Rob saw Marcus and motioned to him, he waved back and we were let in the gate.

A young Marcus greeted us, about my age twenty four. Rob introduced me and he invited us into his house. Marcus looked at me, "se habla espanol?", "pikito", I answered. Marcus then called a woman into the room to interpret; I later learned she was his wife. She spoke perfect English, had a very light complexion, definitely of Spanish ancestors, very pretty. Marcus said to his wife in Spanish and she interpreted to Rob. "Marcus wants to know where the money is you owe?" Rob tried to explain that his old partner up north had burnt him and that it wasn't his fault. Marcus cut him short and in English said "You guys both were using and addicted, why should I trust you?" Marcus turned to me and asked me what I thought. I said, "I don't, this is the first I have heard of this. Rob told me you had coke and that is what I want." At that moment I saw Marcus's coat open slightly and he had a hand gun in his belt. What did Rob get me into I thought. To my relief, Marcus smiled and spoke to his wife in Spanish. She said to us, "Marcus says you can pay him back later, just don't start using again, agree?" Rob agreed.

Marcus was ready to deal now. "When do you need the chiva (heroin)," he asked and looked at me. I told him I wanted coke not chiva. Marcus looked at me and said he would send half pound of coke and half pound of chiva. Again I told him I didn't want the chiva, I didn't have any connections to sell it to. Marcus paused, "okay, a half pound of coke at three hundred dollars an ounce and a free ounce of chiva, you'll see, it will sell," he said. I told him Rob had said he would front it to us. Marcus agreed but only one quarter pound the first time. We were to meet the donkey, the delivery person, the next day. He told us to go to a smut theater in San Diego, sit in the back row on the right and wear a white shirt. A girl would come in and sit next to me and give me the stash. He said for us to call him in the morning and he would let us know what time and what theatre. We then smoked a joint with Marcus, and his wife, before we left. We shook hands and told him we would see him in a week.

Rob and I drove back to Huntington Beach, I dropped him off, then went home myself. I was excited to tell Judy about Marcus. I told her all about his house and family and how the deal was going to go down at a San Diego theatre. I said everything Rob had told us about Marcus was true, except that he left out an important fact, he used to be a junky and owed Marcus money. I explained Rob was an idiot, you don't burn someone like Marcus, you could get killed. I told her about the gun Marcus wore and that he gave Rob a break, he could pay the money back over time but made him promise he wouldn't become a junky again.

The first delivery went off smooth. A young Mexican woman, who looked like an average "Mamasita," not at all what I was expecting, came in the theatre almost immediately after we sat down. I was glad she was there quickly, the theatre was full of old guys sitting by themselves watching nasty porn and doing who knows what else. The Mexican woman sat next to me, reached in her pants and pulled out a packet and handed it to me, down low, I then stuck it in my pants. Five minutes later she got up to leave and motioned for us to wait before leaving. Walking out on the streets in broad daylight, exiting from a raunchy porn flick with a bulge in my pants seemed normal. Rob and I were laughing but we couldn't wait to get back to our car.

While driving back up the five freeway, I pulled the packet out one time to look at it. It was so tightly pressed it looked like a big "dildo" and to top it off it was packaged in a condom. This was unreal, so easy, just a phone call away and Mexico drug prices. We'll be rich! I thought.

When we got back to my house the girls were waiting on pins and needles. I plopped out the packet and the girls just looked at it. "What's that?" they said. I told them it was my dildo. We laughed but the laughter was quieted when we opened the rubber and found two tightly pressed packets, one dark and one light. "What is the dark one?" Judy asked. I told her it was chiva, heroin, and that Marcus insisted on sending it for free. I told her that Rob said he could sell it. "To who?" Rob's wife quickly asked. It was a bit uncomfortable now, she was pissed to say the least. I opened the white packet of coke and suggested we weigh it and try some.

I chopped out eight big lines on a mirror and passed it around, with a twenty dollar bill rolled up as a straw to snort with. I set up my scale and the coke weight was short. I found out that Mexican ounces were twenty five grams; American ounces were twenty eight grams. It was the same with the chiva. We snorted the lines, the coke was good. Rob was anxious to leave, he took the chiva with him, and he didn't want any coke. I told him I would see him the next day at work. We had agreed to partner up for three months, and then we would go our own ways.

Within a week I had sold all the coke, made the money to pay back Marcus, made one thousand dollars profit each and still had an ounce of heroin.

Things went pretty good for the first month, I was making money again. Instead of driving to San Diego, I flew from

Orange County airport to San Diego, rent a car, go to the theatre to pick up my stash and then back to Huntington Beach in four hours. My friendship with Marcus was genuine, he knew I wasn't a junky and respected that. Once a month Judy and I spent a Saturday or Sunday with him, his wife and kids hanging out around the pool, having dinner and drinking shots of Tequila

Marcus started quizzing me about Rob. He wanted to know why he never came down. I tried to make up excuses for him saying he had paid his debt. I told Marcus he was having family problems. Marcus stopped me from saying anymore. In broken English he said, "I know Rob, he's using again," and looked me straight in the eyes. I knew Marcus wouldn't trust me anymore, if I lied, so, I was honest and told him yes, Rob was using. I told him my partnership with Rob was only for three months, which I only had two more trips and the partnership was over. "Good," Marcus said, "We can work together better without Rob, I trust you alone, and I'll make you rich!" he added. I smiled, Judy smiled, Marcus smiled and we sealed it with a shot of strong Tequila.

Marcus told me that my next pick-up he was sending a pound of the best chiva he had. I started to say no and he put his hands up. He told me the number one business was chiva not coke. He told me he was sure I could sell it and if I didn't, he would take it back. "So this is how it is going to be?" I asked. "Si," he replied.

When I got back home Rob called. He started to talk drugs, Marcus and Mexico on the phone, I couldn't believe how lame he was. We weren't really friends, just business partners. He was making two thousand dollars a week, using heroin morning and night, not taking any chances, I did all the work. It was okay; I was just sticking to my word, a three-month partnership. I could tell he thought I was a chump, he was about to get a rude awaking. He only lived fifteen minutes away from me, I said I would be right over and hung up the phone.

As soon as I walked through Rob's door he told me, "don't ever cut me off on the phone again, you get it?" My reply was, "two more times and it's over." I told him I informed Marcus our partnership was over and if he wanted to still do business with Marcus he would have to do it on his own, I turned to walk out the door. Rob stood up, from his rocker, and grabbed me from behind as I was walking out. I turned around and blocked a feeble punch, grabbed him by the shirt, shook him and told him not to ever do that again and then shoved him back into his rocker. "You're just a pathetic junky." I shouted. I told him I would send him some money and told him if he ever came to my house I would kick his ass. I could tell this was a shock to him and his wife. As I walked away I thought to myself that he was a real looser, he'll be dead in a year and that I would never be like him.I paid Rob off the next week. I really didn't owe him anything, I was sticking to my word.

Two weeks had passed since I had last seen Rob, I decided it was time for Judy and me to move. I didn't trust junky Rob. I was afraid he would snitch on me or try to rip me off anyways, I could afford a nicer house. Judy and I found a great house and moved right away. It was melancholy leaving our little downtown house but, it was time.

Marcus was fronting me large quantities of drugs in endless supply. I could get anything I needed by the next day in San Diego. He definitely was making me rich. He told me that I was perfect to sell heroin because I wasn't using it. I really didn't want to sell it but, Marcus insisted. He told me once I started getting connections, the quality would sell itself. The only hard drug I used was coke, but I mostly still smoked pot and hash. Addicts were a different bread of people, I didn't know any and I didn't want to.

The next three months I sold lots of coke and made lots of money. Coke was now the drug of choice and I had a steady source of it. Mexican coke was not the best but I had an excellent connection. The few people I dealt with could always count on me for ounces, which I sold for one thousand dollars. My close friends always bought ten to fifteen grams a weekend at one hundred dollars each, which to me was just icing on the cake. Also, now I was selling heroin for a big profit, just like Marcus had said, it sold it's self. I only sold the heroin to a middle man, who was a good friend, and his people flew in from out of state to buy from him. This heroin was the best.

I was making money so easy, one hundred dollar bills flowed in like water. By the end of the day my pockets were bulging with thousands of dollars. I started having trouble figuring out where to hide the money every day. I started to get very inventive, hollowing out two by four studs with a router big enough to hold ten thousand dollar stacks. I had the richest garage in town. I removed mirrors, opened walls and I had cabinets that were removable with hidden openings for stash. I had a hidden floor safe but I still had drugs and money hidden in shoes and drawers.

I did have one cardinal rule, and stuck to it. I never met someone new through drugs. Sometimes a good friend, I'd known for years, would want to introduce someone to me and I would always tell him or her "no way." Even if they had known that person for years I still did not allow people to break my cardinal rule.

Everybody wanted to be my friend. My house was the place to be, free drugs but, only to my close friends and by invitation only. At night Judy and I would go to fancy restaurant, drink fine wines and then back to our house to snort giant lines of coke. Jon and I were still great friends and sort of celebrities among the Orange County dealers.

My house was an experience in it's self, set up mostly for privacy. It had gradually been decorated with very expensive antiques, carpets, pictures, appliances, collectables such as coins, opals, gold and diamonds. The back rooms were made up like a "sultan's palace," luxurious Persian pillows, expensive Afghan rugs with sixteenth century Persian gold threaded tapestries hung from the walls. This was where massive amounts of coke were snorted. The front rooms were drug free and people free, a safety zone, just in case a stranger knocked on the door.

I started taking vacations to Lake Tahoe for skiing and gambling. Of course I always brought plenty of coke and a little bit of, " Dr. Brown," code name for heroin, to snort for mellowing purposes but, that was all, I was not going to get strung out on that stuff.

Jon's friend from prison arrived with two thousand pounds of Afghanistan hash in New York. He told Jon one thousand pounds would be arriving the next week and told him to be ready.

Like clock work, the hash came in. Jon was staying at high priced hotels in Newport Beach, moving nightly. He had a million dollars of hash and he was careful. I wanted to get fifty pounds of hash but I couldn't get in touch with Jon. I was happy for him but I couldn't understand why he wasn't returning my calls. When he finally did contact me he told me he wanted and ounce of coke, for him, Boris and another guy, to snort and then told me most of the hash was gone. He said he would give me a quarter pound to smoke but, the rest was guaranteed, I couldn't believe my ears. I told him that really sucked and his reply to me was, "you don't need it. Just come to my hotel, I'll introduce you to Boris and bring that ounce okay?" I agreed to meet with him but I wasn't happy about it.

I saw Jon at his hotel and he looked terrible. He introduced me to Boris, a friend from Germany he had been in the nut house with, and he looked terrible too. It was obvious they were snorting coke day and night. Jon told me that they were planning to go to El Salvador in a week and then when they got back they were going to Lake Tahoe to ski and casino hop, Jon suggested I go with them. It was hard talking to Jon around Boris, he was living on the edge and making real big bucks. I left the hotel without any hash, Jon treated me like I didn't matter, and I wondered what was up with him. When I got home I told Judy what an ass Jon had been with his uppity attitude and all. I couldn't figure out what was up with him?

The next time I saw Jon he was alone and apologized for being an idiot. That still didn't make up for him stiffing me on the hash but, I let it go. Jon's smile could get you every time making it impossible to stay mad at him. Then he asked me if I had any of the heroin I called Dr. Brown. He said he was going to Tahoe to meet Boris and they wanted to smoke some. "I hear the Skiing is great, you're going aren't you?" he said. I looked at Judy and asked her what she thought. It sounded good to her, we agreed to meet him there in a couple days.

Three days later we were heading up three ninety five towards Tahoe in a new Mercedes, skis on top, listening to a Steely Dan tape and snorting coke. I had half an ounce of coke and an eighth ounce of, " Dr. Brown," to snort while skiing and gambling for a week. We had plans to meet Jon, Boris, and his wife, that night at Harvey's Casino. I had brought five thousand dollars cash and figured it would be enough and if it wasn't I knew I could always borrow some from Jon.

That week in Tahoe was fantastic! We skied all day, gambled most the night, stayed in luxurious rooms, dined in the most expensive restaurants and drank the finest wines. We snorted coke on the ski lifts through glass vials and then at night smoke Dr. Brown to take off the edge. Money was spent as if we had an endless supply.

I became good friends with Boris, he loved Dr. Brown. He said he was leaving and going back to England and that on his next trip he would bring two thousand pounds of hash, half for me to turn, if I wanted, I told him I would love to. The next morning Jon didn't go skiing with us, he had to take Boris and his wife to the airport. He drove them there in Boris's new Range Rover he had brought over with him.

When I came in from skiing I saw Jon at the black jack table. He told me Boris had given him the Range Rover. I was amazed, that was an expensive vehicle. We left the next morning and headed back to Huntington beach, Judy and I in our new Mercedes and Jon in his new Range Rover.

On the way home we stopped a few times to eat and we decided it was time to recuperate, we had consumed a lot of drugs in the last month. We decided when we got back there would be no drugs, just surfing and smoothies, but for now we all needed a big snort of coke to get home.

Ten hours later, when we finally got home, the phone was ringing. No time to slow down yet, people wanted their drugs and they wanted them now, not tomorrow. I told Judy I needed another line of coke and a puff of Dr. Brown, I couldn't stop using until the next day.

A friend called who had just gotten back from Columbia, he said he had a present and wanted to know if he could come over. When Robbie got there, he pulled out the best Ecuadorian abalone flake coke I had ever seen. He made out a couple of railroad lines and passed me the mirror. "Try this," he said, "you will love it." It was pure flake, way better than what I was getting down in Mexico. We ended up partying and consuming massive amounts of coke before Robbie left. To come down, Judy and I had to smoke more Dr. Brown. It seemed we were on a continuous cycle of money, drugs and parties, we couldn't stop.

The next day, Jon came by and I told him about Robbie's coke. We decided to split a pound between us for personal use, just to have "the kind" after all we deserved the best.

14

*Never do business with a
guy named "Weasel"*

THE NEXT SIX MONTHS IT WAS CONTINUOUS parties between
Huntington Beach and Lake Tahoe. Jon and Robbie rented a
house in Tahoe for the winter. Heavy drug use accompanied
me everywhere I went, just groups of tight scammers. Plates
of coke were passed around constantly, we snorted a quarter
to an ounce of coke a night. I hadn't surfed in months or even
been to the beach. This lifestyle didn't agree with cold-water
mornings.

My business was expanding and now including Ecuador coke scams once a month. Jon, Robbie and I did a joint smuggling scam of seventy two ounces of pure flake each month. We would send a runner, which would take a week, and netted big profits. I still scored from Marcus in Mexico, but my heroin sales were out of state mostly in pounds. Lots of money was coming in, months of cocaine and heroin use were starting to affect my health. Judy and I both had lost a lot of weight and we were experiencing heroin addiction. Each week we would swear we were going to clean up but then the "jones" (withdrawal) would start and it was hard to go through, if you didn't have to. It would always be next week and then we would fail again.

Parties, money, cocaine and heroin every night, we were addicted. I told Judy we needed a break so we planned a trip up to Tahoe. We both agreed we wouldn't take any heroin with us, we would quit cold turkey.

Before we left for Tahoe, a guy I knew called and wanted to buy a pound of coke. I told him all I had was half a pound and he said that would be fine he wanted it and would come over and get it. He then said," Can I bring a friend"? I told him, "absolutely not!"

He told me he didn't have the money, his friend did. I told him I would front the stash to him, I didn't want anyone but him to come and get it. A few minutes later he called me back and asked if I would drive to his house in Anaheim. I told him, "I don't do deliveries." I covered the phone and asked a friend of mine if he wanted to take a drive to Anaheim with me, he said he would. I got back on the phone, told Weasel I would be at his place in Anaheim in forty five minutes. Judy was surprised when I told her, she knew I never did deliveries. I assured her I would be fine, I would sell the half pound and in the morning we would be off for Tahoe.

It was kind of scary, two long hair young adults driving a Mercedes, pulling into a vacant parking lot at night holding one half pound of coke. I looked at my friend Billy and shook my head, "this is why I don't ever do deliveries, it's too unsafe." I stuffed the coke in my pants and we quickly walked down the alley to Weasel's house, taking the back door route. I knocked on the old wooden screen and Weasel came to the door. We entered into the kitchen and then into the living room. There in the room was a stranger, I looked at Weasel and said," what's this?" The stranger then said his name and then said, "you're Dean," and stuck out his hand. Just at that moment someone tried to kick in the door. I thought it was a joke at first, that is, until I saw a black combat boot as the door warped at the bottom. I yelled to Billy to run and we headed for the kitchen back door only to run straight into guns pointed in our faces. "Get up against the wall," they shouted. I did as they said. At least ten more DEA agents came in the kitchen back door outfitted in combat fatigues, guns drawn and shouting to get against the wall. I complied but they pushed their guns against my head as if I was resisting. Again they commanded, "get up against the wall", over and over and each time I yelled back, "I am, I am." "I'm not resisting and you're going to shoot me," I said. Just then the stranger from the living room came into the kitchen, walked up to me smiling, reached in my pants and pulled out the half pound of coke and then said, "you are under arrest for possession with intent to sell cocaine, you'll be going to jail for twenty years," and then laughed.

I was handcuffed behind my back, Billy and Weasel were also handcuffed and were made to sit on the living room floor, but not me. The DEA agent took me from room to room throughout the house using me as their shield while they searched.

These guys were thugs in police fatigues, kicking us while we were handcuffed on the floor and drinking beer out of the refrigerator. We didn't know if they were going to kill us and take the drugs or what. It was like a movie out of New York with crooked cops. Finally they read us our rights and then couldn't make up their mind where to take us. We were going to either Anaheim city jail or San Clemente Federal holding detention center. Eventually they decided on taking us to Anaheim jail.

On the way to jail I began to settle down enough to think. I was always so careful, no strangers, I realized Weasel deceived me. He knew I wouldn't go to his home or sell to him if there was a stranger there. I wanted answers now! Why did he do this? I wanted some answers, I was screwed because of Weasel.

The booking in the small Anaheim city jail didn't take long. We were put in a small holding cell with an old wino. Immediately, I told Billy how sorry I was for asking him to come with me. I told him I would bail him out and pay for his attorney fees. I said to Billy, "I can't believe this idiot," and I pointed to Weasel.

We were given our one phone call. It was Friday night and chances were we wouldn't get out until the following Monday. I had the ugly thought that I would be "jonesing" before I got out of there, I wondered how sick I was going to get. No Tahoe for me, just jail and withdrawals.

I was afraid to call my house, thinking the line was tapped so, I called my Mom, told her I was in jail. She told me not to worry she would bail me out. I hoped she would hurry. Now it was just sit and wait with a drunk and a fucking Idiot. As the hours passes I was so pissed off at Weasel I finally said to him, "come over here and talk quietly, I want some answers."

First I asked him why he tricked me and asked if he was in on it. He said no and that he was tricked just like me. "That's bullshit," I said, "you knew that guy was sitting in your house and that if I knew I wouldn't have come over, you're a fucking asshole, you just wanted the middle money." I told him that no matter what lies he told me he was the reason I was there and if I ever saw him on the street I would fuck him up. "Now get out of my face," I told him. I grabbed him by the nose and twisted it. He was such a punk. He stayed away from me for the rest of the weekend.

I was getting sicker and sicker as the weekend went on. I slipped into the deepest living hell for the next three days in Anaheim jail. I experienced, for the first time, complete heroin withdrawal. I had continuous excruciating pains in every joint, shooting needle pain in every muscle and unbelievable chills. I kept thinking to myself that it couldn't get any worse but, it did, and it did and it did until I was scared to death. If I could only fall asleep, but I couldn't. I knew if I could only take one puff of heroin I would feel fine. I got bailed out on Monday and Billy and Weasel went to court. Billy was released on his own reconnaissance and that idiot Weasel I hoped rotted in jail, no such luck he got bailed out.

When I walked out of the jail, there stood my Mom and Judy. I was really sick and embarrassed to see my Mom but, it was inevitable. I thanked my Mom for bailing me out and hugged Judy. My Mom asked if I was hungry. I told her I just needed a shower, a clean change of clothes and some sleep, I had been awake for three days. She had no idea I was going through withdrawals.

When my Mom dropped Judy and me off at our house her eyes were red from crying. I felt terrible. I kissed her good bye and again told her how sorry I was. She told me to get some rest and we would talk later. We waved as she drove away, I thought to myself what a true disappointment I had become.

When Judy and I got in the house I told her, "get me a big snort of Dr. Brown, I have the "jones" bad." I powered down a big line and smoked some, the flu like symptoms disappeared. I went into the bathroom, threw up and felt much better.

While I was taking a shower, Judy shared her disbelief how this could have happened. I explained that Weasel had set me up. He wanted to be the middle man and make a profit on the half pound, he knew I wouldn't have gone there if there was a stranger there and the stranger turned out to be a DEA agent. "He set me up!" I said. I continued, "I'm going to kick his ass." After I got out of the shower I told Judy we had to clean out the house. "As soon as the DEA finds out where we live they will raid us," we have to get rid of the scales, drugs and paraphernalia. If they found this stuff there is no telling what would happen to me."

I was so paranoid now, any noise on the phone made me think the line was tapped. I was sure I was being watched and that the DEA was out there just waiting for me to score again. I wasn't about to tell Marcus about being busted, I was afraid he would cut me off. I needed my connection with Marcus, I was going to need a lot of money for my defense. Any calls I made to Mexico were going to be from random phone booths and I only would sell in large quantities. There were no more parties at our house. Judy and I were paranoid and determined to be careful, we knew what had to be done and we did it. Now I needed to find a criminal attorney, a good one.

My preliminary hearing was set upon my release, I promised to appear in three weeks. In that time, I needed to find and retain my attorney, which I did for five thousand dollars. He said he would guarantee either a dismissal or minimal probation. He told me there was a chance it could take one to two years and multiple appearances in court maybe once a month. He told me just to go about my life, it would be a long process. He then said he would contact me after he got the arrest report, then he would know more. Lastly, he said I should make sure my house was free of any and all drugs, I couldn't afford to get arrested on drug charges before court. He warned if I did get arrested for drugs the DA would not release me, I would be considered a risk to flea.

I learned quickly that once you get busted anyone who

owes you money doesn't think they have to pay you anymore. You are out of business quickly, you're so called friends think you are out of business so, they rip you off.

When I saw Jon again, I explained how I got busted through that idiot Weasel and also people were stiffing me on their debts. He couldn't believe I had gotten busted, no one in our inner circle ever had. I told him how Weasel set me up and he couldn't figure that out either. " Now the DEA is onto me, I can't believe this is happening, I've always been so careful."

The next week my attorney called, told me he had my arrest record and wanted me to meet him at his office the next day. When Judy and I got to his office we were treated like V.I.P's, You pay for a high price lawyer and they treat you well. My lawyer's name was Sneedy. He sat us down and told me that he had gone over the arrest records and that the DEA had been trying to get me for a year. Judy and I just looked at each other in amazement. Then he asked me who I sold to on the military base at El Toro? I told him I had never had anything to do with that base. He told me the investigation stemmed from the base. Again he asked me if I had ever sold to anyone on the base. I was certain I hadn't. "Well obviously your partner Weasel has," he said. I told him, "wait a minute, Weasel is not my partner, he is just a friend of a very good friend of mine, I hardly ever sold to him and I don't know his associations." Sneedy sat back and thought for a moment. He then said, "You're facing five to fifteen years for possession with intent to sell and they really want your ass for selling on a military base," I told him again, " I did not sell on the base." "They feel you did and this is the biggest bust in Orange County history," he replied. He then told me it would have been better if the DEA would of taken me to the federal detention center and tried me Federal, a half pound bust isn't that big in the federal court. He felt the Orange County DA was trying to make a big name for himself by really going after me as a major drug dealer. He then continued to say that is why he was going to take his time with my case and drag it out over a year or two. He felt in that amount of time there was a chance the DA would cool off, leave his position or the case could get dropped for one reason or another.

Lots of changes took place over the next three and a half months. Court was really stressful, making mandatory appearances to Superior court. To top it off my attorney would hardly return my calls before and after court. I started to realize I had made a mistake paying him in advance, it left me no leverage. Also in this time Judy, Jon and I had gotten really strung out on hard drugs again.

After three months and my fourth court appearance, I was very disgusted with Sneedy and I told him exactly that. He told me to meet him in his office the next morning at ten am and we would discuss my case. When Judy and I arrived at his office the next morning at nine forty five, we were told to sit and wait, that Mr.Sneedy would be with us as soon as he was off an important conference call. This time we weren't offered coffee and donuts or treated like V.I.P's.

At ten thirty his secretary said, "Mr. Sneedy will see you now." "It's about time," I said to Judy, not caring that the secretary heard me. I had paid this guy five thousand dollars, he was my employee. When we entered his office, Sneedy motioned for us to sit down. He said, "I'll get right to what the DA is offering." "He is offering you one to ten years straight to the Joint," he said. "You said you could get me guaranteed probation at the worst and even the chance of the case being dropped," I replied. He looked at Judy and me and said, " sorry," that was all he could do for me. He then said we could go to trial for another five thousand dollars. "What are my chances with a trial?" I asked. His only reply was, "not good." This was all bullshit, I was facing five to fifteen years in prison, life was getting serious now and I realized this attorney was a jerk and he was selling me out. "I'm firing you, you've appeared in court for me four times that's all, I want a refund," I demanded. He told me he didn't give refunds that he would still represent me but he recommended I take the deal the DA was offering, I told him he was full of shit. Four times he had gone to court for me, maybe an hour and a half of his time for five thousand dollars, what a rip-off this guy was. I told him he should be going to court and jail for ripping me off, he had my money and he knew there was nothing I could do about it. I got up and walked out in disgust.

I couldn't wait to get home to do some heroin and mellow out. Judy and I dealt with the stress of life now by being stoned day and night.

The next morning I woke up, took a big snort of coke and headed outside to wash my Mercedes. My giant of a neighbor was outside doing something with his plumbing truck and we started to talk. We had become friends with him and his wife, he would occasionally buy coke from me to sober himself up after a night out at the bar. I told him my attorney had ripped me off and that I had fired him. He said, "Dean, use my attorney, he's gotten me off of multiple DUI'S with no jail time, he's no bullshit." He told me to give his name when I called his attorney. He grabbed me with his enormous hands and fingers and shook me like a puppet. "This attorney will take care of you, he knows lots of judges," he said. He opened up his wallet and gave me the attorney's card. I thought well, maybe things are going to work out after all. I went back into the house, into the back room, pulled out a mirror, rolled up a one hundred dollar bill and called Judy into the room. She came in and I handed her the mirror, filled with a pile of coke chopped up into lines, then proceeded to tell her that Bob, our neighbor, had given me the number of his attorney and that he said he was good. I picked up the phone, dialed the attorney's number, gave Bob's name as a reference and my appointment was set.

The next morning Judy and I walked into a swanky law office in Santa Ana. I approached the receptionist and told her I was there to see Mr. Thornton, that I had an appointment for eleven. She asked us to have a seat and offered us a soft drink. She said Mr. Thornton would be with us shortly. Within five minutes of waiting, a smartly young looking middle aged attorney stepped into the waiting room. The receptionist introduced me as Mr. McCormick and let him know I was there to see him. He walked up and shook my hand. "Are you Dean, Bob's neighbor?" he asked, "Yes," I replied. " My name is Michael. Bob thinks a lot of you, he called me personally.

Come into my office and tell me what's going on," he said. We went into his office, which was luxurious and very comfortable. Right off, I got the feeling of a genuine person, not a fake guy, kind of Ivy League but easy to talk to.

We sat down and he asked me to tell him my situation starting with the arrest. I told him the DEA raided the house I was at, with a half pound of coke, how they thought I had sold drugs on a military base and that I hadn't. I had spent three days in county jail and was bailed out for five thousand dollars, that I had gone to court four times over three months. The attorney I had hired promised probation and in the end it was straight to the Joint, one to ten years, that was it. I fired him and asked for a refund but, the guy refused. "That brings me to you, my neighbor Bob said you're good, what do you think you can do for me?" I asked. Mr. Thornton told me that judging from what I just told him and without seeing the arrest or investigation, the fact that I didn't have any prior arrests and the fact that there had been much bigger busts in Orange County since my case, he felt formal probation and possibly some county time was the best he could do. He then said if I was given county time he would have me moved to the honor farm, which was much better than the county jail. He paused for a couple minutes and then told me if I hired him, at a fee of five thousand dollars, he would go to court on my behalf, ask for a two month extension to give himself time to go over the case, would draw out the case for a year until just the right judge and DA and then make a deal. Judy and I looked at each other in agreement. I pulled ten thousand dollars out of my pocket, broke the bank label and counted out five thousand dollars in one hundred dollar bills. I handed it to him, we shook hands and he said "that's a first". No one had ever paid him cash on the spot like that. Judy and I drove home feeling pretty good and couldn't wait to do some drugs.

That night Jon was over and we told him about my new attorney and the offer he had made me. If I got formal probation I would have to have drug testing so Judy and I were planning to kick our coke and heroin habit, we had been strung out for to long, it was time to clean up. I asked Jon if he wanted to quit with us. He said, "sure," but not today, tomorrow, tonight we'll do our usual, some coke and Dr. Brown. My plan was to flush whatever was left at the end of the night to prove I was serious about cleaning up.

The next day, I was feeling sick, I hadn't smoked Dr. Brown in nearly twelve hours. I told Judy I didn't know if I really wanted to go through this quite yet, she agreed. I went to a phone booth and made a call to Marcus and hopefully could get a delivery to San Diego that day, before I got too sick.

I drove to a phone booth, I was still paranoid my phone was tapped, and got through to the Mexican operator who placed my call. The phone rang three times and Marcus's wife answered the phone. She told me that the Mexico City federally, on a corruption warrant, came to Tijuana and arrested Marcus and the Tijuana police chief the week before. She told me that we had to be very careful. She said that I would have to call Marcus at the prison in Mexicali and gave me his number. I couldn't believe what I was hearing. She told me that Marcus had his own phone in the prison. Immediately I hung up and called the number she had given me, not knowing what to expect. A Mexican answered and I asked to speak with Marcus. Marcus got on the line instantly and I asked him how he got arrested. He said it was no big deal and asked me what I wanted coke or heroin, Again I couldn't believe what I was hearing. He was in jail but he could still deal. I told him I wanted half a pound of coke and half a pound of heroin. Marcus told me to call him back in fifteen minutes and he would tell me where and when to pick it up. I waited around the phone booth anxious, I needed to score, and I was getting really sick. I called back and Marcus answered. He told me the downtown theatre, two pm, back row. This was great, I knew within a few hours I'd feel fine then Judy and I could slowly wean ourselves off the drugs, not cold turkey. What was I thinking?

Within two hours Judy and I were on a plane from Orange County to San Diego to make our pick-up time of two pm. We rented a car at the San Diego airport and drove to the sleazy porn theatre. Our connection was there just as instructed. Judy and I opened the stash as soon as we got back to our rental car and each snorted a little spoon of heroin, within one minute we felt fine.

"That was really stupid trying to quit cold turkey," I said. We stashed the drugs on our bodies, got back to the airport, dropped off the rental car, up and down on the plane in thirty minutes and then back into our car. We had another snort when we got in the car and then went home. When we got home Jon was there and he was sick too. We went into the house and I gave him a big snort and then we sat back and smoked some more heroin. When we were all feeling better, we decided we would wean ourselves gradually, that made a lot more sense.

Within the next two months I started an Electrostatic Painting business in Hawaii. I was a silent partner, a good friend of mine, Randy, would head it up. I bought a franchise, supplies and a new van and had it shipped to Hawaii. My commitment was that I would help support him and his family along with the business until it got going, maybe a year. If my court case went bad in a year, I could skip out, take on a new name and have a going business. This was my back-up plan.

Jon and Robbie moved to Lucadia and were living the high roller life spending money like water and using massive amounts of drugs. Once a month the Ecuadorian coke would come in, it was the best but, in between the shipments I had the middle grade Mexican coke and the strongest heroin in California. My money was steadily building again. Jon was selling pounds of coke to a DJ in San Francisco each time the Ecuador flake came in the Mexican coke wasn't good enough, it sold in ounces and grams, not pounds. Jon was getting way out mentally on the coke and started hanging out with some people he met in Hollywood. I only met these people once, they carried guns, they were east coast people that were definitely criminals. I didn't like these guys, I told Jon just that. I told him not to bring them anywhere around my house, Jon didn't like that, Judy and I couldn't understand why he was hanging out with them.

As months passed I hardly saw Jon, except if he wanted

heroin. He would buy an ounce, which would last him two weeks or so. We had always been such good friends even though we hardly saw each other at times. Things had really changed, Jon was weird. I was in court fighting for my freedom, Jon was hanging out with strange freaks and Judy and I were arguing almost daily. I was smoking heroin daily, snorting large quantities of coke, making large amounts of cash but nothing seemed the same anymore.

I hadn't seen Jon in three weeks. I was over at some friends house, snorting coke, just hanging out, and in came Jon. He didn't look good at all. "Dean, I need to talk to you in private," he said. This was odd, we were all friends, I knew something was up. We excused ourselves to the kitchen, as soon as we were in there Jon grabbed my shoulder and broke down. I had never seen Jon so shaky before, he was always cool under stress. We had been with each other in some hairy spots and he always kept it together. He told me he needed cash now, that these east coast guys were going to kill him, or his family, if he didn't come up with the money within twenty four hours. This was so weird, Jon had lots of cash, I asked him why he didn't have it? He told me all his cash was tied up in twenty pounds of coke. He said he needed ten thousand dollars now. He then went on to say he had made bad investments, was living to high and spending too much. I remembered he had two hundred thousand just the year before, I told him he looked terrible and needed some help. He just begged me to loan him the money, he promised to pay me back the next day. I wanted to think about this, it was all to weird, but Jon just pleaded. I told him to wait there and I went to the other room to talk with Judy. I told her Jon needed a lot of money and I didn't feel good about giving it to him. She looked at me and said, "Loan it to him." Judy handed me her purse and I counted out seven thousand dollars. I went back to Jon in the kitchen and told him that was all I had with me and handed it to him. "Thank you, I'll see you tomorrow," he said then followed me back into the living room and rushed out. I sat next to Judy and we just looked at each other. What else could we do, he was screwing with some bad people and now he was scared for his life.

The next morning, afternoon and then night passed and no Jon. He promised he would be back, where was he? Jon was messing with some pretty creepy people now, I hoped he was alright.

Within the next few days and then weeks to follow I started to find out how serious Jon was abusing cocaine and that he was broke. He had used up all his money on hotels, wine, women, clothes and coke. He was no longer snorting the coke, he was now putting it in a baby syringe, an eighth of an ounce at a time, and taking it anal. Sometimes he added heroin to it, this was known as a speedball, he was out of his mind, literally. Also, I started being contacted by other close dealing associates asking me if I had seen Jon. As it turned out, Jon had borrowed ten, fifteen and twenty thousand dollars from each one of them. Everyone fell for his story of temporarily needing the money, everyone assumed he had a lot of money, so no one hesitated lending him the cash but, as with me, he never showed up the next day to pay the money back.

After a few weeks we, we got startling news that Jon

was in the hospital. He had a terrible accident, rolling his Mercedes, going sixty to seventy miles per hour off a freeway exit. Everybody went to see him in the hospital, including all the people he owed money to. Judy and I went to visit Jon with nothing but sincere good wishes and balloons, he had barely survived the accident. His eye socket and cheekbone had been shattered, his arm was broken in three places, he had been through six hours of surgery to repair his arm and face, and he was bruised from head to toe. The doctor told us he was lucky to be alive. If I didn't know it was Jon in that bed, I would have thought the doctors made a mistake, this guy was skinny and looked fifteen years older than Jon. Unfortunately, it was Jon. The doctor told us he would be in the hospital for at least a week. I looked at Jon, still not believing my eyes, and told him to hang in there and that I would see him when he got released. On our way out Judy and I were still in shock, then the elevator opened and there was Jon's mom and sister. Their eyes were red from crying, I nodded and they walked away towards Jon's room.

A week later Jon showed up at my front door unexpectedly, no call in advance. I invited him in and as he entered he started poking me with his finger, his other arm was in a sling and the bandages on his face made him look like a mummy, or the walking dead. "How dare you come to the hospital demanding money," he said. I told him that was bull, Judy heard the ruckus and came in the room as Jon was still poking me in the chest with his finger. "What's going on in here?" she asked. Jon told Judy to stay out of it and then proceeded to say he was going to kick my ass. "Jon you are a fucker, coming into my house after ripping me off for seven thousand dollars and accusing me of all this bullshit," I shouted." "Where is my money? Now I'm demanding it, not just asking," I said. At that point hate between us peaked and we started to fight. Judy started freaking out and started pulling at us to stop. I told Jon to get out of my house. "When I'm well I'll be back to kick your ass," he told me. I told him to have my money when he came and then slammed the door on him. Judy and I looked at each other in amazement. We never said anything about the money at the hospital. He was surely out of his mind. What was he thinking coming over like that, our friendship was over.

I never saw Jon again after that day, I only heard things about him, only bad. He was still ripping people off and the last I heard was that the freaks, from Hollywood, were going to kill him on site so, he left the state and was on the run.

Life got uglier, Judy and I became full heroin addicts, we used day and night, only lots of money kept us going. I had been supporting the electrostatic painting business, in Hawaii, at the sum of one thousand dollars a month. It had been a year and the business was starting to carry it's self somewhat. Court was definitely scary now, I was getting close to a conviction. I was positively going to run if I couldn't avoid prison. I wasn't going to the joint, they'd have to catch me. I needed the painting business to succeed to fall back on just in case, I had to run.

Over one year of court appearances with the same D.A. my attorney Mr. Thornton was frustrated, he couldn't get the district attorney to offer a plea bargain. He wanted the joint for me. My attorney told me for some reason he had it out for me. One day after court I was with my attorney and he dropped the bomb. " This is it," he said, "plead guilty and you will be guaranteed a ninety day observation at chino prison." He proceeded to tell me that he has had excellent luck with the ninety day observation. During the ninety days in prison the prison psychiatrist, a social behavior counselor and the prison staff would interview me. He told me if I kept my nose clean, meaning no write-ups, and with my clean arrest record he didn't feel they would recommend prison, he felt I would be given a second chance and the courts would abide by that. He told me this was the only way. "The D.A. won't budge, he wants to go to trial, he's got it in for you," he said. "You mean to say you want me to plead guilty to a five to fifteen year prison term and then throw my self on the mercy of the court?" I asked. He told me I was sort of right, he explained this would be the only way to get the D.A. out of the picture. He assured me again that the prison would definitely recommend at the most county time and to overturn my conviction. With all that said he told me otherwise we were going to trial the next week. I told Mr. Thornton I had to think this over and I would give him an answer the next day. He said, if I agreed, I was to be prepared to go to prison at court next week.

That evening Judy and I pondered over what I was up against. I completely trusted Thornton, but prison, I would have to detox immediately or go to prison addicted. Judy and I were smoking heroin right then, how could I quit so soon? I was screwed. My choices were clear, go to prison, go to trial or run from the law. If I pleaded guilty and went to prison, I might skate and only get probation or they might decide to keep me for a five year minimum. I didn't see how I could win going to trial and if I ran, it would be forever, there was no statue of limitation. Judy and I talked over the entire pros and cons. She had a kid, how could she leave? Running was chancy, what if I got caught in ten or twenty years. I decided to go with Thornton's recommendation, I trusted him. Tomorrow I would start to detox, I had just enough time. I was going to prison next week.

I called Thornton the next morning and told him I would go with the ninety day observation and then I added, "I hope you are right," I'm trusting you with my life," I said. He said it would be alright and he felt I had made the right decision.

As each day progressed I got sick and decided just a little brown, just enough to make me well not enough to get high. This situation was daily until court was the next day and I was still hooked. Thornton told me to expect to go immediately to jail after pleading guilty.

15

#279CPI7841B

CLIMBING INTO BED THE NIGHT BEFORE COURT was almost as bad as the next morning. I was going to be pleading guilty to intent to sale cocaine and would be immediately sentenced to a five to fifteen year prison term. To top that off I had a one year heroin addiction and I was going to have to detox in jail beginning that afternoon. I would be taken into custody in court, no stay of execution. This was going to be the worst day of my life, I was flat out scared. The decision to plead guilty was rolling the dice with my life but, I had made my decision and there was no backing out now.

I was in court at nine thirty and the first case called. I stood before the superior court judge, my attorney advised the court of my plea. The Judge addressed me, " Are you aware that a guilty plea is a mandatory prison sentence of five to fifteen years?" I replied, "yes Sir." He then asked, "What do you plea?" "Guilty," I replied as my heart sank. The judge pronounced the sentence, five to fifteen years in the state prison, and the bailiff was ordered to take me into custody. As I was being hand cuffed I turned to look at my Mom and Judy, both were crying. I was booked into Orange County jail at five pm that night and in my cell by twelve midnight. What an ugly day.

I was awake all night, sick. I was scheduled to leave for chino prison the following day but my name wasn't on the convict list, it was Friday so that meant I had to stay in the O.C. jail for the weekend and would be on the chino bus on Monday.

The withdrawals were terrible. I was sick, shaky, sweating, freezing, couldn't sleep, and every position I was in was uncomfortable. I was up and down all night long. This was to last for two to three days and then the worst would be over. I couldn't let the guards in the jail know I was addicted, that would shoot my evaluation down for sure. This was the worst weekend of my life.

On Monday morning I was on the bus to chino, also known as the train to chino. This was most convict's stepping-stone to one of the many prisons in the state, depending on their crime and age. Chino was the prison that decided on your fate in the prison system, it was called the guidance center.

When the bus turned down the final street leading up to chino prison, we slowly rambled past some young kids, maybe nine or ten years old, on their way to school. I thought to myself, how did I end up on this bus going to prison. I was a complete loser. My poor mother, her youngest son a convict and junky. I wondered what the kids outside were thinking. What would I of thought at their age? There go the murders, robbers and bad men.

Suddenly the bus came to a stop, one of the guards up front stood and told us to remain seated, the big gate to the prison opened by remote. There were armed guards in the watchtower, the bus passed through the gate and then it closed behind us. The bus stopped, the air brakes were set and the guards exited. We exited the bus handcuffed to each other, marched inside to the detention orientation center and were strip-searched. The room was freezing, my hair was cut off while I stood there naked, shaking from the cold. I showered, then sprayed with some very cold type if insecticide on my butt and genitals. I was then given old prison clothes, my picture was taken, I was finger printed and then given a number, 279CP17841B, that would follow me throughout the California Penal System. I was given an orientation, an old mattress and a cell number. I was told to do as I was ordered or I would spend my time there in the hole till transferred to another prison. I was told I would be spending twenty three hours in my cell and I would get one hour in the yard. The guard then told us the prison was on twenty four hour lock down because of stabbings, they were averaging two a day. We were now chino prisoners and we were marched to our cells. I was semi-conscious by this time, I didn't think I could take anymore, I had no life left in me.

The prison was old, ugly, dark and freezing. I thought to myself that sands prison might have even been better than this. At least at sands prison there wasn't violence and was fairly safe. This prison was run mostly by Mexicans and tattooed gang prisoners. The guards stood in locked cages, no wonder there was so much violence. If I survived, it would be because of my courage and wits, which I didn't have any at the moment.

I was marched down a cold cellblock lined with dingy cells. What windows there were had been broken out years before letting in chilling howling winds. The deferred maintenance and ghastly living conditions were frightening but I was desperate to get to my cell. I was deathly sick and freezing. I actually felt like I was going to die. My withdrawals were full blown and were getting worse by the forth day.

Halfway down the block, a cell door opened, a voice commanded me to step inside and the door closed behind me. I put my mattress on the top bunk, a sleeping inmate occupied the bottom. So here I was, a deathly sick heroin addict, to sick to fight off anyone, wondering what kind of criminal roommate I was in with.

It didn't take long to find out about my roommate. He turned over, looked at me, swung his feet out slowly and sat up. I was sitting on the edge of the toilet with a blanket wrapped around me sweating and freezing all at the same time. "You look terrible," he said, "how long you been jonesing?" I told him it had been four days and I hadn't had any sleep. I said " my name is Dean, is it freezing here all the time?" He told me it was cold day and night and that we would be in there all the time due to all the murders and stabbings that had happened. He asked me what I was in for. I told him I was in for sales of a half pound of coke and that I was only there for a ninety day observation. He told me to keep that to myself. He said a lot of the guys in there were lifers and they would fuck me up just for the fun of it. "That's how they get their kicks, it gives them something to talk about to their homies for years, how they ruined your chances of getting out," he told me. I thanked him for the advice and knew I would keep it to myself from then on. I then asked him what he was in for. "Murder for hire," he said. I was really screwed, sharing a cell with a convicted murderer. "That's your bed up top," he said.

In the days that followed the "jones" continued. Every night I thought I would definitely sleep, then again I would be up all night freezing and sweating. I would try to read with a dim light at night, to occupy my mind, but it was nearly impossible I could hardly hold my head up because, I was so exhausted and sick.

The sixth day, in chino, was Saturday and I had a visit from my Mom and Judy. When they asked me how I was doing I told them pretty good besides freezing day and night. I didn't tell them I was sharing a cell with a murderer or that I hadn't slept in a week because of heroin withdrawals.

That night as I lay in my bunk, I heard a rustling and whimpering. I didn't get up or look to see what was going on. The next day, word travels even in lockdown, I heard that one Mexican had stabbed another Mexican seventeen times just outside my cell.

As the days went by my cellmate became a friend. We talked about ourselves and our pasts that had gotten us there. In between reading, which he did a lot of, he told me about himself. At seventeen he had joined the marines and was sent to Vietnam. His platoon was in the middle of massive fighting and killing. Rather than take prisoners they would shoot women, kids, grandparents, dogs, it didn't matter. prisoners were problems so they would just kill them instead of capture them.

By the second week, my sweats, chills and a running nose were over but, I still couldn't sleep. I had lost count after ten days, I was living like a zombie, and I was beginning to think I would never sleep again.

My cellmate and I had conversations mostly in the evenings. He told me that Vietnam taught him how to kill. He said killing a human was no different than stepping on a bug. He told me how the guys over there used heroin, opium and smoked pot daily in Vietnam. Men were dying daily and their day could be next so, what the heck.

When he made it out of Vietnam and back on the streets he was totally strung out on heroin and it was no longer cheap, he had to rob and steal to support his habit. He said he knew many other Vietnam vets, personally, throughout the country just like him.

One of his friends took him on a kill for hire targeted at a rip-off drug dealer in Watts. His friend asked if he wanted to do the kill. They pulled up to the corner where the black dealer stood, when he walked over to the car and started to poke his head inside, he put a sawed off shot gun in his face and blew his head off. The shotgun recoiled and hit him above the eye, splitting it open needing twelve stitches. His friend split the one thousand dollars pay off with him. He made his name known from that one killing and soon was asked to do another. His price, five hundred dollars per murder, from then on he was busy.

Once we got to know each other better he told me details about hits he had done in Mexico, Los Angeles and Sacramento. He got arrested in San Francisco for a hit he did on a snitch a year before in Fresno. There was a reward for any information that would lead up to his arrest and conviction. He was ratted out by a junky wanting the reward. He was sentenced to seven years and the dealer that hired him for the hit got life. He then told me that when he gets out in seven years the snitch was as good as dead. I asked him if he was afraid the cops would know he did it and his reply was, "no, I don't care, he's got it coming."

On Friday of my second week, I was told to roll it up, which meant I was being moved on to another place. I said to my murderer roommate, "thanks for being my friend." All my obvious symptoms of being a heroin addict were over. Now, I can go to the ninety day observation not addicted and hope for a good report. After two weeks in this freezing cell I was glad to be leaving. I told my cellmate, "good luck at Soledad," and then waited for my cell door to open. The door opened and I was gone as quick as I had come.

While being booked out to another prison, a guy recognized me from Huntington Beach. He looked at me and said, " don't I know you?" I looked at him and then realized I did know him, he was Sandy's friend. "You're the guy that got popped in Lebanon," he said. I asked him what he was there for. He told me he had gotten three years for sales of one pound of pot, this was his last year and he had been returned to chino, on his way out, from another prison. He was a trustee now and said he hoped he could keep his nose clean and out of trouble, if so, he would be released in six months. He said he first would be going to a half way house but, his dream was to be on a surfboard again, tasting the surf and smelling the sea air. "Me too," I replied. He asked me what I was in for and I told him five to fifteen for sales of coke. He told me that maybe I would get a good recommendation from the observation and then I could go back to court. I just agreed and didn't let on, like the murderer told me.

I walked out into daylight, for the first time in two weeks, to a waiting bus that would transfer eight of us to the observation prison, known as "The White Elephant." We all loaded on for a short one-mile ride there. I was so glad to be leaving that dirty, dim, freezing prison but had no idea what I was going to find in the other prison. I didn't have much time to think about it, we were there. The bus stopped in front of thirty foot white walls with twenty foot doors that were opening slowly. The bus crept in, through the doors, the air brakes locked and we were ordered off the bus. I stepped out into the prison yard, there was a track with inmates walking and jogging around. My first impression was it looked like a modern football field or athletic track facility, only surrounded by thirty foot walls manned by gun towers. We were ushered inside the building and our shackles were removed. In stepped the warden; his first words were "welcome gentlemen." Then he continued, "You are at the observation facility of Chino. This is a no nonsense facility. You are expected to keep your nose clean or we will just get rid of you. Is that clear, is that clear?" we all answered "yes."

He continued, "some of you have mandatory return dates to court after your evaluation and some of you do not. Our evaluation depends on whether some of you go back to court or to prison. For those of you that do not return to court our evaluation and our observation will decide if you go to a minimum or maximum security prison. Everyone has something to gain here by a good evaluation so make the most of it. You will be closely observed sometimes knowingly and sometimes not. During your ninety to one hundred and twenty day stay here you will be seeing a staff psychiatrist, scheduled by your assigned social counselor and you will be given a job. How you do with these three requirements will be in our observation report and help with our evaluation. I am warning you to keep clean and no problems or you will receive a poor evaluation", with that he walked away. A lesser-ranked guard stepped forward and took over the orientation.

Next, we were dismissed to another prison guard who took us to various buildings. I was assigned to building B and was met by the sergeant and given a second orientation. He told me that I would be watched night and day and to avoid any write-ups at all costs. I was assigned to a single man cell, told to keep it clean at all times and told my job would be working in the kitchen, three shifts a day, starting that day. I was then, again, told my work performances would go on my prison evaluation, visits were a privilege and as long as I didn't get any write-ups I would be allowed visitors. Visitation was two days a week, Saturdays and Sundays. On my free time I was expected to keep busy. There was a fully stocked library, games to play in the day room, a basketball gym open daily, baseball games you were encouraged to join, a weight room and an olympic size pool open only on weekends. It was to my advantage to join some type of sports activity, it not only looked good for my evaluation but the inmates respected a good athlete. I was then put in my single cell and awaited my call to report to my kitchen duties.

The next day, Saturday, I was hoping Judy would find me for a visit. She would be happy I had finally made it here, compared to the first prison it was like being at a resort.

Sure enough, on Saturday, my name was called for visiting. Judy had found me, and when I walked into the waiting room there stood Judy with a big smile and then I saw my Mom, with a forced smile. I kissed them both and sat down. I had told them both how terribly cold and dirty chino was and about my two-man cell. Now I enjoyed solitude of a one-man room, clean, no bars, that complete isolation was strange, but I was safe. I decided to tell them about my chino cellmate, a hired murderer but, by the looks of him, you would never think that if you saw him walking down the street. I told my Mom it was a safe place, even though I knew no prison was safe. I realized it was a mistake telling her about the murderer almost immediately by the look on her face. The visit seemed short, I was back working the lunch shift in the kitchen right after they left.

After lunch I wondered the grounds and checked out the gym. When I walked inside there was a basketball game going on between inmates. I went to the library and checked out a book and hung out by the pool. Later went back to my cell and thought, ninety days, I hoped it would go by quick. Soon it was time for the dinner shift; the kitchen was a twelve-hour on call shift from five am to five pm. That night I hung out in the TV. room. I watched guys playing ping-pong, others playing cards and dominos in an adjacent room. I didn't feel comfortable enough yet to ask to join in a game so I just watched TV.

As the week went on I ran the track a little between shifts in the kitchen, watched basketball games at night in the gym and eventually I was asked to play. I tried to play but became winded within five minutes but, did make a shot before the quarter was up. I met a few guys and was asked to play the next day. I got back to my building, took a shower, went back to my cell and dropped on my bunk. I felt good about my day and read until count then my door was locked for the evening. The lights were turned off and I slept well for the first time, since going to prison, and it felt good.

Practically every evening after that I played basketball, read a lot and played a little ping pong. Some of those jailbirds were really good, it made it hard to win a match. The days were slow, like being in slow motion, but the weeks seemed to end quickly and I always looked forward to my visits. A lot of the inmates never got visitors, where were their family and friends? How sad I thought.

It's amazing how fast the young body rejuvenates even after a year of addiction. I was playing basketball daily, baseball on the weekends, swimming and weight training by the pool. Working in the kitchen I gained weight, eating as much as I wanted. Now I looked forward to sleeping again, no tossing and turning, the heroin was out of my system finally, never again! What a fool I had been, it wasn't worth it.

I worked three shifts in the kitchen starting at five am and ending at five pm, seven days a week. I stayed busy all the time but still time passed so slow. There were so many rules to follow. I just kept telling myself "just be patient," over and over again.

I hadn't had my interviews yet, it had been a month. Now I didn't mind being locked up in solitude each night at nine, actually I looked forward to it, it was safe, but when were my interviews going to start. What was the hold-up?

I practiced shooting hoops in the gym for the games each evening. Everyday I was becoming more of an athlete, now that my mind and skills had improved. Judy tried to look good every weekend but I could tell she was still using heroin even though she tried to hide the look, I knew it all to well. She felt bad, I was clean and she wasn't. She wanted to be clean but easier said than done.

The second month I was really getting into good shape, I could play full court basketball and hardly stopped to rest. The burn in my lungs actually felt good now instead of feeling like my lungs were going to burst. I lived as much as possible in the gym. Sports was my outlet, I had played them all my life so I excelled among my criminal team mates. I was always picked first for the team whether it was basketball or baseball. My athletic skills helped me to get along with some of the criminal types that otherwise might have given me problems, being white and a surfer.

There was one crazy looking midget that had massive muscles, a real career criminal type that always looked for trouble. This guy was definitely dangerous and I wondered how he got mixed in the general population. I tried not to ever make eye contact with him, he had a "big chip" on his shoulder, he didn't care about anything except his ego. He ended up stabbing an innocent inmate, with a makeshift ice pick, up the nose. The guy lived, luckily but, it got the midget taken out of the population.

That incident made me anxious. I needed to get my interviews and get the hell out of there. I could be set up by another inmate, just for the heck of it, get a write-up, have to fight for my life, kill or be killed. I'd be kept in prison for sure, anything could happen.

Judy came to visit me the weekend starting my third month. I told her about what had happened and how much I wanted to get out of there. I couldn't understand what they were waiting for. It was all so frustrating, I wanted to leave, I wanted it to all be over and not knowing was driving me crazy. Judy started to cry and asked me to please be patient. She told me she would call my attorney and write me every day, she pleaded with me to be patient and careful. Before she left that day, she told me she had seen Jon at a friend's house and that he was really skinny and acted weird. He was definitely losing it. The visit was miserable for Judy and me. We ended the visit feeling upset and not in control. Before she left I told her she looked bad and to please try to clean up.

The next week, after seventy days in there, I started getting my interviews. They said they were amazed I was even there, that I was not prison material. I was relieved, I was getting good evaluations and they told me that in a week or two I would be sent back to Orange County court.

On day eighty-three my name was called to roll it up, this meant I was leaving and on my way back to Orange County jail. Again, this happened on a Friday which meant no court until the following Monday.

The re-booking into the O.C. jail on a Friday was a nightmare. It took at least twelve hours of sitting on wooden benches, concrete floors, no food and moving at a snails pace. The only good thing was I wasn't going through withdrawals this time. Judy wouldn't know I was back in Orange County until she got to chino to visit me and then by the time she could get back to the Orange County jail it would be to late for a visit but I knew she would try. I wasn't allowed a phone call to let her know I had been moved.

Saturday Judy was a no show but, on Sunday she came. She told me she had spoken to the attorney and he was going to go over my evaluation on Monday and then come and see me. She was glad that I was out of chino. I was bummed, I wanted to go to court on Monday and now I was only getting to talk to my attorney instead. Judy had the heroin sniffles, she hadn't tried to clean up which didn't make me happy but I probably wouldn't of either.

On Monday I saw my attorney, he had read my evaluation and told me it was the best evaluation he had ever seen come back from chino. Their recommendation was no time to be served, probation only. He told me we would be in court the next day, Tuesday, and that he was sure the judge would reinstate my bail and that I would be released with a return date in one month. Tuesday came and I was released, but had to go through the long hours of release process at the O.C. jail. My attorney asked me to see him the next week.

Tuesday evening I felt freedom, I had been to hell and back. I couldn't believe I was back in my Mercedes and driving home. When I pulled up into the driveway I stepped out and took in a big deep breathe of ocean air and thought, " I made it, this is me." When we got in the house, Judy made out a big line of coke and we partied the night away.

I went to see my attorney the next week, he shook my hand and told me I had done a good job. Again he said my evaluation said no time to be served but to expect a possible ninety day slap on the hand and probation. He then warned me to be good for the next month, no arrests or problems of any kind, I couldn't afford any. I assured him I would not cause any problems, shook his hand and said I would see him in court.

Judy drove us home from the attorneys office, we locked the doors, laid out a mirror and put a big spoonful of coke on it and then got out some brown. I was only going to do it that night to celebrate and then I would help Judy clean up. We had a few close friends over, drank expensive wine, snorted expensive coke and smoked heroin until midnight. It was so nice to be home with my friends and Judy.

My first weeks home I celebrated day an night. I spend my time chipping heroin and snorting coke. I was dirty by the third day. Besides seeing my attorney I had done nothing but do drugs and live the high life. I was already into my second week before I knew it. I was using everyday always saying I would clean up tomorrow but days passed by. Everyday different friends would come by wanting to hear what had happened, in jail, what kind of time I was looking at and then we would get out some coke and start all over again for another night.

I made a trip to San Diego to pick up a pound of chiva, my customers needed to be serviced. By the start of my third week, out of prison, I was living in the fast lane and slipped deeper into junk again and my court date was coming closer. I tried to clean up everyday with just a little puff of brown to help the withdrawals at the beginning of every day but ended up using all day and into the night.

Judy and I ended up each night in an argument. "I've got to clean up," I told her. I then continued, " You're not facing the jones in jail, all you want is more dope each day, court is next week, I have no time." All I could do was hope the Judge didn't give me jail time.

My court day came and I was dirty. I got up early and smoked some heroin just to feel okay but I was totally edgy and scared. I ended up smoking more heroin and snorting some coke before heading to Santa Ana Superior Court.

When we walked into the court we headed up to the third floor and there was my attorney, briefcase in hand, wearing an expensive suit looking fresh and clean. We greeted each other and he firmly spoke to me, "be prepared to get sixty or ninety days." I asked him if he could get me a one month stay and he said maybe two weeks but, we would have to see. He told me my case would be one of the first to be called so not to go anywhere.

The bailiff came out to get everyone, introduced Judge Smith, as we all stood and then ordered all to be seated. My case was the first to be called and when I heard my name my heart skipped a beat. I approached the front of the court, the judge was looking over his papers and then when he looked up my attorney started to speak. He informed the judge that I had completed the ninety day observation, at chino prison, and had returned with a clean record and an excellent evaluation. The judge then replied, " I have read the evaluation and the recommendation, which I do not agree with, but I am going to give your client one more chance." The judge then looked at me and asked if I was ready for my sentencing. I looked straight at him and said," yes." "I sentence you to five years formal probation, with regular drug testing, first year spent in the county jail, no time served, I feel you need some time, bailiff, take this man into custody." I was handcuffed and taken into custody. My attorney started to argue for a two week stay and eventually the judge agreed to a one week stay and ordered the bailiff to release me. He told me I was to report to the Orange County jail the next Wednesday at six am to turn myself in. He then added if I didn't report to the jail a bench warrant would be issued, my bail would be revoked and my mom would lose her home. He asked me if I understood and I answered him "yes." He slammed down his hammer and said, "stay granted for one week, bailiff call the next case."

I walked out of that courtroom in shock. I couldn't believe the judge completely disregarded the recommendation from Chino then gave me the maximum he could without prison. Judy asked, "what's wrong? You got probation." "Yeah, five years probation with the first year in county jail," I said. My attorney was amazed, he had never seen a judge reject the prison recommendation. He looked at me said "sorry," one year meant eight and a half months that I would have to serve. Now I had one week to withdrawal from a month of heroin use, then turn myself in for eight and a half month stay. I didn't even want to think about it, I just wanted to get home and smoke some junk.

During the short week I tried to clean up but I couldn't, I used everyday. Each and every day I tried. "I'm not going to jail without some heroin " I said. "Judy I really want you to clean up." She said she would do whatever I wanted. "You're set with fifty thousand dollars cash and ten thousand dollars in heroin and coke. When that is gone I want you to be clean. Please promise me." She said "yes," and we hugged.

16

"State your business"

THE DREADED MORNING CAME FOR ME TO turn myself in, it was one of the hardest things I had ever done. I walked up to the steel door and pushed the button. A voice said, "state your business." "I am here to turn myself in'" I replied. A loud buzzer went off and the door opened. Once inside the doors you are in jail instantly, it's not a gradual process. This was the first moments of a year sentence. Once again I had to go through all the booking process that took hours of finger-printing, showering, strip search, mug shots and hours of waiting in cold cement cells. Here in jail again and addicted to heroin. By the end of the day I couldn't wait to get to my cell, which turned out to be a forty man dorm with bars down one side. The guards would walk by and be able to see every inmate in their bunk, taking showers or watching television. I put my mattress on an empty bunk and sat down. I felt sick and was sweating. I asked the inmate next to me when we were allowed to take showers, "anytime," he replied.

I got up, got a towel and headed for the showers, freezing and sweating at the same time. I hated to pull off my orange jumpsuit but, I had no choice. As soon as I got in the shower I stuck my fingers down my throat, gagging as quietly as I could, and eventually threw up a balloon with two grams of heroin in it. I thought to myself," now what? heroin in jail. If I get caught I will get five to fifteen years for sure." I must be crazy, I couldn't let anyone know. I turned off the shower and dried off clutching the balloon. I was scared of everybody. I needed a snort but where? I was so sick but there was no way I could get a snort without risking the chance of getting caught. The lights were on twenty-four hours a day, I would have to wait until everyone was in their bunks to open the balloon by feel very carefully under my blanket.

I found that at night, under my blanket, I could take a pinch from the balloon, just enough to sleep, and put it directly in my mouth. heroin taste really bad, bitter, but this was the only way I could use and not get caught. After, I'd stash the balloon in a toothpaste tube. This wasn't very safe but it was better than having it on my body, we were searched constantly.

My second week there I switched to trustee, transferred

to an eight-man cell and was assigned to kitchen work. By the end of that week my balloon of heroin was running low but it had worked. My withdrawals were getting further apart and less intense. I was asked by one of the Mexican trustees why my pupils were pinned, a well known sign of heroin use, and why I slept so much. I told him I was just sick. "You're holding aren't you?" he said. My heart skipped a beat and I told him I didn't know what he was talking about, I didn't have anything. About an hour later my cell door opened to be swept by two trustees. They were the same two Mexicans, that had confronted me outside my cell, and they ordered me to give them what I had. I again told them I didn't have anything. This was unbelievable, the last thing I wanted was to be in a fight with two Mexicans and be holding at the same time. One of the guys kept trying to get behind me so I backed up against the wall and the other was rocking back and forth trying to sucker punch me. I could tell it was coming so I stepped forward and spattered the five foot seven inch bastard's nose and lips with a power punch and knocked him to the ground. The other little character punched me in the side of my head. My momentum carried me forward and I grabbed the one on the floor and slammed his head against the steel bunk just as the other guy kicked me in the chin, luckily the jail issues tennis shoes, it jolted my head back but I didn't let go of his friend. The one on my back was grabbing in my pockets and found the balloon, yelled something in Spanish and they both ran out of the cell. They got what I had left, which wasn't much.

I had kicked their little asses but later heard they told

everyone, in their gang, that they had kicked mine. That made it so they didn't have to get revenge. Luckily for me, no one in my cell helped me or I wouldn't have seen the last of those Mexicans. Actually, I was glad the heroin was gone, I was playing a dangerous game in jail and the worst of the withdrawals was over.

Judy came to visit me and immediately noticed the abrasion on my chin and wanted to know what happened. I told her two Mexicans had jumped me and one of them kicked me in the chin with his tennis shoe.

My kitchen work got me out of my cell three times a day and for one hour a day we were allowed to go up on the roof, which was optional. I preferred to stay in my cell. The days were unbelievable slow and I was pasty white, from lack of sun, but I had kicked heroin again.

My attorney had told me that within a month he would have me moved to the honor farm to serve out my sentence but, this was my second month and I hadn't been moved. Jail birds I talked with told me not to get my hopes up, that no one serving time for drugs got to go to the "farm."

The animosity the Mexicans had towards the whites in jail was unbearable. If they decided to kill you, you were dead. The Mexicans controlled the jail. You could get jumped just for being white, it was just a matter of time. I said to Judy, " I need to get out of here."

I was still in Orange County jail starting my third month. I saw thieves, robbers and even murders being sent to the farm, only child molesters and people doing time for drugs weren't. I wrote to my attorney, told him he was my only hope to get to the farm and whatever he was doing wasn't working.

I had been working in the kitchen for three months and I hated it. The worst criminals in the jail worked in the kitchen and the food was terrible. I washed dishes next to a derelict Indian, who slapped me in the back of the head for getting water on him. I looked at him and told him, " don't ever do that again!" and he spit on me. That was it we were on the wet floor fighting. The kitchen guard stopped the fight and threatened to put both of us in the hole. We quit our fight and got back to work but I knew this Indian had it in for me and it wasn't over.

My visits with Judy were never good. Every week I was told to expect to be moved and every week I wasn't. I told Judy the anticipation was killing me and now I had a crazy Indian after me, "what is the problem?" I demanded. She didn't have an answer for me, I was stuck in this awful place and nobody seemed to realize how desperate I was to get out.

The fourth month was terrible, I hated this place. The Mexicans and the guards were the lowest scum of society. The guards were as bad as the gangs, a white guy didn't have a chance in this place. The guards considered you a pussy if you weren't a criminal type or a Mexican gangster. Both would fuck you up for no reason. The jail stories that you hear about the guards is true, it's a crazy world in jail. Some very sadistic guards work in the jail and other guards were aware of it but, keep quiet, so as not to violate their, " code of silence."

Almost daily I would have a shoving match with the

Indian in the kitchen. If only we could get outside, I would kick his ass so he would never want to fight with me again but, being inside I didn't want to take a chance of getting sent to the hole, he didn't seem to care. I was worried he would stab me in the back so, I never took my eyes off of him.

Judy came to visit and told me that my attorney's jail connection wasn't working and he was going to try to get a court order to have me moved. I didn't believe what I was hearing. It's almost the end of the forth month, I had lost hope in my attorney and in Judy, I got up and walked out during my visit.

The first weekend, of my fifth month, Judy came again only this time she had a big smile on her face. She told me my attorney got a judge to sign a court order to have me moved. I told her again I didn't believe it. She said that I was to be moved that day. I really didn't believe her now, it was a Saturday. She explained that if they didn't move me that day they would be in contempt of court and that someone higher in the jail had put a stop every week to my paperwork but, now they couldn't since there was a court order. I told her I hoped she was right but, I wasn't going to get my hopes up.

When I got back to the fourth floor, where I had lived for the past one hundred and twenty plus days, one of the worst sadistic Mexican guards was on duty. When he saw me he ordered me over to him via loudspeaker. "You must know some powerful people, you're being moved to the farm today, roll your shit up and get your ass back out on the bench quick or I'll throw you in the hole," he ordered. I hated this guy but, I just replied calmly, "yes sir!" I hurried as fast as I could back to my cell, rolled up my mattress, sheets and towel together, gave away my cookies and peanuts and barely said good bye to people and was back on that bench. The guard came up to me and ordered to see my mattress, "You better have your sheet and towel in there," I knew he would check. This guard had been trying to get something on me for months and never could and now he wouldn't get the chance, I was moving.

17

Life on the Farm

I REALLY DIDN'T BELIEVE I WAS BEING moved until I was in the sheriffs car going down the five freeway. The drive from Orange County jail to the farm was only about thirty five to forty minutes but, it was like being on another planet. We stopped in front of the farm facility, leading up to the compound, after driving up a winding road past corn stalks, tomatoes vines and orange groves. We approached a one story building with a fence around it like a schoolyard. There weren't any guard towers here. I had heard about the farm many times and now I was actually here. The deputy opened his car door, removed my handcuffs and escorted me into the building, through unlocked doors, handed my paperwork over to the sergeant and left. The farm sergeant said, "welcome, would you please take a seat while I process your papers." I hadn't heard the word please since I had left home, I thought to myself, what a wonderful word it was.

After all the paper work was completed, I was sent to orientation. I was assigned a barracks to live in, a job to report to daily, blue jeans, T-shirt, tennis shoes and a hat. These were clothes fit for a ranch hand not a jumpsuit for a jailbird. I was told the rules there were simple, no fights, no drugs and I was required to work. If I lived by the rules everything would be fine and if not I could be told to roll up any time day or night and taken back to the county jail.

He explained this facility was actually a one hundred acre working ranch that brings a profit growing vegetables, raising poultry and livestock. It is the only county facility that pays for itself by supplying the county jail, juvenal hall, county hospitals and itself with food.

As the orientation continued, I was told I would start work at the bottom level working in the picking fields. It would be hard work but, if I showed good work standards I would be promoted and could get the job of my choice. Visiting would be on Saturday and Sunday, I was allowed one kiss at the beginning of the visit and one kiss at the end and if any other contact was made the visit would be terminated. I was assigned to barracks B, across the compound. I was then told to go get settled and relax until dinner at five pm. " Your orientation is over," he said, "good luck!"

I walked over to the barracks, opened the door and it looked just like an army barracks. There was fifty or sixty army bunks lined up on both sides of the room. An inmate was sweeping the floor and looked up and said, "check your shoes for dirt before entering the barracks, you're on a farm now." After I checked my shoes I noticed his arms were covered in jailbird tattoos. He looked like a human scratch pad. He showed me to my bunk and then spelled out the rules. He told me there would be three counts a day, before breakfast, lunch and dinner, standing in front of your bunk. He said the barracks was run more like the military, not the jail. I told him I had been locked up for months in the jail and this was like Disneyland to me. He told me my time was mine till I heard the announcement for count and that I'd better get back there. I unpacked my few things and then went out to take a walk and check out the compound.

After count I headed for the cafeteria and it was fantastic, for jail. We got as much food as we wanted with fresh veggies, fresh fruit, dessert and we could take our time, no rush to finish, this place was humane. I had made it through Orange County jail and now it was all going to be downhill. I felt pretty good for being in jail.

I slept like a bear in hibernation, in my little army bunk that night. They even turned off most the lights at night; this was truly the "honor farm."

Sunday morning I was called first visit. Judy and I greeted each other with a smile and a kiss. "Well I'm here, I still can't believe it," I said. Everything I've ever heard about the farm is true," I said with a sigh. The guards were normal here and the Mexicans couldn't run this place, if they jump anyone or step out of line they will get rolled up and sent back to county jail. The Farm held up to one hundred and ninety prisoners and fifty percent of the people in there were doing time for DUI's, child support or just winos. They weren't threats to society. Of course there were a few criminal idiots to stay clear of but it was a lot easier to do time here than in the main jail. "Now that I am here, tell me what is happening on the outside?" I asked. Judy said the painting business in Hawaii was doing well and that Jon had been missing for over a week. Everyone thought he was probably in Hollywood with his weird friends from the east coast. She also said he was still ripping people off for money. I just shook my head, I never would have thought he would turn out to be such a psycho. Visiting time was over, I kissed Judy goodbye and she promised to write to me and that she would be there for the first visit next week.

After my visit I went to the library and checked out a book. Some of the inmates were playing cards and dominos in the adjacent game room. I wanted to play but, I didn't, I went to my bunk and read until the evening count. After dinner I returned to my bunk and thought to myself, I could deal with this place for the next four and a half months and closed my eyes.

Morning came early on the farm, at five am a loud horn sounds and everyone gets up, makes up their bunk and stands for morning count. Breakfast was at six am and then off to work between seven and eight, depending what job you are doing. I reported to the Japanese guard and was walked out to the tomato vines, given a box and told to start picking. It was fun at first but, then it started to get really hot. We worked until noon and then we were called back to our barracks to get ready for count, I fell onto my bunk fully fatigued. It was about ninety degrees inside the barracks. Count was announced and then we were called to lunch, then we were called out again for afternoon picking. The afternoon picking was hard, the heat was so intense and the thick smell of the tomato vines didn't make it any easier. We all tried to get shade from the vines for some relief but, it was only possible part of the time.

That afternoon, after work, I was delirious. I couldn't write or read. I barely could make it for evening count or dinner. I made a friend out in the field so, after dinner we went outside and sat under a tree to get some shade. I asked him how he does it day after day. I told him I had worked as a carpenter during the summers but this seemed harder. He told me it would get easier. By the end of the first week the work was getting easier but, I was still ready for the weekend to relax.

I made a few more friends by the end of the week and on Friday after dinner, and a nap, I took a cool shower and then a walk. I passed by the game room and was asked, by a fellow tomato picker, to play some cards, this turned out to be a nightly routine. I learned to play pinochle, the greatest card game I had ever played, the strategies between partners and the absorption in the game was intense.

Judy came to visit Saturday and Sunday. After about twenty minutes, we ran out of things to say to each other. I said, "you need to clean up." That never went over very good and by the end of the visit we were at odds. I told her not to score again, we had plenty of money and I would be out in three months. I asked her to please clean up

The next week I didn't get any letters from Judy. When visiting day came I got called out and the first thing I said to Judy abruptly, "why didn't you write?" Judy put up her hands and I could tell she had been crying. "What's wrong," I asked. She said Jon was found shot in the head twice and dumped on skid row. Instantly a tear rolled down my cheek, how could Jon be dead? How did we get to this point? I could see him alive smiling, surfing, and charming everyone. We had big plans, he didn't deserve to be killed. I couldn't believe he was dead. "Who killed him?" I asked. Judy said she heard the cops said it was an execution style murder, probably a drug deal gone wrong. Our visit ended and I headed back to the barracks like a zombie.

After the news of Jon I vowed never to use drugs again and I wanted Judy to stop too but, she didn't want to. The only way to keep my sanity was to stay busy working like a mad man picking tomatoes, running track in the heat after work and working out with weights daily. The sober reality was sinking in, Jon was dead, Judy was strung out on heroin, and I was in jail. How could it get any worse? Then it did. Weasel showed up at the farm. I was pissed. He came up to me like we were old friends. I told him he had a lot of nerve showing up there, he was the reason I was in there. "Roll your ass up and get the hell out of here or I'll have you fucked up," and I pushed him. He immediately went to the watch and told them I had threatened him. I was called up and questioned, I denied it but, the damage was done. I was told that if anything happened to him I would be rolled up and sent back to county. That guy was a true yellow punk and I told him later his ass was mine on the streets. He just sneered at me. I vowed I would get him on the streets some day. From that moment, I never spoke to him or acknowledged him, as far as I was concerned he didn't exist. I was becoming a physco after Jon's death, Judy not wanting to clean up and looking at Weasel. I had so much built up anger I spent every free moment running the track or in the weight room.

By the end of my sixth month my body was rock hard and I was buffed. I had good friends, which I would never see again once I was out, my running partner, my card partner and my partners for working out. We were partners in jail only, I wasn't taking any part of jail home with me.

Next visiting day Judy never showed up and her letters were coming further and further apart. I was afraid she had gotten busted. Sunday she did show up with blood shot eyes and her hair looking unkept. "Something's up, what is it?" I asked her why she hadn't written to me and didn't show up for our visit the day before. I said, " I live for the letters and the visits." "Nothing is up, you're just stressed," she said. The rest of the visit was very awkward. I felt I was being screwed but, she kept denying it, as she looked me straight in the eyes. The visit ended without a goodbye kiss.

Mentally I was in total turmoil then later that week I received a letter from Judy. I felt good inside holding it, reading the letter changed my feelings. She said she needed time to think things out, that she wouldn't be coming to visit me the next weekend but my friend Robbie would be coming. I wondered what things she had to work out. The week was very hard for me, my mind was preoccupied with Judy, sometimes angry and others times heartbroken.

The emotions inside me were screaming but, I was silent. The weekend finally came and I was filled with anxious thoughts. I was called for first visit and when I walked into the visiting area I saw Robbie and his girlfriend, a pretty red head. We smiled and shook hands. "It's been a long time," I said. As soon as we sat down Robbie looked at me and said, "I hate to be the one to drop a bomb on you but, somebody has to tell you what is going on behind your back. Judy has a boyfriend. She's blowing all your money on him and he's driving your Mercedes." I felt my world coming down, I didn't know what I could do, I wasn't going to be released for a month a half. Robbie told Judy he was going to tell me and she begged him not to. We ended our visit and Robbie told me he would visit the next weekend and I thanked him.

I immediately went to my barracks and started writing Judy a letter asking her how she could do this to me. I couldn't believe what she was doing, how could she after all I had done for her.

Sunday came and went without a visit from anyone. Monday I went to work as a zombie then that afternoon, at mail call, I got a letter from Judy. She denied everything that Robbie had told me. She told me she still loved me and that she would be there to visit me on Saturday. She signed it love, Judy. I felt better after reading her letter but it made me wonder why Robbie would say those things if they weren't true. I thought about escaping but I knew I would get caught before I even got home and escaping from the farm was an automatic year in county. I only had one and half months to go, keep your head, I thought.

My job upgraded to the nursery, which was a great promotion, but I could have cared less. I was so messed up mentally, I hated this place and I wanted out now! I just wanted to talk to Judy, I didn't want to wait till the weekend.

Judy came to visit on Saturday and told me it was over between us, Robbie had lied and she didn't have a boyfriend. I told her I wanted my money and the keys to my Mercedes. She had her own car and the Mercedes was mine. Her reply was, you'll get it when you get out and the money is spent. You're an ass," she said and then she walked out leaving me sitting there. I sat stunned. I was being stabbed in the back by the person I trusted more than anyone. I went to jail seven and a half months ago leaving her with thousands in cash and thousands in heroin and it was now all gone. That was hard to believe. Jon and now Judy had ripped me off, Robbie was telling the truth. From then on I lived with a vengeance. I was pulling hard time, as the old timers would say. I was a heartbroken prisoner.

I spent my time working out like a crazy man, running track morning and night. I was starting the first weekend of my eighth month. I had one month left to go. I hadn't heard anything from Judy in two weeks but I did get a visit from another girl that had heard Judy had dumped me. She came to visit me and asked if she could continue to visit and write to me. I told her "sure," and then laughed, probably for the first time in months. Her name was Sherri and she was a beautiful girl with long brown hair and green eyes. She had a great body I'd seen in a bikini before, big boobs, thin stomach and waist, great tight little butt and shapely legs that were always tan. I thought to myself what a delight finding out about a secret admirer like her. My world started to seem a bit better.

Early the next week I got a letter from my Mom telling me that my attorney was working on the modification of my sentence and that the paperwork was going to be presented to the judge that week. I'd already served ten months, including chino, the normal one year sentence time was eight and a half months. By the end of the week I got word that my modification was approved and my sentence was reduced by twenty days. I was getting out next week, unbelievable.

That weekend my mom came to visit all excited to tell me the news, she didn't know I already heard from the jail. She said she would be there Wednesday morning to pick me up with a smoothie. I couldn't believe this was my last weekend in jail.

Robbie came to visit on Sunday and I told him my good news. He told me he had threatened to kick Judy's boyfriend's, ass for driving my Mercedes. I said, "Judy thinks I have twenty more days, please don't tell her or anyone else I'm getting out. I want to surprise her."

Wednesday morning, six am, first announcement of the day is always prisoner release. Today my name was being called after eight and a half months. I had watched probably one hundred people be released during my five month stay on the farm. My mattress was already rolled up and I was just waiting for my name to be called. I walked up to the watch to get my release papers and signed a promissory note that I would contact my probation officer within seventy two hours. I put on my street clothes and walked out the front door a free man and free of drugs. I could see my mom sitting in her big Lincoln smiling, she was great. I would have never guessed my release after nine months would be like this. No Judy, no Jon and hurting so much inside. I was going to surprise Judy but, right now I was free as a bird.

18

Sober reality

As we drove down the winding road out of the farm, I rolled down the window and felt the wind of freedom on my face. I opened my banana strawberry smoothie and gulped it down. My Mom looked at me and said, "You look really good." I asked her to take me to breakfast, I wanted some real people food, I was tired of jail food. We pulled up to the International House of Pancakes, I ordered ten grain pancakes with orange juice and devoured it like a caveman. Mom told me she knew I was upset but, I shouldn't go after the guy Judy was messing around with. I told her I knew that but, I had to get my car. I asked her to take me to my house after we ate.

When we drove up to my house it was a depressing sight. The plants that lined the driveway were all dead. I went up to the front door and opened it. Judy hadn't even locked the door. The antique rugs were stained and other antiques were broken or missing. I figured Judy must have found out about my release and left. I found a note she left on the kitchen counter telling where to find my Mercedes along with five hundred dollars under the matt. She wrote that was all that was left and she had moved out.

I went back out to my Moms car and we followed the directions to my Mercedes, which we found, abandoned in a Huntington Beach neighborhood. My car was filthy and had a large scrape on the door in the beautiful misty blue paint. I opened the car door and lifted the car matt and there was miscellaneous bills fives, tens and twenties spread around totaling about five hundred dollars. Judy was really out there. It was as if I had never known her. I started the car and told my Mom I would be at her house later, I needed some time to be alone and think.

I drove to downtown Huntington beach, feeling lost and alone, passing by some friend's houses but not stopping. I knew if I stopped there would be lots of questions to answer and I didn't feel like talking. I was a lost soul driving around all evening. I realized I needed some answers and Judy was going to face me the next day like it or not. I headed back to my moms house and found her waiting up for me. "Welcome home," she said. She gave me a hug and a kiss goodnight.

I tossed and turned most of the night, when morning came I had coffee with my Mom and went out for a jog. When I got back I told my Mom I had to go find Judy that I needed some answers and then I had a date with a girl named Sherri that had been visiting me. I hugged her " don't worry about me, I probably wouldn't be back for a few days", but I would call.

It didn't take long to find Judy. I knew she would be in Huntington Beach, all I had to do was visit a few old friends that were now past friends, I found out. She was staying at her new Boyfriend's apartment, a funky old twelve unit complex situated in the low rent district of downtown Huntington. I parked my Mercedes around the corner so she wouldn't see it and walked up to the door and knocked. Judy answered the door surprised and said, " what the fuck do you want?" In the back of my mind I thought, or hoped, she would jump into my arms when she actually saw me but, reality hit, she was living with another guy. It all had been true. I threw up my arms and yelled' "you left me for this? I want some answers". She finally said '"okay what?" I told her for starters I wanted to know where all the money was. "You claim to have spent it all on bills, that's bullshit!" I said. She said she spent it on the painting business in Hawaii and on attorney fees. I told her all the bills had been paid before I left including the attorney. "I know your ripping me off !" Her reply to me was that I deserved it, that my friend's had told her that Jon and I screwed prostitutes all over the world.. "How could you do that to me," she said. All I could say to her was "Your ripping me off for my money, screwing some punk, dumping me while I was in jail, the house is a wreck and you have the nerve to blame this all on me? You are one sorry excuse of a woman." She screamed she had told me all she was going to tell and to get out of her sight. She said she didn't give a fuck what I thought and tried to slam the door but, I stuck my foot in the way. Now reality had really set in, she had turned into a hardened junky bitch, living in a broken down sorry apartment, with an obvious loser boyfriend. I looked her straight in the eyes and told her all that we were was gone and that I would never forgive her for this. I turned away while she was screaming, cussing and spitting. A real class act I thought. I turned, flipped her off and said, "your history bitch!"

I drove straight over to Costa Mesa and picked up Sherri. What a difference, she was a twenty-year-old sweet girl with a dazzling body I couldn't wait to undress and I knew she was ready. I just wanted to go out and have a good time. I told her about my house being a mess so she suggested we go over to her house to take a shower before going out. I told her she was just what I needed. When we got back to her house she undressed in front of me revealing the body of a playboy centerfold. She had full breasts, which were sculpted perfectly. She then removed her little pink panties revealing a goddess. This was sending thrilling chills all through my body. We got in the shower and enjoyed each others bodies until the water went cold, I told her we had to do more of this and she gladly agreed. Later we went to dinner and a movie. My friend Robbie had given me the key to his place and offered for me to stay there for the weekend. Sherri joined me. We had a great couple of days but, Monday came fast and we both needed to deal with responsibilities. I dropped Sherri off and told her I would call her in a couple days.

I drove over to my house, walked in, looked around, turned and walked out and locked the door. I wasn't ready to deal with it just now so I went to my mom's house. When I walked in my mom was waiting for me with a hug. I told her that I saw Judy and that I really didn't know what had happened but, it was over between us. I told her it was time for me to pick up the pieces of my life and my house. She told me she would help me and that she loved me. I could always count on my Mom.

First things first, I needed to first call my probation officer, for an appointment, and then my landlord, to see where I stood with my house. My probation officer wanted me to come in the next day, which was a priority. I then found out the rent on my house had not been paid for three months, the utilities were behind and the phone was turned off. My mom loaned me a few thousand dollars to catch up and to live on, she knew Judy had left me only five hundred dollars out of thousands and this would catch me up, but I realized there was only one thing for me to do. After breakfast I was ready to enjoy my precious freedom at the H.B. Pier surfing and enjoying the beach. I spent the day in the water, it was fantastic, I felt so alive. I was going to leave my troubles behind me.

I went to see my probation officer the next day. I had to give a urine test immediately, he told me I would be drug tested regularly, I had to get a job within the next two weeks and to report bi-weekly to drug test. He then wanted to know where I was living, what I was driving and if I was doing any drugs. I told him, "certainly not, I have learned my lesson." I told him, I already had a job at a candle factory and that I was living at my Mom's house until I got back on my feet. He scheduled me every Tuesday and Thursday for drug testing and said he would see me personally on the first of every month. With all that said I stood up to leave and felt his eyes look at me with suspicion as I walked out of his office.

I drove straight to a phone booth and made a call to Marcus, in Mexico, within one week my financial problems could be over.

My first week I spent cleaning up my house and surfing. I hired two neighborhood kids to clean up my yard, paid my rent up to date, turned the utilities back on and got a new phone number. I started cleaning out the house first of Judy's things. There were clothes, make-up, brushes and pictures. I got rid of anything and everything that reminded me of that snake. Sherri came over with a few other girls and cleaned the house from top to bottom. I loaded up the cabinet with food and stocked the refrigerator. The most important thing, I called a locksmith and had all the locks changed.

By my second week home the house was looking pretty good. I reported to my P.O.'s office for testing as instructed. I wasn't concerned because I wasn't doing any drugs. I showed up in the Wax Castle delivery truck and showed it to my P.O., he didn't know it really belonged to a friend of mine. He was going to be easy to fool. He was an old fart, not to bright.

I dropped the candle truck back off in Costa Mesa, at my friend's shop, got in my Mercedes, picked up Sherri and caught a flight from Orange County to San Diego. At the airport we rented a car and drove into old town. Sherri and I stopped for some Mexican food, parked the rental car and headed out on foot through the sleazy streets of porno book-stores and theatres. We went into the theatre and sat in the back row. After our eyes adjusted, from the bright sunlight, we could see the theatre was sparsely occupied. Within a few minutes a young Mexican girl came in, sat next to me and from under her dress handed me half a pound of heroin and half a pound of coke wrapped in rubber. My heart was pounding, I was really paranoid. I hid the stash in my pants, nodded to the girl and walked out. I was holding twenty years in prison in my pants. We walked through the streets to get to the car. This part of the city has a lot of cops, we passed by two of them working a fender bender and just nodded. When I got to the rental car I looked to make sure no one was around, pulled the stash out of my pants and hid it next to the spare tire.

As we drove out of the parking structure, I asked Sherri if she wanted to go to the San Diego Zoo and we could catch a later afternoon flight back to Orange County. At the zoo we were having a great time looking at all the animals. In the trunk of the car was an easy profit of eight to ten thousand dollars. All I had to do was be really careful and not use.

For the next month I dealt to only a couple different people for big profit. I never used the drugs. Sherri and I enjoyed quietly hanging out, good restaurants, movies, the beach and an occasional trip to San Diego. My money came in by the thousands, especially since I wasn't using anymore. I treated my dealing as a business, no parting.

I was always on time to my probation appointments in Westminster, twice a week for drug testing and my first of the month appointments with my P.O. I really wanted to travel and spend some money but, I knew my P.O. would never let me out of his sight for long.

On Thursday, when I saw my P.O, for drug testing, I told him I had an opportunity to deliver candles in Northern California and Oregon. I told him I could get a lot of overtime if he would allow me to go. He agreed to wave my drug tests for the next two weeks and gave me permission to go but, said I had to be back in two weeks.

I called my business partner Randy, in Hawaii, and he was glad to hear I was out of prison. I told him I was ready for vacation. He asked if I was bringing Judy and I told him "no," she dumped me and robbed me blind. He told me not to worry, he would hook me up with an island girl he thought I would really like. I told him I would be flying over in the morning and he agreed to pick me up at the airport.

By the next afternoon I was walking down the steps of a 747 at Honolulu airport, walked across the tarmac, trade winds blowing, blue skies, a few clouds and scattered rain with Diamond Head in the distance. I thought about how many times I had done this, but never with such a feeling of loneliness.

I was expecting this to be a business trip until I got in the terminal and saw the girl standing next to Randy. He introduced her as Sandy, a beautiful creature from top to bottom. We walked to the baggage area to get my bags and then to Randy's car. As soon as we got in the car Randy lit a joint and handed it to me. I told him I couldn't, I was drug testing. "That's a bummer but, now you're here for two weeks in Hawaii." Sandy just smiled at me from the back seat. She was wearing a tiny Hawaiian see-through dress with golden tan legs leading up to an island style Bikini. "She is yours to enjoy if you decide to party," Randy said. He then looked at Sandy and said, "This guy really knows how to party!" Randy was setting me up with her and she was ready to have fun. I thought for a moment, I had been out of jail for one month but I wasn't really happy. I had two weeks, I could do coke for one week and then clean up the second week. I looked at Randy and then at Sandy and said "Okay' I've got some great flake in my suitcase I've been dying to try."

We pulled onto a short dirt driveway, surfboards on the grass beside a white wooden house up on a hill above Sunset Beach, a North Shore neighborhood. I got out and took a deep breath of the island air. I noticed in the back was the Ford van I had sent Randy, two years earlier, with supplies and electrostatic painting equipment to start our business.

We went into Randy's house, it was great, open windows, Hawaiian cloth curtains and no furniture, just pillows. He showed me to a bedroom where I got out of my traveling clothes and into a bathing suit. I took a couple big rocks of coke out of my bag, put them on a plate, and then the rest back in my bag. I walked into the living room, Randy was putting some music on and Sandy was sitting on a pillow. I sat down next to her and handed her a one hundred dollar bill to roll up, chopped up some big lines and handed the plate first to Sandy and then to Randy and his girlfriend. When the plate got back to me I said, " It's been a long time." I stuck the rolled one hundred dollar up to my nose and snorted two giant lines.

After another couple of snorts I told Randy I needed to get in the water. He asked if I wanted to go surfing. "Not right now," I said. " I'll surf in the morning, right now I just want to get wet." We left the girls with a rock to snort and drove down to Sunset beach. Talk about being amped, no coke for nine months and then snorting four giant lines, I was feeling electric.

Walking onto Sunset beach the grainy sand between my toes was great, but I felt weird and out of sorts being all "coked" out. We got in the water, it was greenish blue, warm and clear. I could see guys surfing the Sunset reefs. I turned to Randy and said," this is me."

After a short swim we headed back to the car and snorted another line. Randy asked about Judy. " I'm pissed at Judy for her ripping me off and leaving me broke", I told him. I was starting over but I needed to very careful since I was on Probation for the next five years, with a suspended sentence of five to fifteen years. Also, I let him know I was planning to move over to the islands in one year, my probation officer would have to let me after one year clean, so keep the business going. Randy said the business was doing okay but, he could use more cash at times for supplies. I said, "It's been two years Randy, it has to start carrying its own weight pretty soon." Randy said it would just take some more time. "We'll talk business later, tonight is all about snorting coke and partying."

When we got back to the house the girls rock was gone. We opened some primo beers, snorted a couple more lines and then I broke out the good stuff. I went back to my suitcase and got out some Dr. Brown. When I returned to the living room Randy was saying that there was going to be a great local band playing at the Del Webb hotel that night and a lot of his friends were going to be there so we all decided to go. "Let's smoke some brown to mellow out before we go", I said. Randy was leery, until he smoked some but Sandy loved it. She had grown up in Miami around hard drugs, she had gotten a taste of brown before. We passed the heroin around the room on tinfoil lighting a lighter under it, causing it to bubble, capturing the smoke through a tube and inhaling. A few more lines of coke, this made a speedball, a great upper and downer.

Sandy took my hand and led me from the living room to the bedroom and shut the door. This was going to be good. She pushed me to the bed, removed her bathing suit bra, right in front of me a beautiful topless girl rubbed her boobs in my face. She started a seductive dance and grind with her body while sitting on my legs. She closed her eyes and reached her arms in to the air keeping rhythm to the Rod Stewart record playing in the other room. That was all I could take, speedball sex at its best was going down now! Later I was back in the living room doing coke lines with Randy while the girls got ready to go out and party some more. I turned to Randy and said, "Thanks, she's great!"

Randy and I smoked more brown waiting for the girls and it was worth the wait. The girls looked great wearing Hawaiian colored wrap skirts, slit up the leg, exposing long tan legs. To think, just one month ago I was in jail, feeling like I was losing it, broken hearted and now I was in paradise. The Del Webb was a huge resort hotel that had been built since I had been there last. It was situated close to the North Shore. It brought Waikiki to the country and was a perfect place to hang out at night. Randy introduced me to his friends as his partner and Sandy introduced me to the girls she was living with, more beauties. It was unspoken but everyone knew I was the man with all the drugs, money and beautiful girls. All the girls wanted to sit at my table, the drinks, money and bundles of coke passed all night.

The next morning, while the girls were sleeping, Randy and I went to Velzeeland to do some surfing. We had a big snort of coke to wake up first. The waves were fun but kicking my ass. I was strong from working out and my lungs were in good shape from running but I wasn't in surfing shape. My shoulders and arms were burning but I loved it. I had a great time except every once and a while I would remember back surfing there with Jon.

Later that morning Randy and I went to Haleiwa's outdoor country store for some carrot juice and some Dr. Bronner's chips. While sitting on the bench eating, Randy told me he had a job on Kauai and wanted to know if I wanted to go with him.

I told him I would pass, this time, asked how long he would be gone. He said it was a good job, a federal job painting some file cabinets and desks for the post office and it would take two or three days. I thought maybe the painting business would start making some money doing Federal work.

"Lets get some waves," I said. Randy drove back to Velzeeland and parked on the dirt road. I chopped out four giant lines to snort and we grabbed our boards and headed for the water. We paddled out among the others to get our share of the beautiful waves. After twenty waves, or so, I saw Sandy on the beach with some girlfriends. "Look at that body," I said to Randy. "I'm heading in." I paddled over into line up and caught an in between set to ride, and paddled up to Sandy on the beach. "Good wave," she said.

I stood there all wet, "I'm going to the car to get a towel, want to come along?" She knew by my grin what that meant. She grabbed me by the waist and said, "sure." When we got to the car I gave her a big rock to chop up while I dried off. I kissed her tits and then her lips. We fondled each other but then saw Randy coming up to the car. Sandy chopped up some more coke for him and then ran off saying, "See you tonight at the club!"

That evening we were back at the hotel lounge doing coke and having soft conversation. Sandy and I were getting tight so I asked her if she wanted to get a room there and stay with me for the next week. We walked up to the front desk and asked for a room with a balcony facing the ocean. I laid out a few hundred dollars and tipped the guy fifty dollars. He offered us some complimentary wine and of course we accepted.

We christened our room with big lines of coke and some Dr. brown. In the back of my mind I was planning to do fewer drugs but here we were in our own room so it was more drugs and more sex. I was worried because I knew it only took three days to get a heroin habit going again, I needed to stop tomorrow.

Randy showed up at the lounge and I told him I had a room and invited him to come up and have a line. We hung out on the balcony overlooking a private beach snorting coke. While we were chopping lines, I told Randy I had promised myself I would never use chemicals again, I wasn't going to end up dead like Jon or a junky like Judy, but I felt I deserved some fun after all I had been through. I told Randy I was going to clean up the next day and I didn't want to ruin anyone's good time. I thanked him for introducing me to Sandy, "girls like her don't pop up every day," I said. I asked him if I could borrow one of his rust buckets and a board while he was gone to Kauai, he didn't mind at all. He asked me to drive him home that night and take his station wagon, which was his best car. We snorted some more coke and then I offered him some Dr. brown, he refused. We went and found Sandy, at the lounge, to ride with us back to Randy's to drop him off. He had to get up early to go to work and would be working all night the next night. Sandy and I returned back to the hotel, skipping the lounge and going to the pool and jacuzzi instead.

The first week there went by to fast, I was surfing everyday, snorting coke and smoking heroin at night. I realized I was a little strung out and it was time to detox. As always, easier said than done. I promised myself to clean up in plenty of time. Each day it didn't happen, Sandy and I used coke and heroin every day. I never used Randy's board once, we just stayed in the hotel room high on drugs.

Randy returned from Kauai after three days. He netted some good bucks painting for the post office and offered me some of the profit. I refused any money and told him to put it back into the business. I told him that Sandy and I were a little strung out and I had to get clean before my drug test the next week who was I kidding, I was getting worse every day . Randy said he was glad to hear that, he knew I didn't want to become a junky again and he didn't like hard drugs. I knew it would take at least three days of no drugs to get my system clean so Sandy and I planned to just hang out on the beach and clean up. By evening we were back at the lounge, with all the music and people wanting to get high, I couldn't stop. Again, I figured I had plenty of time and I would clean up tomorrow. It's always tomorrow.

When I was ready to leave, to go back home, I was more strung out than I had been the week before, I was going to try to go cold turkey. I said good-bye to Sandy and left her with some coke and heroin and told her how to clean out slowly. Randy and I had to talk some business on the way to the airport in private so, I said goodbye to Sandy at Randy's and told her I would call her in two weeks.

On the way to the airport I thanked Randy for a great time, Sandy was fantastic. I told him that I had promised myself never to get strung out again and here I was a mess. I was going to have to dodge my P.O. for a week and get clean before he saw me. I knew the first thing he would do is test me, I had to avoid him at all costs. I could see the airport now so I asked Randy to pull over. We snorted some big lines of coke and I needed to smoke some brown before my five-hour flight back home. I asked Randy to keep the business rolling, I was counting on him. I planned to be back in one month, we high fived and I walked into the airport on my way back to sober reality.

Once on the plane, the heroin was flowing around in my brain. I settled into my seat, closed my eyes and started to daydream. What had I been thinking? I must be crazy to allow myself to get this way again. Sandy was sizzling sexy but she wasn't worth going to jail for. I was expected to report to my P.O. the next day and I wasn't going to show. I hoped to make up some sort of story. Just before I nodded out I thought about Randy and what a great partner he was.

The next thing I knew, the stewardess was waking me with a warm towel before landing. I needed a snort. I went to the tiny airplane bathroom, snorted some coke and then snorted some brown.

I picked up my dirty Mercedes from the long-term parking and headed for home. As I was driving home, on the five freeway, I thought of a good excuse. I called my P.O. and told him my truck was overheating and that I was limping back. The excuse worked, he told me to call when I got back or see him the following Tuesday. Now I had four days to get clean. I knew there was no messing around, now cold turkey was a must. I didn't go to my house, instead I checked into a nice hotel in Newport that had a pool, Jacuzzi, sauna room and room service. I was going to suffer and I knew I had to do it.

I didn't waste any time, I changed into my trunks and went to find the Jacuzzi. I got into the Jacuzzi and thought to myself, "This isn't going to be to bad," I only had a two-week habit but as I sat there I could feel the sickness entering my body. " I've withdrawn from a one year addiction in jail," I thought, I can make it through this. As the next few days dragged on I realized there was nothing to prepare you for the "jones." The threat of jail was the only thing that kept me going.

On Tuesday I walked into my P.O.'s office as scheduled. He handed me a cup to pee in and walked me to the bathroom across the hall. On our return to his office I handed him a phony pay stub showing the money I had made for overtime in the last two weeks. He was impressed and asked if the opportunity would present it's self again. The lights shined in my head and I answered, "definitely, the candle company is growing fast and they need drivers."

For six months I played my P.O. He thought I drove a truck two weeks, out of town, every month and instead I was scoring regularly from Marcus and making thousands and thousands of dollars. I was using coke and heroin between tests and then going cold turkey at the Newport hotel. Finally I got caught, I had a dirty test. I didn't get clean enough, I was living on the edge. My P.O. called me into his office and wanted to know why I had a dirty test. He said if I weren't honest with him he would violate me. I could tell I was caught so I told him I had smoked some opium at a party. "Just once?"

he asked. I told him I had smoked it all weekend. He said he wouldn't violate me, but he was increasing my drug testing to three times a week and I was not allowed any more delivery trips. "I want you in town so I can keep a closer watch on you," he said.

I walked out of his office shaking. He told me if I got another dirty test he would violate me. For the next two months I used an apparatus to fool the drug tests so I was always clean. I could tell my P.O. suspected something. He wanted to know how I afforded a Mercedes and a house like I had on the salary I was bringing home. I told him if I was short of money my Mom would help me. What could he say to that?

I had made it three months since my last dirty test and my P.O. knew I was dirty but he couldn't catch me. I was getting surprise visits, drug tests and searching of my house. One visit I came really close to getting caught. They came in and searched my house and at the time a girlfriend had a pound of heroin in her purse but they didn't search her bag, that was a close one.

I was making big money, about fifteen thousand dollars every other week, from out of town buyers. I was totally strung out and didn't even try to clean up any more. I counted on my apparatus to give me clean tests. Once my P.O. went on vacation but I still had to test with whoever was available in the office. I always showed up right before the office closed. At one appointment I walked in and told the front desk I was there to test and gave my name. After about a five-minute wait a young cocky looking P.O. called me up and escorted me to the bathroom, across the hall, to test. When I turned out of the stall and handed the bottle back to him, he felt it and then looked at me." You're wearing something, this bottle is not warm enough, pull down your pants," he demanded. I did what he asked and tried to pull the apparatus down with my pants but it didn't work, he saw the bottle. "Your Busted!" he shouted. He then ordered me to pull up my pants and to follow him. He opened the door leading across the hallway and then opened the door leading to the office. He thought he had me but I took off running down the hall and outside to the side of the building. I looked back and he wasn't following me so I jumped into my car and drove away. I knew a bench warrant would be put out, I was on the run now.

19

On the Run

I WASN'T ABOUT TO GO BACK TO my house, which would be the first place they would look for me. I knew I couldn't go to my Mom's house either and my car and plates would be hot. I stopped, called my Mom and told her to expect the cops and my probation officer. I told her I hadn't done a crime, I had been violated and they were looking for me. I told her I was okay but, that I was on the run. I told her I would contact her when I got settled and that I loved her.

I sold my Mercedes as soon as I could to a car dealer and took a room at the Newport hotel. I rented a car until I could buy another one. I needed some company and a chauffer for the next couple of days while I acquired a new identity so I called Sherri. "I haven't heard from you since you went to Hawaii," she said with an angry tone, "I'm a little pissed at you." I told her I really needed her and wanted her to come and spend a few days with me. She finally agreed. I told her I was at the Newport hotel on coast highway, just in front of fashion island. She asked me what clothes she should bring and I told her just her body and a driver's license. "What's going on?" she asked. "I'll tell you when you get here, just bring clothes for a few days and a couple of bathing suits," I said. She said she would be there in two hours.

Sherri knew lots of coke, Dr. brown and cash accompanied me. While I was waiting, I smoked some Brown, which accompanied everything I did nowadays, made a list of phone calls and places I needed to go. I called Marcus and set up a score for the next day. My out of state buyers were expected in two days and I needed to service them with two pounds of heroin. When Sherri arrived I would have her drive me to the county records office where I would search death certificates until I could find a child that had died that was my race and approximate age. Once I got that information I would have to drive to the county he was born in, with all the info I had, and get a copy of his birth certificate. Next I needed to get a social security number in his name and a drivers license. I would go to the local library and get a library card, then to the car lot to buy a car in my new name. I hoped to be able to do all this in three days to start another life.

I was paranoid of every car coming and going. I watched

out the window constantly. I saw Sheri when she parked. I watched Sheri as she came up the stairs to where I was standing waiting for her. "What's going on?" she asked. "I'm violated on my probation and I'm not going back to my house," I explained. We went into the hotel where I had some coke all chopped up and ready to snort. We both snorted a couple big lines sitting next to each other. We kissed and she hit me on the shoulder and told me what an idiot I was for getting violated. I told her I was on the run and that I would be moving to Hawaii but I needed to do a few more scams from Mexico and get a new name. I asked her if she had any friends that could move my furniture and belongings into storage. "I can't chance going there and possibly getting caught."

The following day we were on a plane to San Diego and picked up two pounds of the best heroin I had seen. I met my out of town buyers at a Mexican restaurant and made the exchange of two pounds of heroin for thirty thousand dollars. The stash had cost me eight thousand. A couple more scams like that and I could buy a house in Hawaii.

The next few days everything went like clock work, I got a new ID, bought a car and had a perm and hair color change.

The following day I rented a little house in Laguna beach, up the hill on Thalia street, using my new name. A perfect gingerbread house with a sun deck and a peek of the ocean. I furnished it with everything new, bed, refrigerator, stereo, towels, etc. I wasn't going to risk trying to get my old furniture, I felt it was being watched, it was the only trail to me and I was paranoid.

Neighbors I met knew me by my new name only. I told people I was a traveling salesman that worked out of my house. My perm and hair color change had completely changed my look and I had all the proper ID's from the proper agencies and I lived in a different city. This was to be my hideout for the next few months, my identity was complete.

My plan was to deal only large quantities of dr. brown for the next few months and gain mass amounts of cash. I had a sweet little Laguna beach house, a beautiful girl. I only had a five minute walk to the beach, stores and restaurants which kept me from driving the streets. I wasn't going to blow it, I was going to keep a low profile till I moved to the islands.

I phoned Randy in the islands, told him that I was on the run from the law, that my P.O. had violated me for a dirty test. I told him I would be moving over there soon. Randy wanted to know if I was still using the brown stuff and I said, "no." I asked him how the business was doing and he told me it was doing good. Randy cut the call short and hung up and I told Sherri I felt something was weird.

The next month I made a couple big sells. Other than that I stayed in my house with the curtains closed. I kept my car in the garage and spent my days with Sherri smoking heroin, sleeping until noon and walking on the beach in the afternoons.

Over a the next few months, I had cash stashed all over the house. I had ten thousand dollar stacks in shoes, coffee cans and pants. Sherri and I were totally addicted, skinny and unhealthy. We hardly ever saw daylight. I still knew in the back of my mind I was going to go to Hawaii and all this would change. I knew I would become a surfer again, eat avocado sandwiches on the beach, have a great Hawaiian tan and get healthy, this was temporary.

My friendship and partnership with Randy was getting strained. He would rarely return my phone calls and when he did he was very vague about the painting business. When I talked with him he would always tell me it wasn't doing very well.

Somehow Judy got my address and showed up at my door. Talk about a bitch, she was one. "You're my man and you're living with another woman, I want some money and some heroin!" she demanded. I reminded her that she had left me and robbed me blind, that she had some nerve showing up at my house. She changed her tactics at that point. "Okay, I'm sorry, my boyfriend left me and I'm down and out," she cried. I had heard she was scamming to support her habit, I didn't believe it until now. I gave her some money and told her I didn't have any heroin, that I didn't use it anymore. I asked her to leave and never contact me again.

I returned to Sherri after Judy left. I wondered if Sherri thought as badly about me as I thought about Judy as I smoked some more brown. The last thing I wanted from Judy was sex, she was no longer pretty or sexy. I felt bad for her, but she did it to herself by leaving me.

Days passed as I slipped in and out of consciousness, staying high on heroin. I finally forgot about Judy. Nowadays when I phoned Randy he either wasn't there or if he did answer the phone he was evasive. I tried to carry on friendly conversation but it didn't seem we were bros like before. He didn't

talk about business, he said he didn't have the time but that
he did need more money. I refused to send him more money
and he hung up on me. I couldn't believe Randy's attitude,
he had lost complete respect for me. Every night I planned
quitting tomorrow, only it never happened. "What can I do?"
I thought. I couldn't quit. I was a full-blown addict again.

Randy's evasiveness worked, weeks would pass before
I'd call him again. At this point I was just high all the time
and not even taking care of business much less dealing with
Randy.

One evening a friend of mine, in Hawaii, called and said
he saw Randy on Maui doing a painting job. He asked Randy,
"how is yours and Dean's business doing?" Randy stated the
business was doing great but that I was a jerk and he had
gotten rid of me. I was pissed! I had done so much for him
and he thinks he's going to screw me out of the business. I
bought the franchise and supported him and his family for
two years. I own that business, I needed to get back to Hawaii
and settle this!

Sherri and I were on a plane in two days. When our plane
landed in Honolulu I only had one thing on my mind, get to
Randy. We rented a car at the airport and headed straight to
the North Shore.

I turned onto Randy's dirt driveway as he was loading
the painting van with supplies. I walked up to him angrily,
"You've been lying to me about the business," I shouted. He
said, "you're just a druggy loser, look at you, you're a junky,
you're sickening! You just paid the money, I did all the work
and built the business, it's mine!" he shouted. We argued

about all the money I had given him but, he didn't care, he just argued the business was his. Then he offered me ten thousand dollars to buy me out but I refused. "Take it or leave it," he said. "I'll see you in court!" I replied. Randy just laughed, "You, a wanted convict junky is going to take me to court. Get off my property or I'll call the cops." I turned and walked away but let him know he hadn't seen the last of me, but really I knew he had.

Sherri and I drove back to Waikiki in silence. We found a resort hotel and rented a luxurious room facing the beach. We took the elevator up to the 10th floor to our room. We couldn't wait to get inside to get high, Dr. brown was our only peace.

I got up about eleven thirty the next morning, smoked some brown and told Sherri I was going to rent a surfboard and go surfing. I felt self conscious in my bathing suit walking to the beach. I was really pale, skinny, long hair, sideburns and a mustache. I thought to my self I looked like a "ho-dad."

I approached the surfboard rental stand and asked to rent a board. The guy looked me over and asked, "Have you ever surfed before?" When I replied, "Yes," he seemed surprised. He handed me a big old log board and as I walked away with it I stumbled. I heard the guy laugh and I felt embarrassed.

I waxed the board up at the waters edge and then paddled out. I felt uneasy as I paddled out among about one hundred surfers. A small two foot swell built up behind me and knocked me over. I struggled to get back on my board and tried again. The next wave I tried was another two footer and when I stood I immediately fell. I tried a few more waves but the same thing happened, I fell immediately. After twenty minutes I was so winded I paddled in and returned the board to the rental guy.

The next morning Sherri and I packed our bags and caught a flight to Maui. My friend Sonny, the guy who clued me in about Randy, lived there. We rented a car at the airport and drove to Lahaina, on the other side of the island, where he lived. Sonny was a carpet layer by trade but mostly a surfer.

Sonny was happy to see me and we talked about the situation with Randy. He said he had worked in some of the same buildings as Randy and that he had a crew of ten guys and really had the business doing well. He also told me that Randy had talked about dumping me for the past six months. I was so angry I was shaking. Sonny suggested I stay with him for a few days and mellow out. Obviously I looked a mess and he was concerned.

He gave Sherri and I his bedroom for our stay. As soon as we could we went into the bedroom and smoked some Dr. brown. Sonny and his friends didn't mess with coke or heroin, so we hid it.

We had been there for three days and I noticed my equilibrium was off and my speech was becoming slurred. Sherri and I were in the bedroom smoking some brown and I was having a hard time sitting up. I overheard some friends in the kitchen saying, "have you seen Dean? He really looks sick, I hardly recognize him." They continued saying," He is so skinny and pasty white, he looks like he is dying." Others agreed and then one said, "I hope he doesn't die here." They went on saying they couldn't believe what I had done to myself and that I was really heading down a dead end street. As I fell over, onto the bed, I thought to myself, "what's happening?"

20

Conclusion

THE NEXT DAY IT WAS OBVIOUS TO Sherri I needed help from a doctor and my family in California. She asked my friends to drive us across the island to the Maui airport.

I stumbled into the airport and immediately had to sit down. Sherri went to get our boarding passes and pointed to me and asked for wheelchair assistance. The ticket agent asked me if I needed medical assistance and Sherri interjected that wasn't necessary. She explained that she would be accompanying me to California and that my family would be there to meet us when we landed. She told the agent that

I had had a head injury but I was stable for the flight and we only needed assistance boarding.

While I sat there I could see the look on people's faces, they were obviously feeling sorry for me. I could see in their faces, they're thoughts, I was such a young guy and practically an invalid, or a derelict, what a waste.

Boarding the plane I was wheeled on first. The assistant asked me if I was comfortable and I slurred out "pretty good." My mind could think what I wanted to say but I couldn't speak clearly. Once seated I fell in and out of consciousness through out the five hour flight. A few times, when I did wake up, I would try to talk to Sherri but my speech was slurred and I could see a scared look on her face so I would just close my eyes and try to sleep.

When the flight attendant announced that we would be landing soon, I motioned to Sherri I needed to use the restroom. I stood up, holding onto the seat in front of me, took a step toward the restroom and fell flat on my face in the isle. My equilibrium was completely gone. The stewardess ran down the isle to me, held up my head and asked if I was alright. I couldn't form the words to answer, I just pointed to the restroom. Sherri explained that I needed to use the restroom and that she would go with me to help me.

While in the restroom I was standing against the wall while peeing and I happened to look in the mirror and there looking back at me was someone I didn't know. The person I was looking at was really sick looking. I felt really sick to my stomach and finally realized something was really wrong with me, I might even die.

I opened the Restroom door and grabbed Sherri's arm for stability and nodded toward our seats. We moved slowly down the isle with everyone looking at us. When I got back into my seat I saw the lights of LA as I peered out the window. I kept looking out at the lights approaching and kept thinking to myself over and over, "What have I done to myself? What will my mother think? Will I recover?" Finally we landed.

My head was spinning with all these thoughts. I never noticed the passengers leaving the plane. The next thing I knew, Sherri and I were the last people on the plane and the attendant was wheeling up a wheelchair for me to get off the plane. The attendant asked me if she could help me out of my seat into the chair. I nodded and slurred out, "yes."

While being rolled off the aircraft, entering the arrivals terminal, I thought, if only I can recover, I'll never do this again. I made a promise to myself. We emerged from the exit tunnel into the airport bright lights, laughter and excitement of happy travelers. I saw my mother and brother across the way with worried faces. They spotted me being wheeled out and my mother came up and kissed me, as she held back tears, my brother hugged me. They both at the same time said, "don't worry, we'll get you well again."

I hoped they were right.

I promised myself never again.

I hoped it wasn't to late.

About Me

MY MEDICAL CONDITION, AND PHYSICAL STATE WAS finally diagnosed after six months. I was diagnosed with motor nerve damage brought on by massive drug use and addiction. How much I could recover, only time would tell.

Recovery from nerve damage is very slow but, after only eight months, I started showing signs of recovery. After two full years I had recovered to about ninety percent. I could walk, without an aid, I could talk, but still had a slight stammer. I just couldn't seem to get back that last ten percent.

I had used up nearly all my money on medical bills and legal fees. I still had to retain an attorney to negotiate turning myself in. My attorney felt that turning myself in after nearly three years, with no arrests, reinstatement of my probation was probable.

The day came for me to turn myself in and it was the usual formality of finger printing and face the judge. I agreed to three years probation and made arrangements to meet with my new probation officer. It felt good not to be on the run anymore.

I had to find work so I took a job as a salesman, but just couldn't make enough money, so I went to school to become a hairdresser then after some time I got my real estate license, unfortunately the market was very slow. My recovery was maybe ninety eight percent now so I decided to go back to carpentry work and make money.

Age crept up on me, I was in my thirties, my probation was over and it was time to do something for my future before it was too late. I thought to myself, "what?" I was lucky to be alive at this point in my life, I should have a career, a house and kids. Not only I didn't have any of these things, I barely had a pot to pee in. I knew I couldn't work as a carpenter for too many more years so I needed to make some changes. Eventually I got my general contractor license, met my wife and started a business.

We struggled along for a few years until I made enough contacts and completed enough jobs to get myself known. The business has grown strong and now I realize somehow, I survived and got another chance.

Today I am sixty years old. I am a twelve year survivor of colon cancer and I am self-employed as a general and plumbing contractor making a comfortable living. I was lucky enough to be reacquainted with my oldest son when he was sixteen years old; he is now forty and married with three adorable daughters. I married my wife of twenty two years in 1986 and have a wonderful stepdaughter, now thirty-three and mother to our oldest granddaughter, and we were gifted with a son between us who is now ninteen and attends Cal State University Long Beach.

It has been twenty-seven years since the time you have just read about and I have been clean ever since. Unfortunately, most of my friends in my story are gone now due to drugs. I was lucky. As it has been said before, "No one grows up wanting to be a heroin addict." I wrote this book to show just how no one is a winner when it comes to drugs, it is truly a "DEAD END STREET."